MURDER OUT

Of

BOUNDS

By

Colin Holcombe

This book is dedicated to the memory of:

John Cambridge, John Newbury and
Ken Budd.

All three lost their fight against cancer and have
left the world poorer by their absence.

This novel is entirely a work of fiction. Any resemblance to actual persons, living or dead is entirely coincidental apart from the two divers mentioned in the opening chapter who have both given their permission to be included.

Chapter 1

The two divers were attached to each other by means of a buddy line, a ribbon-like strip attached to each of their belts, and a sensible precaution in waters where visibility could alternate between six feet and six inches in the blink of an eye. They approached the boat's superstructure with caution, not wanting to catch any part of their suit or equipment on an unseen and possibly sharp or otherwise hazardous obstacle.

Chris, the elder of the two brothers, used his left hand to rub away at one of the glass windows and shone his torch through it into the cabin, not really expecting to see anything of great interest. There was unlikely to be anything worth the added danger of trying to enter the vessel, even though it seemed likely they were the first to set eyes on it since it had been on the surface and succumbed to whatever chain of events had caused it to founder.

The door to the cabin was shut and remarkably, all the glass still seemed to be intact. Nevertheless the beam of light from his torch disturbed fish that had somehow found their way in, causing silt to swirl around in small eddies and restrict visibility even further.

How the fish and other small marine life had managed to gain access to the cabin was a mystery but they always seemed to find a way. Perhaps the boat was holed below the waterline. That would certainly account for her being where she was rather than on the surface enjoying the sun. Perhaps the water had just leaked in through small gaps, carrying fish eggs with it that had hatched out inside the vessel, the progeny of which were destined maybe to live out their entire lives within the limited environs of the cabin.

Once again Chris swept the beam of his torch from one end of the cabin to the other and just as he was about to signal to his brother that there was nothing inside, something caught his eye. He shone the light once again where he thought he had seen a brief glint of something reflected in the light but there was nothing to be seen. It was easy to imagine all sorts of things under these conditions, especially when all you really want to do is get back to the surface so you can get some hot food or drink inside you.

But no! there it was again; as one of the larger fish darted away to avoid the light's intrusion into its domain, there was the definite glint of something. Chris squinted into the cabin with his mask tight against the glass and his heart missed a beat. He couldn't possibly have seen what he thought his torch had revealed.

He tugged on the buddy line to summon his brother who was beside him in a second, concerned, wondering if there was a problem. Chris pointed through the window excitedly, indicating to Steve, his younger brother and business partner, that he should also examine the cabin's interior.

With two powerful beams of light penetrating the darkness there could be no mistake. The bones of a hand and arm, once held together in life by ligaments and tendons were now tenuously attached by no more than interweaving strands of seaweed. The bones themselves were discoloured and projected from the tattered and partially decomposed cuff of what was once a jacket.

The little tableau would probably have gone unnoticed had it not been for the gold watch that adorned the wrist standing out in the torchlight. The gold bracelet of the watch looked otherworldly in its relatively clean condition against the silt and decay of its surroundings.

The two brothers continued to stare for some time, wondering if their senses were playing tricks on them.   Christopher   and Stephen Foulkes had been commissioned by Royal Marine Insurance for an agreed fee, to try and locate the wreck of, "White Warrior" a ninety-foot-long luxury yacht that had been lost four months earlier.

If located, they were to look for any obvious signs that the owners, who were also the crew at the time the vessel foundered, had given an accurate account of the event leading up to her loss.

The said owners, Mr. and Mrs. Scott-Henderson, had maintained that they were trying the vessel out for the first time after she'd had a major overhaul of the onboard gas and electrical systems. They stated that all four souls on board, the Scott-Henderson's themselves and Mrs. Scott-Henderson's two brothers, had been on deck when there had been a substantial explosion from below and that the boat had sunk so quickly, that they had only just managed to grab their life jackets, launch the boat's tender and board it, before White Warrior disappeared beneath the surface like a slice of cake at a children's birthday party.

If this description of events was indeed the case and the vessel was resting where they said; there could well be obvious visible signs to corroborate their story. If an explosion had caused the vessel to sink as quickly as they had said, there should be substantial damage to the hull.

The White Warrior was insured for a little over ten million pounds, so Royal Marine considered some expenditure to locate the wreck worthwhile.

The company that had carried out the maintenance of the vessel were also keen to show that the yacht had been sunk as part of an insurance fraud, rather than through any negligence on their part, which accounted for the fact that they were part funding the dive.

The vessel the brothers were now exploring was definitely not White Warrior. This vessel was more like thirty-foot-long rather than ninety, with a single inboard motor and a small cabin in both the bow and the aft sections that would contain little more than a couple of cramped berths aft and a berth and galley forward.

They had been lucky to spot it with the equipment they had. It was a far cry from the floating gin palace they were looking for and from which they expected to get a half decent signal if she was located.

But the indications had been that something was down here and they had decided to dive and make sure. There was always the chance that White Warrior had broken in two and the signal they were receiving was from only half a vessel.

Their equipment although quite sophisticated, had been purchased second-hand; there was no way the brothers could have afforded the kind of equipment they needed new. They were in debt to the finance company already, just from purchasing the dive boat.

It was obvious that this vessel had been under water for some years, being half buried in silt and sand. The bits that were still visible were encrusted with barnacles and covered with all kinds of marine growth which made it difficult to make out her exact shape or age in the dark waters. All they could determine initially was that she wasn't a wooden vessel, so probably fairly modern.

After examining the exterior of the wreck a little more closely it was obvious that their initial instincts had been correct and it was not the one they had been looking for. Neither diver was particularly dismayed by this conformation, after all, they would be paid the agreed fee whether they found her or not, and the wreck they had found was in some ways a more interesting discovery, although unlikely to warrant another dive.

This was the Bristol Channel after all, not the Caribbean or the Red Sea. It wasn't somewhere that you would dive for pleasure unless there was a particularly interesting wreck or profitable outcome to look forward to.

Diving is a hazardous business. Even in warm waters with good visibility danger can reach out for the unwary from all directions. Faulty or badly maintained equipment, miscalculations about available air, decompression times or even attack from predators, either annoyed by the invasion of their habitat or simply hungry.

Although unlikely to be attacked by sharks in the Bristol Channel, poor visibility, cold water and strong currents were a constant source of danger, even for experienced divers.

The brothers hovered face to face in the murky water like ballroom dancers in a smoke-filled hall as they each checked their watches and air supplies. Chris pointed skyward to indicate that he thought they should surface and Steve nodded in agreement. They were in 30 metres of water with a strong current and had been down for almost twenty minutes, most of which had been spent trying to locate the source of the signal they had picked up on the dive boat.

Staying any longer would necessitate a decompression stop at six metres if they were to avoid the dreaded bends and there was nothing to be gained by staying longer, better to just mark the wreck's location and report what they had found.

Staying close together they attached a line to one of the moulded hand-grips that were situated along the sides of the wreck. Steve attached the other end of the line to a small buoy that Chris then filled with air from his mouthpiece before releasing it. This would act as a surface marker to indicate the location of the wreak, and now grave, should they wish to dive on it again. The two brothers instinctively looked up as the marker began its ascent to the surface but it soon disappeared from view in the darkness above.

Someone would be sure to want to visit the site and it would be designated as a grave officially. Efforts would be made to identify the body of the unfortunate occupant and determine how the vessel had come to founder.

It was impossible to know what fate had befallen the unfortunate individual inside, but equally impossible not to speculate. What had prevented him from escaping the sinking boat? Was he unconscious as the boat went down or was he somehow trapped inside, terrified and desperate to escape as the waters rose around him?

It was sad to think that the identity of the man may never be discovered or what had befallen him in his last moments of life, but speculation would have to wait, it was time to get back to the friendlier environment of the surface.

With the strong currents, the brothers could easily drift half a mile or so from the dive site as they were ascending but as they did so, they reeled in the line that was attached to a second buoy on the surface, one they had deployed next to the dive boat before descending into what was essentially an alien environment. They followed this line up to surface and next to the dive boat, rather like Theseus following his thread in the Minotaur's labyrinth.

On the surface, Roger Drew, their ever-vigilant colleague in the dive boat, would closely monitor any movement of the buoy until the divers eventually emerged beside it and he would be able to help them aboard.

They were just about to start their ascent when Steve grabbed his brother's arm and pointed.

There was no chance of reading any name that would at one time have been emblazoned on the hull of the vessel, but Steve had spotted what looked like a plaque of some sort on the upper front edge of the canopy that one would have ducked under to enter the forward cabin.

Chris quickly attacked the area with a small hammer and chisel that he retrieved from the tool bag on his hip to clear away the debris. Sure enough, underneath was a brass or bronze plaque.

The writing on the plaque, if any, was indiscernible, so using the same tools again he removed it and placed it in the small string bag that accompanied them on every dive.

On the surface, they could clean and possibly read what was on it. Hopefully it would bear the vessel's name and enable them to identify her, but it could just as easily read, "Mind Your Head."

Anxiously checking their watches once again, acutely aware that they were close to overstaying their welcome in the hostile environment, they headed for the safer surroundings of the surface.

When the brothers finally emerged alongside the buoy, they both felt somewhat relieved. It was always comforting to see the dive boat, even though they were well within swimming distance of land with the aid of their fins and snorkels. With just a head out of the water, the horizon is literally only yards away, and even on a clear sunny day orientation and deciding in which direction the nearest landfall was could be difficult, even with a compass.

Fortunately, Roger had not fallen asleep or suffered a coronary whilst the brothers had been busy below and he was soon helping them aboard the eight-metre-long twin hulled craft and off with their equipment before interrogating them about what they had found.

On the three-hour return journey back to Portishead Marina where their Land-Rover and boat-trailer were waiting, the three men went about their various tasks. Roger piloted the boat while Steve cleaned and stowed away the diving gear and Chris worked on the plaque they had salvaged, eventually cleaning it sufficiently well to be able to just make out what was on it.

Oblivious to the fact that the afternoon August sun was beating down on his bare back and threatening to give him a painful and sleepless night he had worked furiously on the thing. He now turned to Roger and his brother holding the plaque aloft and declared in a somewhat subdued and disappointed tone of voice, "Sylvia," as if he had expected a more exciting or controversial name.

Steve had just closed the lid on the deck locker and looked up when he heard his brothers disappointed declaration.

"What did you expect?" he enquired, grinning "Son of Titanic."

"Oh! I don't know, but Sylvia just seems a bit boring," replied Chris, the disappointment still discernible in his tone.

"It was a boring little boat," said Steve, "apart from its occupant anyway."

"And Sylvia's a nice name," cut in Roger, "I used to go out with a girl called Sylvia."

"I know, but I can't help wondering what the story is? I wonder if anyone has been looking for her?" continued Chris, trying in vain to elicit some excitement from the other two. "Perhaps we've just uncovered the whereabouts of Lord Lucan or something, he would have had a gold watch, wouldn't he?"

Stephen just rolled his eyes and smiled at Roger, who was earwigging the conversation as he steered the boat and folded away the chart on which he had just marked the position of their discovery.

Many theories were cited on the journey back to Portishead, theories as to just how Sylvia had ended up where she was and who the owner of the gold watch could be. One theory even explored the possibility the boat had actually been named after Roger's old girlfriend but it was soon discounted. As things turned out, none of them came even close to the truth.

In the top storey observation room overlooking the Bristol Channel from its vantage point on top of the cliffs, Coast Guard David Cartwright was multi-tasking, at least, that was the way he viewed it. He was manning the phone in event of any emergency call, ready to call out a lifeboat or a rescue helicopter from any of the various stations covering the Bristol Channel. He was also drinking a cup of instant coffee that was rapidly becoming too cold to enjoy, eating a jam doughnut, occasionally scanning the coastline with his binoculars and also searching the computer records for any reference to a lost boat called Sylvia.

When faced with the task of looking through their extensive list of missing small craft he had decided that, instead of starting with the latest and working backwards, he would take a chance based on the divers' description of the state of the wreck and start in 1980 and work forward. If he didn't find anything and had to continue his search he would then work backwards from that same date.

Staring at the screen almost in disbelief, he yelled out in celebration and mentally slapped himself on the back for a job well done. There she was, "Sylvia" a small cabin cruiser thirty-foot-long, nine and a half feet in the beam with single inboard motor, owner, a Mr. David Carver from Clevedon and moored at small privately owned jetty in Portishead. Oh! how he wished his colleagues were there to witness his triumph. His plan had worked well, the Sylvia he had found matched the divers' find perfectly and had gone missing in 1989.

The police had asked the coastguard to keep an eye out for her after she had apparently been used as a getaway vessel after a jeweller and his wife had been held hostage and their shop robbed.

Two men and possibly a third had escaped in the boat and had never been seen again, the men or the boat.

Well it now looked to David Cartwright as if the reason they had never been found, was because the boat had sunk and the men had gone down with her and drowned, simple as that.

David speculated that perhaps it was no more than they deserved if they were the sort of people who robbed and took hostages, at least that meant that the state wouldn't have to pay for their keep at some luxury prison or other where they could play table tennis and watch television all day. He picked up the phone, feeling more than a little pleased with himself and called the police.

Chapter 2

The large room, although normally light and airy in nature, today felt hot and stuffy, almost oppressive, despite the fact that the aluminium casement windows, that ran almost the full length of one wall, were open and the sun was shining in, flooding the room with light and summer warmth.

Inspector Paul Manley looked out of his office and surveyed the room and its occupants. Paul's own office was little more than a partitioned-off area at the end of the large communal office that accommodated twelve desks. It was a sign of the times and the economic realities of modern policing that only nine of the desks were now in permanent use.

He looked at the faces of his team and concluded that they were actually bored. For the last couple of weeks, although inundated with work and run off their feet, they had had nothing of any great interest or importance to get their teeth into. It was a shame to see such a good team just going through the motions.

He mentally gave them all review. The two newbies, Constables Ben Horrocks and Giles Harcombe hadn't been with him long enough for him to get to know them very well but they had settled in quickly and got on with the rest of the team. Constables Peter Cook, nicknamed The Comic for obvious reasons. Derrick Price, who would often take the role of case manager because he was good at coordinating things. Phillip Strange and John Campbell, both highly trained firearm officers. June Kelly, the only woman on the team, an advanced driver and a good detective, and Sergeant Reginald Evans the most experienced of the lot, a father figure and mentor to them all. Full marks to all of them as individuals but the best thing was the fact that they all got on really well. He wasn't aware of any friction between any of them and that made for a formidable team. He was lucky to have them.

Morale had suffered to the extent that lately his Sergeant, Reginald Evans, a forty-eight-year-old widower, who had immersed himself entirely in his work since the untimely death of his wife five years earlier, had been openly talking about going on holiday somewhere. Although none of the team took his holiday comments seriously, it was an indicator of the state of morale that they were actually suggesting places he could go rather than trying to dissuade him.

Paul and his team had been fortunate enough in the past year to clear up two high profile cases and gain some considerable respect amongst their colleagues, plus some recognition from higher up. It had also seen Constable June Kelly receive a commendation for bravery after tackling a man armed with a knife. Now they were back to investigating the rather mundane burglaries and muggings that are the bread and butter of urban policing. Now everything, even closing a case, felt like an anti-climax.

Hopefully the news he had now would cheer them all up.

He left his office and called out "Listen up everyone," before wiping clean one of the larger white boards that screened of his office window from the main room.

Paul had positioned the boards there because there were no blinds on his window and they gave him at least the semblance of some privacy on those rare occasions he deemed it necessary.

He took up a position to one side of the board and his actions created an air of expectancy in the room. Everyone stopped what they were doing to listen.

"Now I know life hasn't been as exciting lately as we have become accustomed to but hopefully that has just changed and we now have something not only interesting but also somewhat out of the ordinary to investigate." Looking over towards Reg, Paul continued, "I'm sorry Reg, but I think this means you'll have to put your holiday plans on hold for a while."

Reg tried his best to look disappointed.

"Can't we send him away somewhere anyway Guv?" quipped John Campbell, to a general smattering of laughter and approval, "we were hoping to be rid of the grumpy old sod for a while," he continued, giving Paul cause to wonder in how many other teams a constable would dare to refer to his sergeant in such a way.

June held up a plastic tub that had once contained the rice from a Chinese takeaway, on the side of which someone had written, "Sending Reg away somewhere fund," and a couple of people contributed a few more coins as the mood in the room took on an air of expectancy.

Paul smiled but put his hands in the air, indicating that everyone should be quiet but then elicited another round of laughter by starting off saying, "Although I share your disappointment John, I think we may need Reg for his......ah...his," He looked over at June Kelly and asked frowning, "remind me June, what is it need Reg for?"

"We need someone to blame if we get something wrong Guv," replied June, smiling broadly.

"Ah yes...of course, that was it....I knew there was a reason we needed him, thanks June."

The fact that Reg was the most experienced officer in the room and a well-liked and respected member of the team didn't stop them taking the micky out of him whenever the opportunity arose. He was sitting casually on the edge of his desk in silence, listening to the banter with a somewhat aloof expression on his face. In truth, the genuine friendship of his work colleagues had stopped him from falling into the abyss of depression when his wife had died, and he regarded them all as family.

Paul had to raise his hand a second time to quell the new-found mirth in the room and they soon fell silent again, anxious to hear what he had to say.

"A couple of days ago," he began, "two divers came across the wreck of a small boat at the bottom of the Bristol Channel. That boat has now been identified as a small pleasure craft by the name of "Sylvia." Now, the boat went missing in 1989 after being used as a rather unusual getaway vehicle, but I suppose I had better start the story from the very beginning.

"On 31st May 1989 the joint owner of a jewellery business in Clevedon, one David Carver was taken hostage along with his wife and business partner Sylvia Carver."

Paul pinned a photograph of a man on the board and wrote the name David Carver below it.

A second picture, this time of a woman, joined the first. "This is Sylvia Carver," Paul continued, "after whom we assume the boat was named. Now according to Mr. Carver at the time, three armed men wearing masks entered his house when he answered the door the evening before, that's the 30th. He said that they tied his wife in a chair and threatened to cripple her with a baseball bat if he didn't do what they said."

"They sound nice," commented Phillip.

"Just the sort you want dropping in unexpected," replied Derrick.

"Can I continue now?" cut in Paul, trying to sound annoyed at the interruption but secretly pleased by the banter. This was just how the team behaved when they were interested. "They stayed several hours and at approximately 2:00am the following morning, one of the men stayed in the house with his wife while he was forced to drive the others to his shop well before any staff arrived.

"Once again he was told that his wife would be hurt if he didn't open the safe for them. He did as he was told and after filling a couple of metal boxes and some velvet bags with the contents of three safes and a couple of cabinets, they took him in his car to Portishead where Mr. Carver moored his boat, Sylvia. His car was later found abandoned beside the mooring. He said that they forced him to go with them on board and that they made their way out into the Bristol Channel. Once they had reached the middle of the channel he says that they hit him over the head and threw him overboard."

"Blimey! He was lucky to survive that and tell the tale?" observed June.

"Well yes, he does appear to have been lucky in that respect, but apparently our jeweller is an experienced open water swimmer who regularly swam in the sea all year round back then."

Several of the team looked at each other and shivered.

"He maintains," Paul continued, "that the shock of hitting the cold water brought him round and he managed to make landfall at Weston-super-Mare."

"That sounds like quite a swim Guv." murmured Peter.

"Yes, it is. Now unfortunately his wife was not so lucky and when the police got to the house they found her dead, still tied in the chair but now with a plastic bag over her head."

"That's a cruel way to do it," observed June.

Paul pinned up a police photograph of the dead woman bound in a wooden chair, her head slumped forward with the bag obscuring her face. He then drew a line between the two pictures of her so there was no mistake that the dead woman in the second photograph was the same woman as in the first.

"So, it looks as if they'd intended to kill them both from the start, Guv?" stated Derrick Price, who was now stood beside Paul pinning up an underwater picture of a sunken boat that Paul had just handed him.

"Apparently so Derrick, they must have assumed David Carver would drown after being thrown unconscious into the sea like that."

"Did we catch the men responsible Guv?" asked June.

"No June, no trace was ever found of the men or the jewellery or the boat until now."

"What are our chances of finding them after all this time if they couldn't be found then?" asked Reg. "Presumably they sank the boat so that we wouldn't know where they made it to shore, but just knowing where they sank the boat isn't going to help us very much, we still don't know how or where they made it ashore,"

"That's true Reg."

"You say the boat was found sunk Guv. So, how could they have made it ashore? Don't tell me they were all open water swimmers as well?" asked Phillip, "or do we think somebody else met them with another boat? Seems a rather clumsy and elaborate get away if that's the case, why didn't they just make their getaway in a car like any other self-respecting low-life."

"Just one question of many that need answering Phillip. But the fact is that one of them may not have made it to shore, the divers who located the boat said they saw part of a skeleton in the main cabin."

"So, a falling out among thieves maybe Guv. Perhaps one of the men didn't agree with killing the jeweler and his wife and they had a fight about it; but we still don't have anything that we didn't have back then," observed Reg, "except the boat of coarse...well, and a body if the divers are right. Has the body been retrieved?"

Just as Reg finished speaking Detective Chief Inspector Blake entered the room accompanied by another officer in uniform.

"Sorry to interrupt you Paul," said Chief Inspector Blake, "but this is Sergeant Mike Jones, he's in charge of the police dive team that have just been down to inspect our boat, I see you have the photographs already," then turning to Sergeant Jones he continued, "I'll leave you to update Inspector Manley and his team Mike," then turning back to Paul, "Keep me updated Paul, I've got a meeting to attend now but I'll be back before you leave, make sure we meet, yes."

"Yes of course Sir," said Paul before holding out his hand to the newcomer, "Welcome Mike, what can you tell us?"

DCI Blake watched the two men shake hands, before saying, "I'll leave you to it then." and leaving the room.

Paul turned back to the new arrival. Mike Jones would have been cast as an action man by any director or producer worthy of the name. He was tall, well-built and sported a complexion that could only have come about by spending much of his time outdoors. June was most impressed.

"We've been down to the boat a couple of times now Sir," Mike began, "and we've recovered the remains of two bodies."

"Two bodies?" queried Paul.

"That's right Sir, both male."

The silence in the room was only broken when June enquired, "Did you find any jewellery while you were down there?"

Mike grinned. "Trust a woman to think about jewellery at a time like this," he said smiling and causing June to revise her appraisal of him a little.

"Neither the jewels, nor the metal boxes they were supposed to be in, just the two bodies I'm afraid."

June looked at Paul, "If we assume the two men who threw our jeweller over the side are the two who went down with the boat, then what happened to the jewels?"

"That's a good question June, and it needs an answer for sure," said Paul, now resting himself on the corner of another desk and looking around the room waiting for other questions or comments.

"Has anyone looked at the remains yet?" asked Reg. "Do we know how they died, because I'm assuming that if they were alive when the boat sank they would have at least tried to get off, not shut themselves in the cabin. Maybe there was a third person on the boat who locked them in the cabin and then sank the boat."

All eyes were on Sergeant Jones. "I don't think anyone has had time to examine the bodies yet and I wouldn't get your hopes up anyway if I were you, all we brought up were bones, the remains of a couple of wallets, some keys and two watches, one of which was a gold Rolex."

"So, you didn't find any kind of a weapon down there either, no gun or knife or anything?" asked Paul.

"There were some knives, but they were all together in a pile under what remained of the galley cabinets, together with other cutlery, nothing suspicious but one of them could have been the murder weapon I suppose. We felt around looking for a possible bullet, but we were searching amongst silt and debris, in the dark, with gloves on and now the cabin's interior is exposed to the outside, currents are constantly swirling around and moving everything. It's not a stable environment to search in."

"What about the third man?" asked Derrick. "The nasty piece of work that stayed behind with Sylvia and presumably put her head in a bag? Perhaps they picked him up somewhere after dumping the jeweller overboard and he double crossed them. Maybe he killed his accomplices as well as the wife and made off with all the goodies for himself."

"Same question," said Paul. "How would he have got ashore after sinking the boat? I feel sure that whatever happened out there, there has to be another boat involved somewhere."

"Well they have to have had another boat Guv," queried John, "unless perhaps they picked the third man up from shore somewhere; he killed them, then made a hole in the boat, tied the wheel and just let it sail out into the channel on its own until it filled with water and sank."

"That's another one of the possibilities that we'll have to look into," answered Paul, "because there was no mention of a tender in the jeweller's statement. That doesn't mean there wasn't one of course and it would provide a means for whoever killed our two victims to get ashore."

"One other thing that puzzles me Guv," said June.

"What's that?"

"Well, why did they stay so long at the Carver's house? Why wait all that time at the house? In fact......why not carry out the robbery earlier in the night if they knew David Carver would have the keys?"

"Perhaps they needed daylight to handle the boat," suggested Reg.

"Blimey Reg," smiled June, "that's quick thinking, perhaps we do need you after all."

"It still doesn't explain why they entered the night before."

Derrick suggested, "Maybe they went in early so that someone would open the door to them, if the couple had gone to bed they may not have heard or answered the door and the perpetrators would have had to break in."

"Yes, that might explain it."

Mike Jones cut in. "I might be able to explain why they waited till early morning Sir."

Everyone turned to look at the new-comer in their midst, who shuffled his feet a little and looked a bit uncomfortable now. "I'd have to check the times of course, but if they were intending to use a boat to get away in, they would have had to take the tides into account."

Reg and June both looked at each other smiling and repeated accusingly at one another in unison, "The tide! *you* should have thought of that."

"Guv." This time it was Peter Cook who spoke up. "You said that the three men wore masks; but if we think the intention from the start was to do away with both Mr. and Mrs. Carver, why bother with hiding their faces?"

"Another good question Peter; even if one or more of them were known to the Carver's, they couldn't identify them if they were dead, I agree."

Paul got up from the desk and put an end to the round of speculations by stating, "It's obvious at the moment that we have a lot of questions and no real answers. Let's see if we can turn that round. I am however surprised that no-one has suggested another possible interpretation of the events."

"You think there's another possibility Guv?" asked Reg.

"Well, isn't it possible our jeweller friend, David Carver, has been telling porkies all along and that he was in on the whole thing. I can't believe none of you suggested that. Perhaps it was an insurance scam and he killed the men in the boat, made off with the jewels and collected on the insurance as well. It would also explain the anomaly of the masks"

"How would it do that Guv?" asked Reg. frowning.

"Well, if Carver was in on it, there need not have been a third man at all, or he could be the third man, and if he was making the story up, perhaps he described them as being masked simply because that's what you expect robbers to be. It also eliminates the need for them to have to pick anyone up from shore, if we discount Carver's version of events the third man, if he existed, could have been with them all along. I think the discovery of two bodies on board the boat drops our Mr. Carver right in the frame."

"You think he organized the robbery and arranged for his wife to be killed, or killed her himself before they left the house, Guv?"

"That's right June....why not?" Paul shrugged his shoulders, "who is normally the prime suspect when a wife is murdered?"

"OK Guv, so where do you want us to start?"

"Well you can start by tracking down the present whereabouts of Mr. Carver so we can give him the good news, I'd certainly like to see his reaction when we tell him we've found his boat.

"Reg, I'd like you to see if the Pathologist has any idea what killed the two men in the boat or who they were. At the moment, we have to assume they are the two men who robbed the shop but let's see if we can identify them before jumping to any conclusions. I can't imagine the Pathologist will have much for us but as there was a gold watch recovered with the bodies, perhaps it has an inscription of some kind. John; can you have a word with the rest of the officers who dived on the boat and recovered the bodies. See if they noticed anything else of interest; anything at all and speak to the divers who found the boat; they may have overlooked something when they were first interviewed......get the exact position of the boat from them, let's see just how far our jeweller had to swim to reach shore."

John walked across to speak to Sergeant Jones, who supplied him with the names of the rest of the dive team.

"They may have taken the boat out further to sink it, Guv. After they threw Carver overboard I mean." said June.

"You're right of course June, but it will be nice to have the boat's resting place anyway. The rest of you.... I want everyone who was interviewed at the time, re-interviewed. If our Jeweller was involved and an accomplice in the murder of his wife, then their marriage must have been in trouble, so let's find out, contact friend and neighbours of theirs back then, see if there were any rumours of an affair.

"Someone find out more about the boat as well, where exactly it was being kept back then...and speak to people who were there at the time, if there are any after all this time, see if they remember if there was ever a tender or life-boat with it.

"Peter, see if you can locate whoever sorted out Mrs. Carver's estate, let's see just how well off or otherwise our Mr. Carver came out the whole business. Obviously, there was the insurance money but see how much he inherited from his wife and how the business was divided up. And see if we can get a list from the insurance company of the items they paid out on."

Paul turned to another original member of his team, Constable Phillip Strange. "Phillip, I'm sorry but I want you to familiarise yourself with all the original case files and get them into some sort of order of priority based on what we know now. Keep an eye out for anything that was said by anyone back then that doesn't fit in with our new information."

Paul looked at the team in front of him and spread his arms wide. "Well come on......tomorrow I want to see this filled with information," he almost shouted, indicating the sparsely adorned white board behind him. "You wanted something to get your teeth into....so start biting."

Paul watched as the team set about their various allotted tasks, wondering how on earth they were going to discover the truth of what happened on board a small boat, in the middle of the Bristol Channel, over 26 years ago.

* * * * * * * * * * * *

June had lived in her present flat for eighteen months. Situated in the Redland area of Bristol, it was a typical large Victorian terraced house that had been converted into two flats. The disadvantage of living where she did was that June had to park on the road outside along with the rest of her neighbours and that meant she seldom managed to get close to the house. The advantage was that it was near the centre of town and only a short car journey to work each day.

She had the downstairs garden flat. The first floor was occupied by a man who June placed in his mid-thirties, John Stubbs. He lived alone and had obviously taken a shine to June, not that she was particularly concerned about it, in fact, when she had turned down his request for a date he had taken it in good spirit and since then had kept his attempts at conversation on a friendly but less personal level. He seemed OK, he just wasn't June's type.

This morning however he stopped her as she left the house, trying to remember how far away she'd parked her car the night before.

"June," he called, "Good morning, off to work, is it?"

"Yes, no rest for the wicked is there."

"You never said what it was you did for a living, all I know is that you don't work regular hours, shifts is it?" he asked.

June had always found it best not to let on to casual acquaintances and neighbours that she was in the police, so she'd slipped into the habit of lying.

"Journalist," she replied.

"Oh great! Will I have seen anything of yours, do you do national or local news?"

"Both, but you're unlikely to have read any of my stuff unless you're into flower shows or fetes."

"Ah! no, not my thing at all." John shuffled from one foot to the other. "Look, can I ask you what perfume you wear...it's just that I have contacts in the trade, my brother is a retailer in fact and I could get you some very cheap, if you're interested."

June sighed expecting another chat-up line, "Look John, I have a boyfriend, and I'm not sure what he would make of me accepting offers of discount perfume from another man, I'm sorry, it's nothing personal."

"No, listen June, you misunderstand, I'm not looking to chat you up this time, I'm not going to pester you or anything I promise. I ask a girl out once and if she turns me down then that's that, I'm not a stalker for God's sake. No, I really do have contacts in the cosmetics trade and to be honest, I make a little bit on the side by selling it, so I'm not doing you any particular favour. I'm actually trying to make a buck."

June smelt a rat. John had a part time job at some shop or other in Cabot Circus, one of the many shopping centres in Bristol, and he may well have contacts in the retail perfume trade, but in her experience, cheap perfume is usually either knocked off or fake.

"What ones can you get?" she asked casually, thinking she should really just let it drop. What was she going to do if it did turn out be stolen or iffy in any way, arrest a neighbour?

"Tell me what you use."

"Coco Chanel."

"Perfume? Eau de toilette? What size?"

"I normally buy eau de toilette in a 50 ml spray," replied June, "can you get that?" June kicked herself mentally for asking and thought, I've just asked a neighbour to get me some iffy gear!

"I can probably get that for you, I think it's probably seventy or eighty pounds in the shops but I reckon I could do it for around thirty-five, forty tops. Do you want some?"

"Wow! That sounds really cheap. Can you really get it for that price?" she asked, torn between wanting to investigate a possible crime and yet not wanting to have to inform on a neighbour.

"Let me see what I can do for you."

"OK, look I have to go or I shall be late for work." June said turning away to walk to her car.

John Stubbs watched her as she walked off, kicking himself for his stupidity. He had liked June from the first time he'd seen her and still had hopes that she might consent to go out with him if she knew him better. Offering to get her cheap perfume now seemed extremely stupid, she was a clever woman...a journalist for God's sake, she would be sure to think it was dodgy goods and if she did, that wouldn't exactly impress her, would it? Perhaps he would be better off telling her he couldn't get it after all, or maybe he should fork out and buy some genuine stuff from Boots and just cut his losses.

"John Stubbs," he told himself, "you can be an idiot sometimes, especially when it involves a woman."

Chapter 3

The day after Paul had outlined their new case, having traced the present whereabouts of David Carver, Detective Constable June Kelly pulled onto the tarmac driveway of Fairway View and remarked to Inspector Manley in the passenger seat, "Mr. Carver seems to have come out of things OK Guv, judging by the house anyway."

The house June was referring to was in fact a Georgian manor house that had been converted into a small hotel in the 1960s after falling into disrepair.

The rendered front still looked very much as it had always done. It still had the original square windows to the upper floors and the ground floor still boasted the imposing tall elegant ones that came down almost to ground level. It wasn't until you viewed the back of the property that you could see changes. The whole of the ground floor had been extended and it incorporated a brand new state of the art kitchen on one side and a very large and beautiful conservatory on the other.

"Still having to earn a living by the look of it though, June, running a hotel, even a small one, has got to be hard work, it's not something I would care to do when I finish fighting crime."

"Wow!" June stared at Paul and smiled, "Inspector Paul Manley....crime fighter. Is that how you think of yourself Guv, rather than as a detective or a policeman I mean?"

Paul grinned back, "You should show a bit more respect Constable and don't be so sarcastic if you don't want to find yourself back in uniform," he replied. "You've only been out of it a while so don't blow the opportunity by taking the mickey out of your superiors. And as a matter of fact, seeing as you asked, I see myself as all three of those things, don't you?"

June contemplated the question for a minute, also grinning as she pulled up outside the impressive ten-bedroom property.

"I'm not being disrespectful Guv, it's just that I think of you as a detective, detecting things, working things out, not as a crime fighter as such. Crime fighter conjures up images of gun fights and car chases. I guess I see you more as a Hercule Poirot or a Morse rather than a Dirty Harry."

Paul opened the car door to get out saying, "You can continue trying to dig yourself out of the hole you've started after we've spoken to our jeweller-cum-hotel proprietor and done some detecting. But while we're on the subject, I seem to remember you taking on an armed man recently, and didn't we chase someone in a helicopter a month or two back? Sounds a bit like crime fighting to me; I can be Dirty Harry if the need arises," said Paul, squaring his shoulders.

"Yes Guv," said June mimicking Paul's stance as they strolled towards the building.

The tarmac drive had given way to a wide gravel path that surrounded the house and looked newly laid. It ended several feet from the entrance and was replaced by square concrete slabs which were much easier and quieter to walk on. It was almost as if whoever designed the approach to the front couldn't make up their mind as to what material to use so incorporated all three. June had to scuff her shoes on the slabs to remove a piece of the sharp gravel that had embedded itself in the soft sole of her shoe.

"Damn, I hate gravel," she muttered to herself and then pushed open one of the large mahogany double doors with one hand while using the other to retrieve her warrant card from the leather bag she carried over her shoulder. Paul produced his from the inside pocket of his coat as they walked through the doors to be greeted by a smartly dressed woman who looked to be in her fifties and stood about five foot six.

"Welcome to Fairway View," she greeted, with a smile that June thought looked practiced, "are you looking for accommodation?" she asked cheerfully before spotting the jointly proffered warrant cards.

Paul caught a slight trace of West Country in the woman's voice and he thought she had probably tried hard to lose it.

"No.....I'm Inspector Paul Manley and this is Constable June Kelly," answered Paul, "we were hoping to have a word with David Carver, we understand he's the owner of the property."

The woman appeared a little miffed at Paul's remark, "It's our property Inspector, I'm Mrs. Sandra Carver, joint owner and proprietor of Fairway View with my husband. Can I ask what you wish to see him about?"

"Yes of course, Mrs. Carver." Paul saw no point in not telling her the reason for their visit. "It's concerning the robbery at his jewellery shop in 1989, there's been a development."

The new Mrs. Carver seemed taken aback by Paul's statement. "Good Lord! After all this time, well you'd better come in Inspector."

Mrs. Carver stepped aside to allow June and Paul to walk beside her. "My husband is in the office, we can talk in there," she said, leading them through into a large room, the door of which was situated behind a modern glass and stainless-steel reception counter that curved out in an arc from the far side of the office door.

The desk supported a telephone and computer and could have graced the lobby of a five-star hotel, but June thought its ultra-modern design, although impressive, clashed with, rather than complemented the Georgian grace of the building's exterior. Behind the desk, to the right of the office door was a large painting of a golfer playing his ball out of a bunker. Paul recognised the golfer's face but couldn't put a name to it, something that would bug him until he remembered, the painting itself was obviously an original artwork and looked expensive; business couldn't be too bad.

Inside the office, David Carver was seated behind yet another impressive desk but this time of antique design. Indeed, the whole office was much more traditionally furnished than the reception area and even Paul felt it was more in keeping with the rest of the property. It occurred to him that perhaps the Carvers had very different tastes from each other.

Carver appeared engrossed in whatever it was he was doing and didn't look up until his wife announced, "There are some police officers here to see us David, I said we could talk in here, I think there are guests in the lounge and the conservatory."

Paul and June exchanged glances and smiled at the way Mrs. Carver had told her husband they were there to see them both rather than just her husband as they had stated.

David Carver looked up smiling but Paul had the feeling he was not best pleased to be interrupted.

"Yes of course, do sit down, how can I help you.....ah"

"Inspector Paul Manley, and this is Constable Kelly," Paul finished for him.

Paul had introduced himself and June to Mr. Carver as Mrs. Carver had failed to do so. He didn't take to the woman but wasn't sure why; perhaps it was because she assumed that they were there to see the two of them, even though he had clearly stated that it was Mr. Carver they wanted to see or perhaps it was because she referred to them as "some police officers," even though she knew both their names and rank. Whatever it was, Paul sensed hostility from her beneath the outward cheerfulness.

There was an imposing leather chair to the left of the desk and Mrs. Carver took up residence in it and looked at them expectantly while they sat in the two reproduction Chippendale chairs that were in front of and facing the desk. June rested her bag on the floor beside her chair after retrieving a notebook and pen from it.

"Firstly," began Paul, "I'd like to verify that you are the David Carver who was joint owner of a jewellery business with your wife in Clevedon in 1989."

"That's right, yes, I was in business with my first wife Sylvia. Is this to do with the robbery? It was a very long time ago."

"The robbery yes......And the murder of your wife, Mr. Carver."

"Well yes of course.....that to. It was a horrible time for me Inspector, I've tried hard to put it all behind me; I don't have the nightmares anymore but the horror of it is still there, lurking below the surface. I almost died myself you understand."

"My husband was under the doctor for depression for some time after it happened Inspector," interjected Mrs. Carver in defence of her husband.

Paul had the feeling she had spoken more to remind every one of her presence rather than to give her husband support.

Carver looked nervously at his second wife as she spoke, irked that she felt it necessary to speak of his depression, but her face showed no emotion.

"When did the two of you first meet?" enquired Paul.

Is when my husband and I met important inspector?"

"No Mrs. Carver, probably not but I'm a policeman, I ask questions, it's my job," he replied, interpreting their reluctance to answer the question as confirmation they had been seeing each other before Sylvia's death.

Paul glanced sideways at her as he spoke, trying unsuccessfully to size the woman up. He wasn't sure whether the hostility he sensed was aimed towards them or her husband. The interview had not started the way he had expected. He'd imagined that David Carver would have been excited and full of questions along the lines of, "Does this mean you've found the men that killed my wife?" but instead, he seemed guarded, uncertain of how he should react, and possibly a little resentful that his new wife had involved herself.

"Aren't you curious to know why we're here Mr. Carver? I thought you would have been full of question for me."

"Well of course I'm curious Inspector, but you've caught me off guard as it were, I'm trying to get the staff wages sorted out and this is the last thing I was expecting after all this time. So why are you here? What developments have there been? Have you found the jewels?"

Paul watch the man carefully as he said, "No, not the jewels, but we have found your boat."

"What....you....what makes you think it's my boat you've found? I mean how can you tell after all this time?"

"Well we're pretty sure it's yours, but you could help us with that if you would. Do you have any photographs of the boat at all?"

"No....I don't think so."

"Yes, of course you have David." Mrs. Carver cut in once again. "Your old photograph album's are upstairs, I'm sure there are lots of pictures of it in there, my word, this does seem to have knocked you for six dear." she said, smiling somewhat awkwardly at her husband, "I'll go and get it, shall I? I know where it is."

Mrs. Carver stood up and walked towards the door quickening her steps half way as if suddenly realising that she might miss something if she took too long.

So the hostility wasn't aimed solely at them thought Paul, glancing at June, it was split between them, some of it clearly aimed her husband's way. Perhaps all wasn't sweetness and light in the new Carver household.

"Yes...yes of course, thank you dear, that would be great," said Carver, but his wife had already left the room before he had finished speaking.

He looked at Paul after his wife had left the room and continued, "I sorry Inspector, this has taken me aback a bit, I'll get my head in gear in a minute. Where did you find her.....the boat."

"Was there anything distinctive about her that could help us to identify her?" asked Paul, not wishing to answer David Carver's question just yet.

"No, not that I can think of, to tell the truth, I've almost forgotten what she looked like, where did you say you found her?

"At the time, after the robbery, were you surprised that she was never recovered?"

"No not really......it's easy enough to give a boat a new coat of paint and re-name her, the bastards probably got a good price for her."

"Maybe so Mr. Carver but thieves don't usually bother too much about their getaway vehicle; cars are usually found burnt out....your boat wasn't found at all....until now."

"Well I can't say that I thought about it at the time and you still haven't told me where she was found."

Mrs. Carver returned to the room, triumphantly clutching a large brown photograph album that she handed directly to Paul, opened to a page containing what were obviously holiday snaps. The pictures were several group shots, taken either with a small boat in the background or with the people actually standing on the boat. Most of the pictures included images of Sylvia, some with David in shot, the others probably taken by David. The ones with David in mostly had him standing beside his wife with his arm around her and they looked like a happy couple. One in particular caught Paul's eye. He stood up and turning the album around, showed the picture to David Caver.

"Can you tell what that is, Mr. Carver?" Paul asked pointing, "I can't quite make it out."

Paul placed the album on the desk in front of Carver who stood up and leaned over to inspect the photograph more closely. Paul had been indicating a small plaque that was just visible behind the couple being photographed. They were stood either side of the door leading into the boat's interior, turned slightly towards each other and smiling at the camera.

After a considerable hesitation during which Paul thought the man was contemplating a lie, David Carver replied, "Oh, that's a small plaque with my wife's name on it Inspector. Apparently, it was a name plate that she had on her bedroom door when she was a teenager living with her parents. She'd always kept it and when we named the boat after her we screwed it there, just above the cabin door. Don't tell me that's still on her."

"Yes it is......And I think that removes any doubt about the boat we have being yours, don't you agree Mr. Carver?"

"Well I suppose it does Inspector. You still haven't said where you found it, is it a secret or something?"

"No, no secret, it's at the bottom of the Bristol Channel," confirmed Paul.

"Oh...right, yes, I suppose those bastards must have scuttled her after dumping me overboard, no wonder she was never found."

"Why do you think they would have scuttled her?"

"Well I don't know, I can't think of any reason, but you said she was at the bottom of the channel, so I suppose they must have, mustn't they?"

"Unless you think she hit an iceberg Inspector," cut in Mrs. Carver sarcastically, "but I suppose they sank her for the same reason you find getaway cars burnt out inspector, to destroy evidence."

"Your right Mrs. Carver and no, I don't think she struck an iceberg but neither do I think the two men who took your husband hostage scuttled her either, because there's a little more to it than that."

"How do mean, more to it?" asked David.

"Well if they scuttled her after dumping you overboard, how would they have made it to shore?"

"Well perhaps they had another boat. Yes that's it! They must have met up with someone else in another boat."

"But why scuttle her at all? They could have just left her drifting, there wouldn't have been any more evidence on the boat than at the shop."

"Well who knows what goes on in the criminal mind Inspector, they just thought it would be better if she wasn't found I suppose. I doubt there's any more to it than that."

"Oh I'm afraid there's a lot more to it than that Mr. Carver and we can rule out any thought that the two men you spoke of sank her deliberately."

Carver's brow furrowed with lines. "Why do you say that?"

"Because they were both still in the boat when we found it, that's why."

There was a definite intake of breath from Mrs. Carver at Paul's words. "But....that doesn't make any sense Inspector, how could they still be on board?" Mrs. Carver looked as if she had just smelt something nasty. "It must have been an accident of some sort then, they must have got into some difficulties and the boat sank, surely," she insisted, obviously aware of the implications.

"The men were found in the cabin of the boat, Mrs. Carver and I can't think of any scenario where they would stay on board if she was sinking, can you? And there's the other thing."

"What other thing?"

"If the boat sank with the two men still on board, where is the jewellery that they stole? It's not on the boat with them."

Mrs. Carver stared at Paul and then turned to her husband, a long list of questions etched on her face. "David?"

Her husband returned her gaze and shrugged his shoulders. "Well I don't know, I was in the water swimming for my life! remember. Perhaps the one they left behind with my wife met up with them, they would have had to get together some time to split up the takings wouldn't they? He must have double-crossed them when they came ashore to pick him up, he must have shot them and then taken the boat out to sea again and sunk it with their bodies on board."

Mr. Carver took up residence in his chair again trying to appear relaxed but not fooling anyone.

"I didn't mention anything about them being shot," observed Paul, staring intently at Carver.

"They were armed Inspector, one of them anyway, It's natural for me to assume they were shot."

Carver's wife seemed genuinely relieved, "Yes of course....there you are Inspector, David's solved the mystery for you. The two men you found in the boat didn't choose their accomplice very carefully, did they? He shot them and then sank the boat."

"And how did he get ashore with the jewels?"

"Oh! now wait a minute......I can't believe I forgot about it, there was a small inflatable life raft in the deck locker, only a small thing, but he could have made it ashore with the jewels in that."

It was a lie, but Carver was desperate to find an explanation that would satisfy the Inspector, the only trouble was that everyone in the room could tell it was lie. Carver looked at their faces and knew they didn't believe him.

"That's the only explanation I can think of Inspector," he said lowering his gaze.

"Well, that's if he knew it was there, of course," pointed out Paul.

"Well I think that explains everything Inspector....don't you?" snapped Mrs. Carver. Anxious now for their visitors to leave and stop questioning her husband. She had some questions of her own for him but they could wait until the police had gone.

"It's possible," answered Paul, "but the whole operation seems odd right from the beginning. Why choose a boat as a getaway vehicle in the first place, they're not exactly going to outrun anyone in it are they, no, I don't think we have any of the answers yet Mrs. Carver but we'll get them, you can count on that."

"Well if you ask me Inspector," said Mrs. Carver, her West Country accent becoming more evident now, "They chose to use the boat simply so that they could throw poor David overboard, surely you can see that."

"We're going to be looking at all the possible scenarios Mrs. Carver, you can bank on that."

Carver stood up abruptly. "Thank you for letting me know my boat has turned up Inspector but if there's nothing else I really do have to get these wages sorted."

Sandra Carver stood as soon as her husband was on his feet,

"Well I think that's all for now," said Paul, also standing and nodding to them both in turn. "Mr. Carver......Mrs. Carver. We'll keep you informed of any future developments as and when."

"Well that's very reassuring Inspector," said Mrs. Carver already on her feet and indicating the door.

June was the last to stand and she put her notebook back in her bag as Mrs. Carver ushered them towards the door.

As Paul and June retraced their steps to the car and drove back to the station June asked, "Do you really think he was involved, Guv?"

"It seems the most likely scenario to me June, and I got the impression that he was a little reluctant to identify the boat and it was an obvious lie about the inflatable, you could see it in his face, but I'm keeping an open mind at the moment. Let's get back and see if the team have got anything interesting to tell us."

* * * * * * * * * *

Back at the station Paul was pleased to see that everyone had at least something to add to their pool of knowledge. After electing to give the hot-chocolate from the machine a go, rather than the brown liquid that tried to impersonate coffee, he stood in front of the white boards expectantly, polystyrene cup in one hand and black marker pen in the other.

"Well who's going to start.....Reg. Have you got anything?"

"Nothing much I'm afraid Guv. They can't even give us a cause of death; if they were shot it wasn't in the head and as we know the divers didn't find any bullets or shell casings in the boat. The only slight ray of light is the gold watch found on one of the bodies, it's an old Rolex. They managed to get the serial number from it and I've contacted Goldsmiths, they're our nearest Rolex supplier and a very helpful manager there is contacting Rolex for me to see who first purchased the watch. Of course, our friend on the boat may not have been the first owner, lots of Rolex watches change hands on the second-hand market, in which case we could be up a creek so to speak, but fingers crossed Guv."

"Nothing else at all Reg?"

"Sorry Guv, that's it, there was no inscription or anything and even if there had been, it may not have related to our victim, as I say, it may have had several owners."

"John, anything from the divers?"

"Nothing from the two who found it and as you know the police divers, as Reg. just said, had a good feel around for any possible weapons or bullet casings but found nothing, and they failed to find any reason that would account for the boat sinking either.

Don't you just open sea-cocks or something?" asked Derrick.

"That's right but they said the conditions down there were pretty bad and they failed to get to the sea-cocks. They say that the only way to find out any more would be to bring her up and unless we all have a wip-round for the money I can't see anything happening on that front....unless Reg is willing to dig into his savings."

"Or we could use Reg's holiday fund to pay for it," joked Phillip.

"Has anyone got anything useful for me?" pleaded Paul.

"Not sure Guv, but maybe," answered Peter, "I traced Carver's solicitor, also a Peter...Peter Edwards, he's Carver's solicitor now, although at the time of the robbery it would have been his father Adrian Edwards. They're based here in town but his secretary said he's gone away for a couple of days and won't be back until Monday; I've made an appointment for someone to see him that morning."

"Well that's something......Phillip... did you turn up anything in the old files?"

"Nothing new really, unless you count a more detailed history of Sylvia's side of the family. Wealthy by all accounts, her father was German of Jewish decent, Karl Wagner, a diamond merchant and jeweller. His first wife died young in Germany and Karl must have seen the ways things were going and had the right connections. He managed to get out of Germany late in 1935 and set up in business over here. He married his second wife Anne, Sylvia's mother, in 1952 but although Anne was much younger than Karl she died before him in 1980 aged 43. Either he was very unlucky in his choice of life partner or he was quietly bumping them off. Sylvia herself was born in 1962 but she had an elder brother, Marcus, who was born three years earlier in 1959. Sylvia married our Mr. Carver in 1981."

"So....Carver may have been on to inherit a large sum if there was money in his wife's family. We certainly need to clarify things with his solicitor."

June passed Paul some papers, "What's this June?" he asked.

"A list of all the items stolen from the shop Guv...or at least, all the items the insurers paid out on. Sylvia seems to have had quite a collection of antique jewellery entirely separate from the shops stock, museum quality a lot of it Guv, and that's got to have been hard for them to shift."

"It may well have all been broken down and sold in bits, June, but go through the list and check to see if any of it has ever surfaced at any time since then."

"Did anyone find out about where the boat was kept or if there was ever a tender?" asked Paul as he pinned up the list of stolen items.

One of the new men on the team, Ben Horrocks spoke up, "Giles and I asked around Guv, but everything has changed since then, it was before the new marina was built and we couldn't even find anyone who remembered the old jetty. The house the jetty belonged to is owned by new people who don't use the boathouse and say they know nothing about any jetty."

"OK, that's good work so far, but let's keep at it," finished Paul., and with the briefing over everyone set about their tasks.

Paul noticed the mood amongst the team had brightened

considerably now they had something to get their teeth into, it would seem that murder is good for moral.

Chapter 4

June was in the kitchen looking though her cupboards, desperate to find something tasty to eat that wouldn't take hours to cook. It wasn't looking promising and she was just considering opting for yet another take-away when there was a knock at her door.

She knew it had to be John from upstairs. They shared the front door to the house and anyone visiting would have rung one of the two bells outside. Inside the front door there was a small lobby that originally would have opened onto a hallway and a flight of stairs.

When the property had been split into flats, the stairs had been partitioned off from the hall and a front door fitted at the bottom that provided access to the upstairs flat. Access to June's flat was through what would have been the door into the original front room and at the end of the stairs the hallway had been blocked across completely separating the two flats.

June opened the door. "Hello June," greeted John, smiling.

He had decided in the end not to go to the expense of purchasing the genuine article. "I've managed to get hold of the perfume you wanted," he declared, looking over June's shoulder into her flat. "Do you want to see it?"

It was obvious from his manner that he expected to be invited in and it would have been rude not to, so June stepped aside, "Come in John," she said, in as friendly a voice as she could muster.

John walked in and after a brief perusal of the room, took a package out of his pocket and presented it to June. "Thirty-Eight I'm afraid, but it's over sixty in the shops, is that OK?"

June accepted the package from him and opened it. She took off the cap and sprayed a little of the contents on her wrist before holding it up to her nose and inhaling the fragrance.

June had always prided herself on having a good palate and a keen sense of smell. The aroma was pleasant and she did think it was the same or at least very similar to what she had in her handbag but she just wasn't sure if it smelt exactly the same or not. Maybe the doubt she had about the product to start with was clouding her judgement.

"Unfortunately, I think I might be going down with a bit of a cold," she said, "but it seems OK, how on earth did you get it so cheap?"

"I've a brother in the trade," he said.

It was only a white lie, his brother ran a market stall and basically sold anything he could get hold of, including the odd fake perfume.

June went over to her bag which was on the dining table at the back of what had originally been two large separate rooms, but now served as a lounge cum kitchen diner.

She looked in her purse and was please that she had just enough to pay for the perfume, "That's really great John, thank you," she said, as she passed him the money.

"Have you eaten yet this evening?" asked John. "If not, perhaps we could try that new restaurant that's opened on the Fishponds Road."

June just looked back at him blankly and he got the message. "Sorry June, force of habit if I'm with an attractive woman."

June ushered him towards the door. "I'm sorry John, thank you for getting the perfume but I think you should leave now."

For a moment, June wondered whether she was going to have trouble getting him to leave but he walked to the door with no hesitation, only turning back when he was in the hall to say, "Please don't hold my persistence against me June, I'm not a bad guy. Let me know when you run out of perfume, I'll get you some more."

June closed the door behind her neighbour then turned and leaned backwards against it, unable to make up her mind what to think of him. On the surface he seemed pleasant enough but he was obviously up to no good somewhere. She felt a slight tinge of guilt but she was definitely going to tell Paul of her suspicions. She would have liked to have done a bit of investigating herself but they were very busy with the Carver investigation at the moment and she was sure Paul would simply tell her to pass on what she knew to Trading Standards and perhaps that was her best course of action.

* * * * * * * * * * *

Roland Ratchford was into his third week of following the man, and he was becoming bored, although it was by no means the longest he had ever followed anyone. He had once stayed on the trail of a woman for ten weeks before seeing anything significant, but this chap was an accountant with what was beginning to look like the most uneventful life imaginable, he almost felt sorry for the man.

The target had been in the block of flats for three hours, far longer than he would normally spend with any of his clients so maybe the man's wife had been right to have him followed by a private enquiry agent.

Ratchford had to grab his camera off the passenger seat quickly as the man emerged from the entrance to the flats in the company of another man, a young man. He had expected a woman and at first Ratchford thought his vigilance was to be in vain once again, but then he noticed how close the two men were, and as his target opened the door of his car to get in the two men kissed, quickly and discreetly, but not so quickly as to prevent Ratchford's camera capturing the moment.

Got you, thought Ratchford smiling to himself. He reached for his mobile phone and called the man's wife, not to share the husband's secret with her, not yet anyway, but to tell her he had news and to make an appointment to see her.

Ratchford ran his private enquiry business from home and today the wife who had employed him to discover whether or not her husband was seeing another woman was sitting opposite him, anxiously awaiting his report.

"Well, go on, give me the bad news," pleaded Mrs. Bryant, on the edge of tears, "is she very young?"

"You want the bad news you say," said Ratchford handing her a single sheet of A4 paper.

"Yes.....what's this," she asked, extending a shaky left hand to take it from him while wiping away a tear with her right.

"It's your invoice for my services over the past month, it comes to £3,400, plus VAT of course. I think you'll find that that is in line with the agreement we had."

"Yes, I'm sure your bill is correct Mr. Ratchford, but what about the details of my husband's affair, that was bad news I as referring to, who is the woman?"

"I will supply you with a written report of my findings if you want, of course, but I can assure you, Mrs. Bryant, your husband is most certainly not having an affair."

Mrs. Bryant looked puzzled, "But I was sure there was something going on, I could sense that he was hiding something from me.....are you absolutely sure he's not seeing anyone?...I can pay you for longer if needs be."

"That really won't be necessary. Look Mrs. Bryant, I didn't say your husband wasn't keeping anything from you, it's just that it's not an affair."

"What then?" she exclaimed, not sure now whether to be pleased or alarmed by the new development.

"Your husband is in the habit of meeting up with some old friends from college, they visit a club together and play poker, they're all very discreet about it. I imagine that he doesn't think the image of a gambling accountant would be good for business. Now, I have a contact in the club and he assures me that although the stakes are quite high, it is nothing that your husband can't afford. He's not an addict or anything like that, he just enjoys playing poker.

"Now I suspect that he feels you would disapprove of him playing cards for money and that is why he has kept it from you."

"Is he getting into debt?" she asked, taking another tissue from her bag.

"Good Lord no. My contact tells me that, like most gamblers, he loses more than he wins and although, as I said, the stakes are quite high, it is nothing he can't afford, and the club is a very respectable one with a lot of highly influential and high profile people as members. They wouldn't allow any of their members to get in over their heads. There really is nothing for you to worry about.

"Now I suggest you go home, have a nice strong cup of coffee and put all these silly fears behind you."

Mrs. Bryant stood up and looked for somewhere to dispose of the damp tissue she held in her hand. Ratchford picked up his waste paper basket and held it out as dropped the tissue delicately into it.

She extended her hand for Ratchford to shake, "That you Roland, do you mind me calling you Roland, you have been a big help to me and I appreciate it."

"I'm only too pleased to have been of help, but there is one way you could possibly help me in return."

"Of course.......just name it."

"Well, if you ever hear of anyone who would or could benefit from my services....."

Mrs. Bryant spoke before Ratchford could finish his sentence, "I will recommend you, of course......now how would you like me to settle my account?......personally I would prefer to pay in cash, but that would have to be in two or three instalments I'm afraid, would that be OK?"

"Yes of course," said Ratchford, rising from his chair to show Mrs. Bryant to the door. "You can just drop an envelope through the door if I'm not here," he said grabbing the door handle with his right hand and gently resting his left on Mrs. Bryant's arm to guide her.

After being shown her out of the front door Mrs. Bryant shook Ratchford's hand and thanked him again.

Closing the door behind her, Ratchford returned to the room he used as an office and pressed a button on the intercom machine, "Would you like to join me in my office now Mr. Bryant, I trust that you heard your wife and I clearly in there?"

Ratchford sat and waited for his client's husband to join him. Mrs. Bryant was in her early thirties, five foot four and attractive, the man who now entered the room was mid-forties, six-foot-tall with narrow features and a somewhat gaunt appearance. He was one of those people who just never look completely well.

He sat opposite Ratchford with a puzzled look on his face and asked, "Why would you do that?"

"Why would I do what?"

"Accept money from my wife to follow me and see if I was having an affair...and then lie to her about your findings."

"Well, to protect your marriage and your reputation as a trustworthy accountant of course."

"I repeat my question Mr. Ratchford, I'm not stupid....Why? You must want something?"

"We are both business men Mr. Bryant, your business deals with money, my business on the other hand deals with information. You have a very extensive and influential clientele. Now there will be times when it would be useful for me to know something about those people's finances, or private lives and you could furnish me with that information."

"Oh I see! And if I refuse to give you this information on my clients, you will tell my wife I'm having an affair. Well I'm not going to do it, I'm not doing anything illegal and I think my wife will forgive me, our marriage is a strong one, we love each other you see. So not to put too fine a point it, you can take your dirty little proposition and shove it where the sun doesn't shine."

John Bryant got up to leave.

"But it's not just an affair is it John? How old are you? Mid-forties is it? How old is Peter? He doesn't look more than nineteen or twenty to me. How long have you and Peter been seeing each other I wonder, must have been a while if you've set him up in his own little flat and are paying his rent.

"You may be right when you say your wife would forgive you an affair...an affair with another woman maybe but a young man, maybe a very young man if you've been seeing him a few years.......Do you think she'll forgive that...and the tabloids will have a field day with it. I think you had better sit down again, don't you?"

Bryant's face looked even more haggard than usual as he re-took his seat.

"That's more sensible, now the first thing I want is a complete list of your present and any past clients, and you will of course keep it updated if you acquire any more. Now cheer up, it's always possible that you'll not hear from me again for ages....of course, it is always possible I shall ring you tomorrow, it just depends how things pan out. Oh I almost forgot, the other thing I shall require is a regular payment of.....what shall we say.....hundred pounds a month. That's not a lot to keep your marriage and your reputation, is it."

Bryant was stunned. "My God! What are you...a bargain basement blackmailer, one hundred pounds a month," Bryant started to laugh, "what sort of blackmailer askes for one hundred pounds a month. That's less than twenty five a week....Good God! I tip more than that if I go out for the night."

Ratchford was angered by Bryant's reaction, "I suggest you run your business and let me run mine Mr. Bryant, I don't take kindly to perverts laughing at me...I might start asking for more if you keep it up. Now I think that concludes our business for today." He rose from his chair to see Bryant out. "Get that list to me in the next couple of days together with your first payment and the world can stay oblivious to your dirty little secret."

Ratchford saw Bryant to the door and went into the front room. He poured himself a whiskey and sitting in his favorite wing chair, picked up the paper to read, feeling rather satisfied with the day's outcome.

As he turned over the first page of the newspaper his interest was instantly aroused by an article on page two. Two bodies had been discovered in a sunken cabin cruiser in the Bristol Channel, and police were linking it to the murder of Sylvia Carver and the attempted murder of David Carver some twenty six years ago.

Well, well, thought Ratchford, Sylvia and David Carver, there were names from the past.

* * * * * * * * * *

David Carver rose from his desk to attend to the reception bell that had just rung. As he left the office and took his place behind the reception desk, he adjusted the position of the guest book that was open on the counter hoping that his action looked natural. In fact, he took the opportunity to check the name of the last guest to sign in because he was the one who had rung the bell and was now standing at the desk. The man was smiling in a way that Carver felt was forced. Carver's wife had been the one who had signed him in early that morning, She had shown him to his room, but although she had told her husband the man's name he had completely forgotten it.

"Good morning, Mr. Ratchford isn't it, is there something I can help you with? I hope you've settled in all right."

"Yes, hello David," Ratchford replied.

Carver was taken off guard by the use of his first name and he studied the man's face more intently to see if recognition would kick in, but no, the man didn't seem familiar at all.

"I realise that you don't remember me David, but I actually knew you and your wife some years ago."

Carver's brow furrowed, "I'm sorry, you say you know Sandra and I? Have you stayed here before?"

Roland Ratchford smiled back at David Carver with some

satisfaction and said, "No, no David, you misunderstand, not your present wife Sandra, your first wife, Sylvia; that was such a tragedy what happened to her...appalling....it must have taken you a long time to get over it."

Carver felt a little uneasy and was somewhat irked by the man's attitude but was at a loss to reason exactly why. "Oh, I see....were you in the jewellery business or something, is that how you knew us?"

"More of the "or something," really, I'm a private inquiry agent, missing people, divorces, that kind of thing, you know. I was hoping to have a word with you in private actually, on a rather delicate matter. Maybe now that your present wife is out, this would be a good time."

Carver just looked back blankly. "It's concerning the fact that the police appear to have discovered the whereabouts of your old boat," Ratchford continued, "Unbelievable after all this time, isn't it? I suppose it came as quite a shock to you when you found out."

Carver was taken aback and his mood changed. "Well I fail to understand what any of this has to do with you...Mr." He had to look at the reception book a second time....."Ratchford...I don't recognise you and I don't recall having dealings with anyone of your name or profession, if that's what it is."

"Look, we seem to have got off on the wrong foot," said Ratchford, trying to get things back onto a more friendly footing. "I know it must have been a bit of a shock for you after all this time, a nasty shock I imagine, the police finding it like that," said Ratchford, who, after studying the puzzled expression on Carvers face continued,

"It must have brought back all those dreadful memories of the attempt on your life and the brutal murder of your wife and all. I can't begin to imagine what must be going through your head right now. Is there somewhere we could chat, your office perhaps," continued Ratchford, indicating the room Carver had emerged from. "Now might be a good time for both of us. You, because your present good lady is at the hairdresser's and me because I want to get down to business as quickly as possible."

"Business? What business?"

Carver thought briefly about throwing the man out. His general manner was very irritating, but he wondered whether it would be better to hear what he had to say. What the hell could this man know about the discovery of his boat, or it's disappearance for that matter? If he had known them back then, in what capacity had it been and why didn't he remember the man. He decided it would be prudent to hear what he had to say, despite the fact that the man's manner annoyed him. He could always have the satisfaction of throwing him out afterwards.

"You can have ten minutes to say what you have to say and then I would like you to leave," said Carver as he turned and retraced his steps into the office, allowing Ratchford to follow.

"Good decision David," said Ratchford, reinforcing Carver's perception of a most disagreeable man. "I'm sure you would prefer me to speak to you about the photographs I have and the identity of the bodies found in your boat, rather than to the police."

As Ratchford followed David behind the reception desk to get to his office he ran his finger along the edge of the desk and then examined it approvingly, "I have to say you do keep the place nice and clean, David or is that Sandra's influence?"

Carver ignored the remark and took up residence in the chair behind his office desk before indicating that his rude and unwelcome guest should sit in one of the two wooden chairs facing it.

Ratchford however, ignored the suggestion and sat in the more comfortable looking leather chair to the side of it, crossing his legs in a relaxed manner that in no way matched Carver's somewhat angry state of mind.

"Come on then, let's hear what you think the police would be so interested in," barked Carver, the desire to hear what the man had to say temporarily overcoming the irritation that the man's demeanor caused in him.

"OK David, I'll start at the beginning." Ratchford leaned back in the chair and re-crossed his legs. "I've already told you that I am a private enquiry agent. Well back in 1989, you remember that year I expect, your wife Sylvia employed me to keep an eye on you for a while. She was suspicious that you were seeing someone on the side, so she wanted me to follow you and see what you were up to."

The colour had drained somewhat from Carvers face as he sat in silence and listened to the man speak. It was bringing back memories that he would prefer not to recall and he adjusted his position in the chair several times but failed to find a more comfortable position.

"On the nights you were supposed to be at your club playing bridge, you were in fact in the company of a lady, a lady who I believe is now the new Mrs. Carver."

There was a pause during which Ratchford waited for Carver to reply but he showed no signs of doing so.

Ratchford continued, "There were however, a couple of club nights when instead of seeing your, what shall we call her, bit on the side, you had meetings with a couple of rather unsavoury looking gentlemen in a pub. Now it's true that I was never within earshot of those meetings but I was in the habit of photographing everything when I was on surveillance, so I snapped, not only quite a few of you and your lady friend, but I also took some good pics of the men in the pub."

Carver was astonished to hear that Sylvia had been having him followed but decided to call Ratchford's bluff. "So I met some friends in a pub for a drink, wow! the police won't know what's hit them when they hear about that. Is that really what you've wasted my time over? Some pictures of me with the woman who later became my wife and a couple of me having a drink in a pub with a couple of acquaintances. Goodbye Mr. Ratchford."

Carver stood up, ready to show his unwelcome visitor the door.

Ratchford however, showed no signs of moving, "Oh believe me there's more to it than that. I was curious at the time, the meetings didn't seem the way you describe them, as friends having a drink, they appeared much more clandestine and conspiratorial then that to me, even back then I thought it looked as if the three of you were planning something.

"So the second time you met I followed them after your meeting was over and discovered their names, Adrian Fellows and Clive Lowe; do the names ring any bells? Then I did some asking around and found out that one of them had a criminal record for burglary and shop lifting.

Who would have thought....Adrian and Clive....posh sounding names for low-lifes don't you think? What on earth could the three of you be planning? You with your bit on the side and a rich wife, meeting with two known criminals, well I can tell you, it all smelt a bit fishy to me."

Carver sat down again and listened in silence.

"Now these meetings took place only a month before the robbery at your shop and I was going to come and see you when things had quietened down and you had the insurance money sorted.

" I was a little confused by the apparent attempt on your life though, that threw me a bit.

"You didn't have to stage that, although I suppose it did give the whole thing a more authentic feel but it was pretty dangerous nevertheless, well unless you had a dinghy or something of course. As for having your wife killed, that was a bit ruthless and over the top in my opinion but I suppose it meant that you didn't have to share the insurance money with her, and you'd get full control of the business and her money and of course you wouldn't have to go through a costly divorce before marrying your bit on the side. A win win for you wasn't it?

"Anyway, I kept a pretty close eye on you after that for a long time, waiting for you to meet those two again and do the splitting up of the spoils and all, but they never showed up. I began to suspect that they had double crossed you and that the attempt on your life hadn't been staged at all but was a genuine attempt. I almost felt sorry for you at one time. That of course meant that you weren't going to get your pay-out from the sale of the jewels, just the insurance money."

"If you're implying that I had anything to do with the robbery or my wife's murder you must be barking mad!"

"Well I wasn't sure what to do then, was I? I could still of approached you for some cash of course but I had expected you to have the insurance money and a share of the lute and an inheritance.

"You were lucky, at that time I wasn't too badly off myself, business was going well, I do find people with secrets to keep can be very generous, so I decided to leave you on the back burner for a while and see how things would pan out. After that, I guess I just had so many other lucrative deals going down, you sort of got, not forgotten exactly, but pushed down lower in the list as it were, put on hold if you like and then I forgot about you altogether, until I read the news about your boat being found.

But now, wow! what a turn up. Seems like you weren't the one double crossed after all, you crafty old sod. You not only had the whole thing planned from the beginning but you turned the tables on them and got away with the whole bloody lot, the jewels, the insurance money, you rid yourself of your wife and I bet you even had a pay-out on her life insurance. I thought you'd been double-crossed and all the time you'd been laughing all the way to the bank. Well done you, I say!

"Well now you can share some of your good fortune with me. We'll start with a small payment, twenty grand shall we say, that shouldn't be too difficult for you to put your hands on quick and we can see how we go from there."

All this time Carver had sat and listened in silence to what Ratchford had to say. Now he stood up and placed the palms of both hands flat on the desk, leaned forward and said, "You're stark staring raving mad! Twenty grand! You're not going to get one penny out of me for a cock-and-bull story like that. If you don't go and pack your bag and get out of my house before my wife returns, I'm going to be the one calling the police. Blackmail is a serious offence and from what I've just heard it sounds like something you make a habit of. And just so that we are clear on the point, I had nothing to do with the robbery, and I certainly didn't plan my wife's murder; but if I ever see your stupid face again I may well murder you..... *now get out!*"

Carver now came around from behind the desk and approached Ratchford who also stood up, thinking for a moment that Carver was going to physically attack him, not that that would have been a problem. Ratchford was used to being physically attacked and could handle himself pretty well, even against people who were trained in fighting. Carver would have been no problem but it didn't come to that.

Realising that he had overstayed his welcome Ratchford started towards the door but said as he walked, "Good performance David, you almost have me believing you, but we both know the truth really. I'll leave you to think about things for a day or two and then we can speak again, when you've calmed down and thought about how much you have to lose if the police match the identity of the men in your boat to the photographs I took of you and your friends. I'm sure you'll see things more clearly."

Ratchford was almost at the door and Carver put a hand on his back between his shoulder blades and pushed him though it sharply, catching Ratchford unawares and causing him to stumble.

Ratchford put both hands in the air as he recovered as if someone was holding a gun on him, "All right, all right. Keep your shirt on, I'm going, but I hope you take the time to reconsider your rash decision today. It'll be in both our interests to come to an arrangement."

Carver pushed him again, this time towards the stairs. "Just pack your stuff and go."

A man and a woman emerged cautiously from the front lounge, curious to see what the commotion was and the man enquired, "Is everything all right Mr. Carver?"

"Nothing to worry yourselves about Mr. Clark...Mrs. Clark, this gentleman was just leaving."

The couple looked at Ratchford, sizing him up and deciding, that in this case discretion was the better part of valour, and they prepared to return to the room they had just left. "If you're sure Mr. Carver."

Ratchford doffed an imaginary hat at the couple and continued upstairs for his things while Carver led Mr. and Mrs. Clark back into the lounge. "I'm sorry about that but I'm afraid not all our guests are as nice as you. I hope you are both enjoying your stay, I expected you both to be out on the golf-course this morning."

"Oh no, Ernest is taking me into Bath shopping after lunch, but we have both arranged a game for tomorrow. How about you Mr. Carver, you play don't you?"

"When I can find the time, which isn't too often these days I'm afraid."

Carver and the Clarks continued their conversation in the lounge for a while longer until Carver heard Ratchford descend the stairs again and exit the front door, at which time he made his excuses and returned to the office deep in thought.

This was turning into a most unpleasant week with a series of unexpected and unwelcome news and events.

Although this Ratchford was gone for now, Carver was under no illusions about the probability that he would turn up again with more threats and demands for money. He had to give some serious thought to how best to handle the man.

Two hours after Ratchford had packed his bags and left Fairway View, Carver's wife Sandra returned from the hairdresser's, carrying bags.

"I've bought some new coat hangers on the way home and picked up some more sausages and bacon from the farm shop," she told her husband as he took one of the bags from her and followed her into the kitchen. "I think some of our guests think we supply complimentary coat hangers along with the shower gel and shampoo, perhaps you could distribute the new ones out as and when this lot leave. Has anything happened while I've been out? You seem a bit flustered."

Carver filled the kettle preparing to make them both a cup of coffee. "As a matter of fact, there is something you should know about," he said, wondering how best to explain the situation regarding Ratchford to his wife.

He loved her dearly, far more than he had ever loved Sylvia and he believed she loved him but she wasn't an easy woman to keep happy. She needed everything to run smoothly and could easily get angry and upset if it didn't. The situation with Ratchford would upset her for sure, they rarely talked about their lives before they married. Although he had been seeing Sandra since before the robbery and she knew all about the events of 1989, it had always been a taboo subject for discussion.

Because they had been seeing each other when Sylvia was murdered, Sandra had felt as if they were in some way responsible and it had been some time before she was able to put the feeling of guilt behind her and agree to marry David.

Over coffee, David filled his wife in with the events that had taken place and tried to prepare her for the fact that he believed they had not seen the last of Ratchford.

"Swear to me you had nothing to do with any of it," Sandra demanded.

David Carver was shocked. Sandra had never asked him about any possible involvement before, he knew the idea that he might have been involved had never entered her head. Everything had changed now the boat had been discovered. He looked at his wife with a strained pleading expression, "Sandra......you can't possibly believe I had anything to do with Sylvia's death....you know me, I thought you loved me."

Sandra began to cry, it all too much for her. she got up from her chair and ran from the room leaving David heart-broken and upset. He sat at the table staring blankly at the still unfilled coffee mugs wondering if the damage that had been done could ever be repaired.

Chapter 5

Roland Ratchford was sick and tired of trying to find parking spaces in Bristol, not only were they few and far between but if you found one the charges were exorbitant. Today, he decided to use the multi-story car-park rather than waste precious time driving around looking in vain for a space on a meter. His destination was in the centre of the city and he had no idea how long he was going to be or even if the man he sought, Peter Edwards, would be in his office.

He parked his six-month old Ford Mondeo on the third floor and made his way to the lift deep in thought. The response he had received from David Carver had not been what he had expected. Hostility and anger were the normal response when he told people he wanted money or information in return for keeping their secrets but few showed total disregard for his divulging what he knew. Could he have been wrong about Carver's role in the events of that night? He thought not, but it would do no harm to check things out further.

He was so engrossed in his thoughts that he wasn't fully aware of his immediate surroundings and he collided with a young woman returning to her car in a hurry and like him, not looking where she was going.

"Sorry," he blurted out, aware of his situation suddenly. He looked back to make sure she hadn't dropped any of the bundle of papers and files that she was carrying; only to see her glaring back at him, obviously convinced that he had contrived the collision on purpose for some obscure reason.

He pressed the button for the lift, but when a group of four others joined him in the wait he changed his mind and hastened down the stairs, once again returning to his earlier train of thought. Carver had just thrown him out, seemingly oblivious to his threats of going to the police and protesting his innocence in a rather convincing manner.

Surely he couldn't be wrong about Carver, it all fitted too well. First there was the meeting with the two men and later discovery that one of them was a thief who specialised in jewellery.

Then there was the coincidence of him being an experienced open-water swimmer and the men apparently trying to kill him by drowning; no, that whole business of using a boat to get away was just too contrived to be true, surely they would have just used a car like any other gang of villains, there was no reason for the boat. It didn't make any sense. And then there was the wife's murder, that was way too convenient for Carver. With a divorce, he would only have received half the business, if that, but with his wife dead he would get the lot. No, he was guilty all right but there was something not quite right and his solicitor friend, Peter, would be the man to shed some light on things.

Newspaper reports at the time of the robbery, all of which Roland Ratchford had on file, showed David Carver leaving the police station after being interviewed; he was reluctant to speak to reporters and said that any communication had to be done through his solicitor, Adrian Edwards.

Well, that was handy. Ratchford not only knew that Adrian Edwards had retired but he was also well acquainted with his son, Peter Edwards, who would undoubtedly have taken over his father's clients. In Ratchford speak, "Well acquainted" simply meant he had something on him.

The walk from the car park to Peter Edward's office was a short one but it was just beginning to spot with rain and Ratchford cursed himself for not bringing an umbrella and for not checking that Peter would be there. The reason he hadn't rung was because he knew that Peter would have tried to avoid him; people he had information on were seldom pleased to see him when he turned up.

As it turned out, Peter Edwards was in and had just finished with a client so agreed, rather reluctantly, to see him. The pretty receptionist who showed him into the office was curious, her boss didn't usually see people who just turned up out of the blue.

"I've not seen you before, have I Mr. Ratchford," she asked "are you a friend or client of Peter's."

Ratchford made a mental note of the fact that she had referred to her boss by his first name and wondered if Peter had acquired another little secret he should know about. "A bit of both I suppose, Miss....?"

"Mrs. actually, Roberts....Susan" she smiled, then knocked twice and opened the door for Ratchford to enter Mr. Edwards office.

"Roland, come in, have seat," said Peter politely and then after the receptionist had closed the door behind her, "What makes you think you have the right to turn up unannounced just when you feel like it, I thought we had agreed that I had seen the last of you."

The room was large and well-lit by a huge window that looked out on the city from the tenth floor. The furnishings were expensive and modern; it was the office of a successful man.

Peter Edwards had neither risen from his chair nor offered his visitor a seat so Ratchford chose to sit, not in one of the two seats in front of Peter's desk but in a spare one to one side so that the two men were almost side by side.

"Make yourself at home, why don't you," sneered Peter, "and then get to the point, why are you here?"

Ratchford looked out of the window over the cityscape and admired the view, "I don't think I've ever told you how much I like your office Peter, it's nice looking down on people isn't it?"

"Just get to the point will you, I have clients to see."

"Very well, I want you to tell me all you know about a certain David Carver."

"Carver, who is he? The name rings a bell but I can't place him, and what's your business with him?"

"I'm the one with the questions, Peter," said Ratchford, leaning back in the chair and crossing his legs.

"And what are these questions exactly?"

"I need all the information you have about David Carver, his wife Sylvia and his father-in-law Karl Wagner, oh and the mother-in-law Anne Wagner, anything you have about the whole family in fact. I know your father was their solicitor so it can't be difficult to get the files. I'm sure you can do that for me."

"All right, I'll see what I can find out and I'll let you know."

"I was rather hoping you could get the files now Peter, you know how impatient I am."

Peter Edwards sighed and reluctantly pressed the button on the intercom that would connect him to his secretary, "Kelly, could you please bring me everything we have on Karl Wagner and David Carver."

The reply came back confirming the request, "Everything on Karl Wagner and David Carver, of course Mr. Edwards but the names are not familiar to me, will they be pending files?"

"No, I'm sorry, they'll be with my father's files in the archives."

"Oh right, it will take me a couple of minutes to locate them and I'll bring them straight to your office Sir, is that right?"

"Yes, thank you Kelly, as fast as you can please."

The two men sat waiting for a good ten minutes before Kelly knocked on the door and entered with an armful of files. Ratchford had made several light-hearted attempts at conversation during the wait, mostly about the young receptionist Mrs. Susan Roberts but Peter had not responded at all. He couldn't wait for Ratchford to leave; his mere presencs reminded him of his frailties and vulnerability, of how stupid he had been in the past.

After entering the room his secretary, Kelly, stood just inside the door with the large collection of files she was clutching and asked where she should put them.

"Just pop them on the desk there please Kelly," said Peter nodding in that direction, "and could you tell Susan that I am not to be disturbed until I have finished in here."

"Certainly Mr. Edwards."

It was obvious that Kelly had picked up on the atmosphere in the room and before closing the door behind her she looked at her employer closely and asked, "Is there anything else I can do Sir? Organize some tea or coffee perhaps?"

"No, that's all Kelly, thank you, just make sure I'm not disturbed until we've finished here."

As Kelly left the room Peter and Ratchford both reached for the top file. In frustration Peter asked, "Do you want me to go through them with you or are you going to sit there and try to decipher them yourself?"

"Do you know what, there's a lot more here than I thought, I think it would be best if I took them away and let you have them back when I've finished with them. No need for any of this to concern you."

"I can't just let you walk out of here with confidential files for God's sake, you'll have to go through them in my father's old office. What exactly is this all about anyway, why does Carver's name ring a bell?"

Ratchford gathered up the files and preparing to leave, remembered that it had been threatening to rain. "Have you got something I can transport these in, it was beginning to rain outside and I wouldn't want you to accuse me of not looking after your files."

"I can't let you take them."

"Well I'm sorry Peter but for the life of me, I can't think how you are going to stop me, you're surly not going to make a fuss and have you're staff asking questions."

Peter realised that Ratchford was right, there was no way he could stop this odious man doing just what he wanted, not unless he was willing to have his dirty laundry hung out for all to see and be struck off into the bargain.

Reluctantly he reached into the bottom drawer of his desk and retrieved a roll of black plastic bags. Tearing one off he handed it to Ratchford and sneered, "There, that'll have to do you, now just go."

Placing the files in the bag Ratchford tucked them under his arm and left the office smiling warmly at Susan, who smiled back, wondering what on earth he was carrying in a black bin liner.

The rain held off as Ratchford made his way back to the carpark, a journey that saw a little more spring in his step than his earlier one. He did enjoy his visits with Peter.

Back at his house, Ratchford spent several hours going over the files. They were of great interest and Ratchford kicked himself for not having obtained them earlier. His gut instinct was still that David Carver had killed his wife and robbed his own shop but the files did present other possibilities, possibilities he would have to pursue.

* * * * * * * * * * * *

When June arrived at work after a particularly gruelling journey she sat at her desk and resumed her research into the history of the new Mrs. Carver, trying to see if there was any evidence pointing to an affair between her and David Carver, before the murder of the first Mrs. Carver.

Paul and Reg were huddled over the newspaper reports covering the robbery and murder of Sylvia Carver in 1989 when Phillip

Strange ended the call he'd just taken, "We're on our way now Sir," he said and put down the phone.

"That was the DCI sir," he called across the room, "looks like we have a new case on our hands Guv. A body's been found up on the golf-course at Lansdown, SOCO and uniform are on the scene now."

Paul straightened up, "Right, Reg..June....Philip, with me, the rest of you keep going on what you're doing at the moment, I want to know who those two men were on Carver's boat and I want a connection between them and Carver...get me something we can work on."

As they moved quickly towards the door Paul suggested, "Reg you go with Phillip, June can drive me...Lansdown...isn't that the course opposite Carver's place?"

"That's the one Guv," answered Reg "Bit of a coincidence don't you think, given that you and June were there a couple of days ago."

"That's all it can be though, Reg," said June. "The Carver thing was years ago and if he was somehow involved in another murder now, he'd be pretty stupid to leave the body across the road from his own house."

"Have it your way June but I'll bet you a tenner we find some kind of connection between Carver and our body on the golf course before this case is closed."

"I'll have some of that Reg," butted in Phillip. "Tenner says there's no connection right, how about you Guv, what do you think?"

"I think I'm with you and June but I'm not going to bet on it and I don't think Reg should accept any bets on it either, if everyone gets in on it and Reg turns out to be wrong, it could bankrupt him."

"No, Reg is good for a bob or two Guv," said Phillip, "He's got a fair bit salted away somewhere, I'm sure of it, probably an off-shore account somewhere exotic. You've only got to look at the way he dresses to know that, that's a top end suit he's got on and no mistake."

"That's right," agreed June, smiling as they left the building, "but top end Primark Phillip, not Saville Row." June eyed Phillip up and down as they walked to the cars. "Anyway, what on earth made you think you were a judge of good clothes?"

Reg kept a straight face throughout the exchange but was smiling inwardly. He knew that despite the banter and rude comments he was constantly receiving, the team respected both his experience and his authority, and he had a hunch he would be proved right about the connection between the two cases, it was far too much of a coincidence.

Paul, opened the car door to get in and put an end to things by saying, "OK...that's enough squabbling children, let's see if can solve a murder or two shall we, that is our job after all."

Paul turned developments over in his mind as they headed to Lansdown once more. He had mixed feelings about it; on the one hand, they had been handed what could well turn out to be another murder to solve but on the other, it had come at a bad time. The team were really beginning to get to grips with the Carver case, hopefully there would be nothing suspicious about this one.

If this did turn out to be another murder, they would have to draft in more manpower from elsewhere, the team wasn't big enough to handle two big cases the size it was at the moment.

It would mean working with colleagues they didn't know, and the new case would take priority over a case that was years old, just as they were getting their teeth into it. He found himself hoping that Reg's connection would prove to be right.

A few minutes later, as June manoeuvred Paul's car though the early morning traffic, siren blazing, a sound that she still found as exciting now as she did when she first joined the police, she commented, "You've gone quiet Guv."

"Sorry June, but Reg is right, isn't he? It's one hell of a coincidence, a body turning up here now."

"I suppose it's possible, are you hoping there is one Guv?"

My God, thought Paul, is she reading my mind now?

Even with the siren and flashing lights it took them nearly twenty minutes to reach Lansdown. Some five hundred metres before the entrance to Lansdown golf-course a uniformed officer was standing in front of a sign indicating the entrance to Bath racecourse on the right. He was waving his arms frantically in the air and signaling to June and the others that they should turn onto the road into the racecourse.

"I thought our body was on the golf-course?" commented Paul.

June, followed by Reg and Phillip in the car behind, did as they were bid and it soon became obvious that the road they were on, although leading to the racecourse entrance, crossed the golf-course. As they passed him the constable pointed in the direction of a small copse of trees some four or five hundred yards to their right and across what was obviously a fairway. Parked alongside the trees were two marked police cars and two white vans. Paul was no golfer but he could imagine the kind of remarks the presence of the vehicles would extract from members of the club, fearful for the fate of their precious fairway. He also wondered how many cars destined for the race track were struck by flying golf balls. It seemed like a recipe for disaster.

As they approached the trees it became obvious to Paul that it had not been possible to erect the usual white tent over the immediate crime scene, due the proximity of the trees surrounding the body. A makeshift arrangement of sheets had been put in place instead, draped between the lower branches of the trees themselves to screen it off from prying eyes and shelter it from the elements.

Paul and Reg were encouraged by an eager young constable to don paper overalls and over-shoes before entering the area, which they did with each other's help. June and Phillip both seemed to manage the same task on their own however, much to Paul's embarrassment. He'd had to steady himself against Reg while slipping on the shoes and hoped he didn't look too unsteady on his feet.

"Need a hand there Guv?" smiled June, picking up on her Inspector's unease.

"I've got it, thank you June," he replied, irked that she had brought his predicament to the attention of all and sundry, but also reminded of why they got on so well. June was turning into a good detective; she was also good company and her sometimes playful manner detracted from the sometimes unpleasant situations they found themselves in.

"What have we got?" asked Paul, aiming his question at the man in similar attire to his own who was bending over the body.

He was answered however, by young woman who was stood close by, and who Paul had also taken at first to be a man because of the overalls and the fact that she had the hood pulled up covering all but her face. She passed him a man's wallet. "This was in the victim's pocket Sir. He seems to be a Roland Ratchford and he has a SIA licence in there Sir...seems he's a, or rather was, a private enquiry agent."

Reg tutted and rolled his eyes. "Private dicks I call them," at which the young officer suppressed a smile.

"Do we know what killed him?" asked Paul.

The man who Paul had addressed initially appeared to be finished with what he was doing and stood up to answer Paul himself. "Well now.... Inspector, is it?"

"Yes, I'm sorry, I'm Inspector Paul Manley and this is Sergeant Reginald Evans, I know it's early days but any information you can give us will be helpful."

"Well Inspector, let me see....you have his wallet I see, so you know who he is and what he appears to have done for a living. He appears to have been in his mid-fifties, quite fit until he was shot in the face. The bullet is, I think, still in there, at least I can't see any signs of an exit wound, although there is some damage to the back of the skull.

"There also appears to be some material imbedded around the bullet hole itself. I've no idea what that is at the moment but it's embedded quite deep so I am assuming that the bullet passed through something before it entered our victim and transferred part of it into the wound."

"What...you think he was shot through something?"

"I'm only speculating at the moment Inspector but it looks that way to me at the moment, just don't hold me to it, I should be able to give you more information about it after the autopsy."

"Time of death?"

"Best guess at the moment would be sometime yesterday afternoon or early evening but again, I'll be able to narrow it down a bit more for you after the autopsy. There is one thing I am sure of that might help."

"What's that?"

"He didn't die here."

"And you know that how?"

"Lividity inspector, the blood settles according to gravity after death and shows up as dark patches on the skin. Our man here is lying on his back but the lividity is mostly on his side. I would guess our victim spent some time after his death curled up on his side."

"Like in the back of a van or the boot of a car you think?"

"That's your job Inspector but that would certainly account for it being where it is."

Paul turned back to the young woman who had handed him the wallet. "Any sign of a vehicle track?"

The woman appeared a little embarrassed by the question. "We're trying to sort that out now Sir, but the ground is quite firm......and..."

"And what?"

"Well the first vehicles here were a police car and van and they drove right past the site by mistake, it was still dark then, so we have to try and eliminate their tracks first, but any tracks are only flattened grass anyway because the ground is dry and firm and the grass has been kept quite short everywhere, except between the trees where a vehicle wouldn't fit anyway, Sir. I don't think we're going to get any impression of tyre treads."

"Anything else in the victim's pockets?"

"A handkerchief, some loose change and a bunch of keys, that and the wallet was all we found."

"Can I see the keys?"

The woman handed Paul a clear evidence bag containing the victim's keys and Paul had a quick look. "Nothing on here that looks like a car key and I would assume he owned a car, so either he had it on a separate ring or someone removed it. Can you make sure these are tested for prints, if someone did take a car key off this ring they may have left a print on one of the other keys."

"Will do Sir," she replied taking the evidence bag back.

"Who found the body?"

"A Mr. Smith Sir, he lives a couple of miles away and drives up here early most mornings to walk his dog and look for lost golf balls."

"Where is he now?"

"One of the groundsmen has taken him and WPC Thatcher over to the clubhouse Sir, he was quite upset and the groundsman had an electric golf buggy thing, so they have taken him to the clubhouse for a cup of tea to settle him a bit. WPC Thatcher said she would take a statement from him there. That was all right wasn't it Sir…to let him go I mean."

"Yes, no reason to keep him here. Where exactly is the clubhouse?"

The constable pointed and said, "If you drive back out to the main road and turn right, the clubhouse and golf-club carpark are the first entrance on the right Sir."

"Thank you, constable," said Paul, as he began removing his overalls and turned back to his colleagues, "All right, June can drive me and Phillip back to the station after we've spoken to Mr. Smith. Reg you had better stay on until they finish here, make sure there are no more cock-ups. Well I don't have to tell you what to do really Reg you've been to more murder scenes than June and I put together. Ring me if anything turns up that I should know."

"Sure thing Guv."

At the clubhouse, WPC Thatcher was sat taking a statement from Mr. Arnold Smith in the club secretary's office while the two of them enjoyed a cup of tea. The constable had just finished taking the statement when Paul and the others joined her but there was nothing of any great interest in it.

Mr. Smith was in the habit of driving up to the golf club every morning come rain or shine. He parked on an area of grass just outside the club carpark because although it was possible to enter the park, exiting could only be achieved if you had a code or card to lower a bollard.

That morning he had parked his car as usual and let Howard his dog off his lead. They mostly followed the same route and that morning had been no exception.

It was Howard that had found the body and he had whined and barked until Arnold had got there, knowing that something was very wrong. Arnold and Howard had walked back to the car as Arnold called the police not wanting to stay in the vicinity of the body. They hadn't seen or heard anything out of the ordinary on their way there or while they had been there, except the body of course.

After a brief and uninformative conversation with Arnold and a few kisses from Howard, June drove Paul and Phillip back to the station.

As soon as they entered Paul said, "Phillip....trace this Roland Ratchford, find out where he lived and where he worked, see if he worked alone or if he was part of a team or partnership. When you've located his home and place of work I want a team to go over each with a fine-tooth comb. June, I want you to find his next of kin and as soon as you've done that you can take me to see them."

Paul needed to sit and think, so he headed for his office after persuading the vending machine to part with some of the dark brown liquid that passed for coffee.

Paul drank the last of his coffee, more to be able to dispose of the paper cup than from any enjoyment he derived from it. His wife Margaret, often offered to make him a thermos of coffee to take to work but the one time he had taken her up on the offer it had remained untouched all day. It had become a sort of office ritual for members of the team, if they visited the vending machine, to automatically get a coffee for Paul. Paul liked the ritual, even though he hated the coffee, it somehow made him feel part of the team rather than its head.

There had been times when he had considered abandoning his office in favour of one of the unoccupied desks in the main room but had decided against it simply because there was the odd occasion when he needed some privacy.

Screwing up the cup and throwing it in the waste bin he looked up to see Giles leaning in, "Sorry Guv. DCI Blake would like to see you."

Chapter 6

Half an hour after getting back from the golf course Paul walked along the corridor leading to the DCI's office, more aware than usual of the noise around him. It was as if all the separate noises of the station, the talking, the footsteps and the hum of computers had somehow combined into one unique cocktail of sound that came from all directions. It was strangely calming but not very conducive to rational thought.

He needed to brief the DCI on the current state of affairs, both as far as their cold case was concerned and the new murder enquiry but he was undecided as to whether he should tell him about the teams, and his suspicion that the two cases may be linked.

Paul brought him up to date on the body at the golf course and in the end, it was the DCI who asked, "You and June were in that part of the world only the other day Paul, do you think there can be any connection between the case you're working on and this new one?"

Paul sometimes thought that the DCI had too many things on his plate to be able to really keep in touch with all aspects of every case, but he was certainly on top of what Paul and his team were up to. DCI Blake may have been the butt of some jokes around the station but the man was no fool, that was for sure. Paul didn't know much about his DCIs career but he suspected that he had been and still was a good detective.

When Paul returned to his office, Phillip Strange had just put down the telephone he'd been talking on for the last half hour and tapped on the door of Paul's office that was almost always open.

Paul looked up from trying to decide if he would be risking serious illness by eating the sandwich that had sat on his desk since the day before. He had brought it back from the canteen fully intending to eat it then, but something had side-tracked him as usual.

Phillip rested one hand against the door jamb and leaned ever so slightly into the room, "Looks as if our murder victim was a bit of a loner Guv. June has found out that both his parents are dead and he was an only child; she is still looking to see if she can find any other relatives but it's not looking promising at the moment. As for work, it seems he preferred to do that alone as well and from home; he's been a private investigator since 1984 and appears to have contacts from just about everywhere. Unmarried, no children and both parents dead, that's one lonely guy. Address is a house in Rodney Place, Clifton, number 7."

"I know Rodney Place, Guv," announced June who now also occupied the doorway to Paul's office, having ducked under Phillip's arm. "I've got a friend who lives in a flat there, in fact I thought they were all flats, big Georgian places, expensive too. My friend is an insurance broker and earns good money but even she says the rents are astronomical."

Paul decided the sandwich was too big a risk and left it on his desk as he made for the door. "June, Phillip, let's have a look at this expensive pad, have we got the keys? And where's Reg?"

"He's gone to see the pathologist, Guv." said June, entering Paul's office to retrieve the sandwich from his desk and drop it in the bin.

"The pathologist, I didn't think he was that bad, I thought a doctor would be able to help him," quipped Phillip, making even Paul smile.

Paul turned to Derrick Price, as they made their way through the main office to the exit. "Derrick, you be office manager on this, ring Reg and tell him that he's to meet us at Rodney Place as soon as he's finished with the pathologist. You'll need to give him the address."

Derrick picked up the phone to call Reg as the three of them left the office.

Philip Strange opened a clear plastic bag that he retrieved from his desk and that contained the contents of the murdered man's pockets; he picked out a bunch of keys and held them aloft. "I've got the keys Guv. Do you want me to drive us there?"

"That's all right Phillip, we'll let June do the driving as she knows where this place is and in any case, I've seen the number of dents on your car, so you can keep your muddy paws off mine thank you very much."

June tried to hide her grin from Phillip as they left the room but Phillip muttered something about his car having fallen down the stairs while in custody, which caused her to laugh out loud instead.

Paul grimaced, "It's like working with a bunch of kids, I swear it is."

"I didn't know you'd ever worked with kids, Guv, when was that?" queried June.

"Just get in the car and drive June."

"Yes Guv."

Rodney Place turned out to be a short row of three storey Georgian terraced houses tucked back off the main road and separated from it by a well-kept, long narrow garden that had gated railings to keep out all those except the privileged residents of Rodney Place itself.

Paul could see that most of the front doors had more than one bell push beside them, indicating that June had been right in her assumption that most had been converted into flats. Number 7 was the exception. Not only did it lack the assortment of bells and name plates the other properties sported, number 7 had what Paul took to be the original bell pull consisting of a round ceramic knob that one pulled out from the wall.

Both Paul and June instinctively looked up at the front of the building as Phillip inserted the most likely looking key into the lock and let them all in.

"June, you and Phillip start at the top, I'll see what I can find of interest down here and we should meet on the first floor."

"Are we looking for anything in particular, Guv?" asked Phillip.

"Well, we don't yet know where our victim was killed, only where he ended up, so if you find any signs of a struggle or a trace of blood, or anything that suggest this might be where he was killed we'll have to call a halt and get SOCO in. Other than that, anything that looks suspicious or out of place, any diary or documents that might tell us where he spent his last hours or who he spent them with.

"Let's also not forget the coincidence of where he was found either, so keep an eye out for anything that indicates he may have known David Carver, everyone keeps telling me this is linked to him in some way."

As June and Phillip ascended the stairs, Paul pushed open the front room door and looked about. The room was large with a high ceiling and it was well lit from the tall sash window that looked across the road outside to the private gardens. It was a pleasant room, well-furnished in a very masculine style but it seemed somehow unkempt. There were newspapers discarded on the floor next to a wing-chair that had a coffee table beside it, on which was an empty wine glass. Paul thought the chair looked well used and he formed a mental picture of Ratchford sitting there reading with a glass of wine in his hand.

The next room along the corridor was more office-like and actually had a large antique desk as its main piece of furniture. Paul assumed this was the room Ratchford reserved for seeing clients. The desk was set at a slight angle to the large window that looked out onto the small back garden. It was positioned so that Ratchford would have his back to the window when working. There were several chairs dotted about, anyone of which could be placed before the desk for meetings, and two of the walls were lined with a combination of bookcases and filing cabinets.

One and a half hours after entering Rodney Place Paul, Phillip and June were finishing up on the first floor when the bell rang announcing the arrival of Reg who June let in.

"Anything interesting from the pathologist?" asked Paul expectantly as Reg ascended the stairs.

"Couple of things, Guv. Firstly, the gun shot wasn't what killed our victim, it was the whack on the back of his head, quite a hard whack actually, with something flat and heavy."

"Why would the killer shoot him if he was already dead? It doesn't make any sense."

"Perhaps the killer didn't know he was dead Guv, or maybe he just wanted to make sure," answered June.

"Yeah....Maybe, anything else Reg?"

"Yes Guv, the bits that were found in the wound turned out to be bits of a plastic bottle."

"So the bullet passed through a plastic bottle before entering our victim's head, perhaps he was drinking from a bottle when he was shot?"

"It may have been as simple as that, Guv. But the pathologist did have another possible theory about it. He said he thought it was possible the killer tried to silence the gun by taping a plastic bottle over the barrel. After I'd left him I had a word with one of the ballistic boys. He told me that he had heard of that being done, but said that whoever it was would have been disappointed with the result. He was of the opinion that any suppression of sound would have been minimal."

"OK, thanks Reg, but as far as I can see this new information gives us more questions and still no answers."

"Have you found anything here, Guv?" asked Reg.

"Only that our Ratchford was a real piece of work. Two of the rooms on the top floor are completely full of files on all sorts of people...some of them quite prominent and influential. We need to get them brought in so we can go through them with a fine-tooth-comb. It seems as if our victim was not averse to a bit of blackmail, may even of made a living out of it. There must be any number of people listed there who would benefit from our Mr. Ratchford's demise. He's got an account book that lists dozens of names with amounts of money next to them. I think our Mr. Ratchford had a lucrative business receiving regular small amounts from lots of important and wealthy people."

"Sounds as if we could be opening quite a can of worms, Guv. Is there anybody we know on his list?"

"Couple of names I recognise already and I've only had a brief skip through. There's also a laptop but we need a password to get in; have one of our computer boys come over and get into it for us. Make sure he comes to us though; I don't want the laptop out of our sight until we know exactly who and what is on it. This Ratchford seems to have compiled a pretty extensive list of people to blackmail and any one of them has got to be a suspect. It's going to take a lot of time unless we get some help, and from what I've seen, we will have to be very careful who we enlist help from."

"Wow! That list really did hit home; I'll make sure the computer stays with us, Guv. No worries."

"Thanks Reg. I'm really concerned about what we are going to find on there."

Paul handed Reg the laptop, "Leave it to me, Guv. I'll make sure it stays with us all the time."

Reg turned to leave, but stopped and turned back, causing his three colleagues to look at him questioningly, "Sorry Guv....but my names not on there is it?" he asked smiling.

Paul smiled back, "Just go, Reg."

* * * * * * * * * * * * * * * * * *

As Paul and June pulled into the car park of Fairway View for the second time June asked, "How are you going to play this, Guv. We didn't find anything at Ratchford's place to connect him to Carver."

"I know June, I think I'm just going to ask him straight out whether he knows anyone by the name of Roland Ratchford and watch his reaction. I think it would be useful if his wife Sandra was present, so we can judge her reaction to the name as well."

"Do you think he was seeing Sandra before his wife died......do you think maybe she was in on it as well?"

"If he is responsible for his first wife's death, then the marriage was in trouble and it would seem likely that Sandra was the cause of that trouble, but whether she would have been involved in the robbery and murder, I don't know."

They both got out of the car and began walking to the front of the house when June suddenly stopped in her tracks and caught hold of Paul's arm.

Paul turned to her, wondering what had caused her reaction. "Are you all right June?" he asked, concerned.

"Tell me Guv, what car did the DVLA say Ratchford owned?"

"A Ford Mondeo.....Blue, WR something, something, MLO if my memory.......bloody hell!"

Both Paul and June turned to look back at where they had parked, and there, three spaces to the right of their car was a Blue Ford Mondeo registration, WR65 MLO.

"Christ, that's actually it isn't it, that's Ratchford's car," said Paul staring at June for confirmation that he wasn't seeing things.

"Yes Guv."

"Call Reg....tell him to get SOCO and a recovery truck over here, I want an initial inspection of the car here in situ and then I want it recovered and gone over thoroughly. Tell him to let the DCI know and get a search warrant for this place. I want the warrant to cover as much as we can get, not just anything pertaining to Ratchford's death, but Sylvia's murder and the robbery in 1989 as well."

Paul left June calling Reg and strolled up to the front doors, one of which was open wide. Paul walked up to the reception desk and rang the bell.

David Carver emerged from his office and looked perturbed. "Inspector Manley, what can I do for you today....or do have some more news for me perchance?"

Carver approach Paul and the two men stood facing each other in the centre of the reception hall, "I'm interested to know if you have ever heard of a man by the name of Roland Ratchford?"

Carver's face paled and his demeanour changed from one of curiosity to one of deep concern.

"Well as a matter of fact Inspector I have, if it's the same Roland Ratchford that booked in here a few days ago. He tried to blackmail me with some absurd story about my having planned the robbery of my shop and the murder of my wife back in '89. I kicked him out Inspector, and I expect he's now come to you with his stupid suspicions and his bloody photographs. Well I'm sorry, but there is no truth in any of it."

"Kicked him out, you say."

"That's right, Inspector. I sent him packing, along with his bags and his smug smile."

"Then how do you explain the fact that his car is still in your car park?"

"What are you talking about? He left with a flea in in his ear I can assure you, I can produce witnesses if you like, a couple of residents saw him leave."

June came through the front door at the same time that Sandra Carver emerged from the dining room. "What's going on now?" Sandra enquired of anyone who would answer.

"The SOCO team are on their way Guv." informed June, "and the other thing should be here soon."

"What team? What other thing?" demanded Sandra Carver, obviously annoyed that things were happening that she knew nothing about and had no control over. "Is anyone going to tell me what's happening here?" she demanded, and for a moment, June thought she was actually going to stamp her foot.

"We have a team on the way over to examine the car that's in your car park and then it will be taken away for a complete forensic check; we are also awaiting the arrival of a warrant to search these premises and grounds."

"A search for what exactly?" This time it was David Carver who asked the question.

"Well, we'll know that when we find it Mr. Carver. In the meantime, I would like you to come to the station with us so that you can be interviewed under caution."

"You make it sound as if I need a solicitor Inspector, am I under arrest?"

"No, you're not under arrest, at the moment anyway, but we do need to ask you some questions; you're entitled to have your solicitor there if you have one, or you can have the duty solicitor, it's up to you."

"My solicitor's name is Peter Edwards but he's not a criminal solicitor, so I'll have the duty solicitor as it seems I need one." He turned to his wife, "Try not to worry about all this love, I've got nothing to hide and I have no idea why Ratchford left his car here, in fact, I'm sure he didn't, someone must have brought it back."

"Ratchford? That odious man who was here the other day?"

"Yes...apparently his car is still in the carpark....did you know?"

"No, I did notice a car there this morning but I assumed one of our guests had hired it, or had visitors. Is that man back here? I thought you'd kicked him out."

"No, he's not back Mrs. Carver," said Paul, "in fact he's dead, his body was discovered on the golf course in the early hours of this morning."

Both Mr. and Mrs. Carver appeared genuinely shocked at the news of Ratchford's death and Sandra Carver put her hands to her face and stared at her husband as June led him out to the car in silence.

Paul followed them out when he heard other cars pulling up outside. He looked back as he exited the doors, just in time to see Sandra Carver burst into tears and run into the office.

As Paul left Fairway View, Reg, who was with the new arrivals, strolled over to see him. "Bit of a turn-up this Guv, Ratchford's car being here. Even though I have to point out that I predicted a connection between Carver and Ratchford's death all along. I'm not complaining you understand, Guv, but I could have won some serious money if you hadn't stopped the betting on it."

"At the moment Reg, all we have is a connection between Carver and Ratchford himself, we have nothing at the moment to link him to Ratchford's death. Anyway, we're taking Carver in for a proper interview. "Paul stopped and thought for a moment, then said to June, "I'd like to have Reg with me for the interview June, can I trust you to sort things out here when the warrant arrives?"

"Yes of course, Guv."

June caught Reg looking quizzically at Paul, he would never question Paul's decision but it was obvious from his expression that he was surprised that Paul was putting her in charge of the search.

"Good," said Paul.... "Get Phillip out to give you a hand, he's been involved in lots of searches and is regarded as a bit of an expert. It's quite a responsibility June, so make use of Phillip, don't be afraid to ask for his advice and make sure you leave no stone unturned. We'll only get the one chance to do this so it has to be done thoroughly."

"Trust me Guv, I can do it," said June excitedly; thrilled at being trusted with such an important task but also concerned that she might miss something significant. She was pleased Phillip would be on hand. She wondered if Reg would express his concerns to Paul.

"I wouldn't give you the job if I didn't think you could do it, June," Paul confided, almost as if he'd read her mind.

Paul and Reg got into the car with a somewhat worried-looking David Carver. June turned towards the forensic team that had already began examining Ratchford's car, trying to look as confident and in charge as she possibly could.

June found the atmosphere inside the large house a little claustrophobic with so many people milling about and found it easier to concentrate while sitting on a small bench that was situated on the front lawn facing the house.

She was pleased with the way she had organized things. She put all the staff and residents in the Carver's large office while the team searched the lounge and put everybody in there while the rest of the house was searched. That way she had the lounge free quickly so that those residents of the hotel that were present had somewhere to sit and take refreshments while the house was turned upside down around them. Mrs. Carver and the few staff were also asked to remain in the lounge while the search was being conducted but asked June if she could sit in the office and work instead because she didn't want to keep answering questions from concerned guests. June agreed, but only if a constable sat with her to ensure she didn't access the computer. June couldn't take the risk that she might delete files.

Studying her clip-board and ticking tasks off as they were completed June became aware that a man from the forensic team had approached and was handing her a clear evidence bag.

"This was in the waste bin waiting for collection, ma'am," he said, obviously unsure how he should address a constable who was in charge.

June smiled, "What is it?"

"Plastic bottle, Ma'am, my colleague thinks it's been made into a silencer for a gun. You asked if I could alert you to anything odd, and I reckon that's pretty odd."

"Please stop calling me Ma'am my name's June and I agree that it's odd, leave it with me, would you?" The man began to walk away and June called after him, "Where's the man in charge?"

He pointed, "Over at the car ma....June."

"Thank you." June carried the evidence bag containing the bottle over to Ratchford's car where a man was writing notes. "Who's in charge?" she asked.

The man turned and looked at her, "Well I was told you were," he said smiling, "you're the constable June Kelly that I have heard so much about, are you not."

June took to the man's cheery disposition straight away and replied, "I am she....you are?"

"My name's Cavall...David Cavall...spelt with an a rather than an e, the theory is that one of our ancestors was dyslectic.

June held up the evidence bag, "Well Mr. Cavall with an a, what do you make of this?"

David took the bag and held it out in front of him. "Ah...well this is your typical "I saw it in a movie once so it must work," mistake."

replied David, wondering why he had not met June before. "Someone has stuffed bubble wrap into a plastic bottle in the mistaken idea that it would act like a noise suppressor. They will have been very disappointed I fear."

"You're saying it wouldn't have worked?"

"Hardly at all I would think. We could do some tests to find out but my instinct says it would be next to useless."

"We have a body with some plastic in the gunshot wound, do you think this could be the source of the plastic?"

"You'd have to match the plastic to say for sure, but if this was used as a DIY silencer then I'd say it was a strong possibility."

"Great. What have you found here?"

"Not much I afraid, we really need to get it back to the lab. We have got samples of hair and fibre from the driving seat, so we should be able to confirm who has driven the vehicle if you give us someone to match them to. We've also got grass cutting galore in the wheel arches."

"The body we have was found on the golf course just across the road from here."

"Yeah, I heard about that, do you want me to see if we can match these samples to the grass over there."

"I'd be very pleased if you could, thank you David," said June, and then hesitated during which time David just stood and smiled at her, aware that she was having difficulty forming her next question.

"Tell me," continued June, "if I were to give you some perfume, could you get it analysed to see if it's genuine?"

David's smile broadened. "If you were to give me some perfume I'd think you were coming on a bit strong, we have only just met after all, but yes, if you also gave me some genuine stuff as well...why?....this doesn't sound like the same case to me."

"It's not the same case....to be honest it's not a case at all at the moment, it would have to be on the quiet, would you mind, I mean I don't want you to do it if it will get you into trouble.... Oh look, forget I even asked, OK."

June turned to walk away but David stopped her. "No look, I can do it, but you'll have to give me your number so I can give you the results."

June gave him her card. "Be careful, yeah? I don't want you to get in any trouble for doing we a favour."

"Of course," David looked at June's card, "but this is your work number, I'll need your private number."

"Why?"

"Well, because I think we have already spent enough time talking about things that are not related to this case on works time, don't you, and I don't think it would be appropriate for me to ask you out while we're at work, so I need your private number to do that."

June was taken aback a little, she had taken to David from the off and it now looked as if he liked her as well and wanted to see her outside work. She wondered what she was getting herself into and whether she would regret it, but she hadn't been on a date in ages and he did seem nice. She took her card back and wrote her mobile number on the reverse.

As he took June's card back David made a point of looking purposely over her shoulder indicating that she should turn around.

When she did so she saw Phillip striding towards them purposefully and grinning from ear to ear. For a moment June thought he must have overheard her conversation with David, he was grinning so much but as he approached, June realised that the grin on Phillip's face was nothing to do with her conversation but was more to do with whatever it was he was hiding behind his back.

"What have you got behind your back, Phillip?" she asked expectantly.

Phillip withdrew his hand and held aloft an evidence back containing a heavy object. "Only a bloody gun, that's all," he cried in triumph.

"Where was it?" June asked excitedly.

"Hidden under insulation in the loft."

June and Phillip started to walk away but June turned back to David, "You'll let us know as soon as you match those grass cuttings ...yes?"

"Will do, June."

"What grass cuttings?" asked Phillip.

Chapter 7

The interview room was bare except for a table and four chairs and the usual recording device. Sat opposite Paul and Reg. were David Carver and his solicitor Peter Edwards.

"Before I start the tape Mr. Carver," said Paul, "it was my understanding that you intended to make use of the duty solicitor because Mr. Edwards here is not a criminal lawyer, may I ask what changed your mind?"

"I can answer that for you, Inspector," cut in Edwards. "Mrs. Carver rang me after you arrested her husband and asked me to be here. She felt it would be better to have someone who's only interest was David's welfare, and David now agrees."

"I see, but I must point out that your client is not currently under arrest...he's being questioned under caution, so I hope they have made the right choice for their sake."

"I'm happy to have Peter represent me Inspector....can we just get on now," said Carver, clearly on edge.

"Very well," Paul said as he indicated to Reg to switch on the recorder. "Interview with David Carver, started at 2.00 pm. Also present are Detective Inspector Paul Manley, Detective Sergeant Reginald Evans and Solicitor Peter Edwards. Well Mr. Carver," continued Paul, "for the benefit of the tape I would like you to confirm that you have been formally cautioned and that you understand why you are here."

Carver looked directly at Paul, his hands gripping the edge of the interview room table, "Yes, I understand all right, a man that stayed at my hotel.....well booked in anyway....he didn't actually stay in the end because I threw him out....this man has been murdered and because his car has for some reason turned up in my hotel's car park again you think I did it."

Carver leaned further over the table and his solicitor put a gentle but restraining hand on his arm, not wishing his client to become angry, "Well I can assure you Inspector," Carver continued, "that I did not kill this Ratchford, although I can imagine there are a few who would have liked to. I have never killed anybody and before you ask, that includes my late wife!"

"Can you tell us exactly what happened and what was said when Mr. Ratchford booked into your hotel the other day, that's the Monday the 14th August. Take your time, we'd like as much detail as possible."

Carver was finding it difficult to remain calm and his solicitor put his hand on David's arm a second time.

"Certainly....my wife actually booked him in, I didn't see him until later, after my wife had gone to her hairdresser's. He said that he knew my first wife Sylvia, and that she had been suspicious I was having an affair and that she had employed him to follow me. He said he was....how did he put it.....a private enquiry agent and that he had photographs of me meeting a couple of men in a pub and that the meeting looked suspicious in some way."

"And was he right? Did you have secret meetings with two men?"

"Yes I did, all right.....Look, Sylvia was the brains of the business Inspector, not me. She knew stones inside out, learned it all from her dad at an early age. If truth be known, I had difficulty distinguishing between a diamond and an ice cube, so she ran the antique and second hand side of things and I bought the new stuff from wholesalers, stuck a couple of hundred percent on it and put it on the shelves. I had no idea whether I was buying and selling good stuff or rubbish. All I knew was what I paid for it and what I sold it for.

"Well one day, when Sylvia was out of the shop, I was approached by someone who had briefly worked for one of the wholesalers I dealt with. He said he could get me some real quality stuff at unbelievably low prices. Well I was keen to show Sylvia that I could do a good deal and make lots of money, so I agreed to meet him and an associate of his at a pub."

"You're saying that these two men were the men Ratchford photographed you with?"

"That's right, they must have been."

"What were their names?"

"It was a long time ago Inspector, the one I dealt with was called Clive something, I can't remember his surname, if I ever knew it, and I was never given a name for his associate. I think that the one I knew from before used to work for Rohan and Pitt, but that's all I can remember about them. Oh.... but Ratchford knew who they were, he told me he followed them after the meeting and found out about them."

"Did Ratchford mention their names when he spoke to you?"

"Yes briefly," Carver put his hand up, palm facing Paul and Reg to indicate that he was trying to think, "posh sounding names.....he said that....I think the other one may have been Adrian something, but I'm not sure. I wasn't really listening to the rubbish he was spotting, I was angry."

"Did you end up buying the stuff, which I am presuming was knocked off?"

"No Inspector, I did agree to look at it but the last meeting I had with them was just before the robbery. I never heard from them again."

"Did Ratchford show you the photographs?"

"No...and I didn't ask to see them, he put two and two together and made five the same as you're doing. Because you found two bodies in the wreck of my boat, he assumed they were the two men I'd met with. He'd got the idea in his head that I'd plotted the robbery of my own shop and the murder of my wife with those men and that I had then killed them and sunk the boat. It's ludicrous!"

"OK, can you tell us what you were doing on the afternoon and evening of Wednesday the 16th August?"

"Not in any great detail minute by minute, no. I was at the hotel all day and all evening, I seldom go anywhere Inspector, I have a hotel to run."

There was a knock on the interview room door and Phillip Strange entered, "Sorry Guv but you need to hear this," he said, indicating that Paul was wanted outside.

"Interview suspended at 2.20 pm," said Paul and switched off the tape recorder, irked at having to suspend the interview. "Excuse me for a moment," he said as he left the room with Phillip Strange. As they left the room a young uniformed constable entered and stood expressionless next to the door.

"What is it?" asked Paul as he got outside, irritated that the interview had been interrupted.

"June has been on the phone Guv. They've found both a gun and what looks as if it might have been a homemade silencer at Carver's place. She's bringing them in as we speak."

Paul's mood improved, "OK, that's good, we'll let Carver stew for a while until June gets here."

"There's more, Guv."

"What?"

"I've been going through the files that we retrieved from Ratchford's house and you'll never guess who I found a file on."

"You'd better tell me then."

"Our friend in there," said Phillip indicating the interview room.

"Well we already know he had a file on Carver, he was following the man on behalf of his wife."

"No Guv......the file's not on Carver, it's on his solicitor....Peter Edwards!"

"What!" Paul thought for just a moment, "Right Phillip....get the duty solicitor up here to take over from our Mr. Edwards and put Edwards in another interview room. Let's see why he didn't mention that he was acquainted with the deceased."

"The fact that Ratchford had a file on him doesn't necessarily mean Edwards knew him, Guv."

"No that's true. What did you get from the file? Have you been through it?"

"Not fully, I thought you ought to be made aware of its existence as soon as possible. What I have gleaned is that it would seem our solicitor is a bit of a lady's man, tries it on with anything in a skirt, married or not. It would seem that Ratchford knew all about his affairs and was threatening, not just to tell various husbands, but to get him struck off because many of the women were either clients or the wives of clients.

"It would also appear that instead of the usual money blackmailers normally ask for, Ratchford was pumping Edwards for the dirty on his more influential clients. Our stiff from the golf-course was a real piece of work and no mistake."

"OK Phillip, that's good work. I'm going to grab a coffee in the canteen and see if I can make any sense of the new developments. Have June come and find me there the moment she gets back. And don't forget to find Edwards a nice comfy interview room all of his own. Oh! and I suppose you had better ask him if he wants a solicitor."

Paul and Phillip grinned at each other as they parted and unbeknown to them both, June was just pulling in to the station car park.

In the canteen, Paul was staring into his second cup of coffee deep in thought as June came through the door but he looked up in time to see her to gesture that she was desperate for a drink. Paul nodded his head and allowed her to get her own much-needed coffee before joining him at his table. As she sat down Paul's gaze fell on the individual Bakewell tart that she had brought with her as well as a coffee.

"I like to give myself a little treat if I've done good work," she volunteered, seeing the direction of Paul's gaze.

"So, tell me about today's good work."

"Several things, Guv. Firstly, Ratchford's car is now in our workshops being taken apart and David said they could certainly put Ratchford's body in the boot at some time if the hair and fibres they have match. It also looks as if grass found in the wheel arches of the car is the same type as they use on the golf-course fairways and David is going to check the length and type of cut against samples from the course. So, we should have Ratchford in the boot of the car and the car on the golf-course, "June saw a smile appear on Paul's face. "I knew you'd be pleased, Guv. Oh! And there was a briefcase in the back of the car that is probably Ratchford's but it's locked, so no idea what is inside yet. Now the next thing."

Paul put up his hand to indicate that she should pause and take a breath, "David said? Who is David?" Paul asked questioningly.

June lowered her gaze to the Bakewell tart that she now divided in two with a fork as she replied, "Oh I'm sorry Guv, I should have said, David is one of the SOCO team that turned up at Fairway View and he was very helpful. He's seems a very clever and intelligent chap and he certainly has the most impeccable taste."

"Meaning?"

"Meaning I think I might have a date for the weekend and our case is much advanced."

Paul rolled his eyes. He enjoyed working with June, she was good fun as well as being attractive but he sometimes wondered how his wife Margaret looked on the closeness of their working relationship. Perhaps it would be a good thing if June was in a relationship outside work.

"Go on," he said.

"Well, in the wheelie bin, waiting for collection in the refuse area, we found the remains of a clear plastic bottle. David had a brief look at it for me and said it looked as if someone had cut the bottom off, stuffed it with bubble wrap, wedged the bottom back on and taped it in place, he speculated that it had been done in the mistaken belief that it would muffle the sound of a gun being fired. I told him it looked like the gun that killed Ratchford had been fired through something and he thought the bottle was a good candidate."

"Phillip said you had a gun as well."

"Yeah.... that was down to uniform, a Constable Wainwright, He put his head up in the loft and apparently, it's like an Aladdin's cave up there, it's going to take forever to go through it all. But, bright boy that he is, he had a rummage under the insulation around the loft hatch and found a gun wrapped in a cloth. Forensics are looking at it now and as soon as we have the bullet out of Ratchford they'll do a comparison. How about this end, Guv? Have you got anywhere with Carver?"

June began demolishing her cake as she looked expectantly at Paul, pleased that he hadn't been angry that she'd half arranged a date while searching for evidence.

"Well, he's very convincing, and I know we have a mounting pile of evidence against him but I'm very confused; I have serious doubts about his guilt now."

"Why..... he had motive and opportunity. We've got Ratchford's car in his carpark, plus a possible murder weapon and silencer recovered from his house, surely if the ballistics report confirms it's the murder weapon, we've got more than enough to charge him, certainly with Ratchford's murder and maybe even his first wife's."

Paul leaned back in his chair. "But therein lies my problem, June. If, as seems likely, he killed Ratchford, it almost certainly means he killed his first wife. But if he planned the robbery of his shop and the murder of his first wife, he almost got away with it, and why, because it was well planned and thought through. If the man that planned that killed Ratchford, why did he leave his car in such an incriminating place....why did he dump the silencer in his own bin....and why oh why, did he hang on to the gun, and why did he dump the body virtually opposite his own property? If he did the first murder he's a criminal genius, if he did the second he's an idiot! The two crimes don't match."

"I see what you mean, Guv. But perhaps it's just that he had lots of time to plan the first one, but he may not have had time to plan the second, he may have had to do it practically on the spur of the moment when Ratchford turned up out of the blue."

"Yes, I know, you could be right June, it could be as easy an explanation as that. It's just that there is so much evidence against him it's too good to be true, and if it's too good to be true......"

Paul stood up. "Finish your cake June, you've earned it. I'm going to see just what is in Ratchford's brief case and then I have a solicitor in interview, I forgot to mention, our victim had a file on our suspect's solicitor. I'm beginning to worry if we're going to find he had a file on me."

"On you Guv? Why, what have you been up to? Are there any skeletons in the Manley family?"

"I don't think so June, my dad was a chef for most of his life and he and mum now run a little tea rooms down in Brixham, but I suppose he could have been leading a double life without me finding out. We'll have to see if a file turns up to find out. What about you?"

"Me! Oh no, my life's been really boring, until I met you and Reg that is, although my dad had quite an exciting career in both the military and the police, I suppose that's why I joined the service really. Do you want me in on the interview with Edwards, Guv?"

"No, I'll get Phillip to sit in with me on that one. I'd like you to assist Reg with finishing Carver's interview, I don't want to charge him just yet but we can't keep him forever; although I have a feeling we will be charging him rather than letting him go. I'd like to know what you and Reg make of him."

* * * * * * * *

David Carver and the duty solicitor had been chatting for some time when Reg and June entered the room to resume his interview.

Carver eyed them expectantly as they sat opposite. "You told my Inspector that you only met Ratchford on the one occasion and that you had no idea his car was still in your car park....is that correct?"

"Yesss....that's right....why is my solicitor not here?"

"It seems that Mr. Edwards has not been entirely up front with us and he is now to be interviewed about his relationship with Ratchford."

"What.....Peter knew Ratchford....how?"

"Let's just get on with your interview, shall we?"

Reg turned to June and as he did so she placed a clear plastic evidence bag on the table in front of Carver. Reg asked, "Do you recognise that?"

Carver stared at the bag, assessing the contents with a puzzled look on his face. "It looks like bits of a plastic bottle....do I get some sort of a prize if I'm right?"

"Have you ever seen it before?"

"Have I ever seen what before? A plastic bottle or that particular plastic bottle? Because they all look very similar to me, sergeant."

"It was found in one of your rubbish bins awaiting collection."

"Good, the maids are obviously doing their job and getting rid of the rubbish.....what is all this about?"

"We believe that that particular bottle was used as a home-made silencer for the gun that was used to shoot Roland Ratchford. Can you explain how it ended up in your rubbish bin?"

"No....I can't. Perhaps one of your men put it there because I didn't.... in fact, I can't remember the last time I put anything in the bins...we have staff for that! Oh! here's a thought, perhaps whoever drove Ratchford's car into our carpark and left it there, also dumped the bottle in the rubbish, had you thought of that? No, you hadn't, because you're all so convinced it was me aren't you, but I can tell you that anybody and everybody has access to those bins."

June produced a second evidence bag and placed it alongside the first.

"Do you recognise that?" asked Reg.

Carver sighed and made a show of staring at the bag and puzzling over it. "Well now let me see.....Oh!.. I know what that is!" he stated sarcastically. "That's the gun I used to shoot Ratchford with obviously.....I'm surprised you didn't realise that yourself, sergeant! You've got me dead to rights haven't you....where did you find it, in the other bin was it? I shall have to have a word with the maids about that one, the green bin is only supposed to be for garden rubbish."

"Very funny David, I'm glad to see you've managed to keep your sense of humour but as you well know, it wasn't in the bin, it was wrapped in a cloth and hidden under the insulation in your loft."

Carver looked towards the duty solicitor who had listened with interest but not spoken a word. "This is all bullshit," said Carver angrily, sounding uncertain and scared for the first time. "They're planting stuff on me....I've never seen that gun before in my life.....perhaps one of our guests murdered Ratchford and stashed the gun in the loft.

"It would have been easy for them to do; sometimes hours go by when there's nobody on the top floor and the loft hatch isn't locked.

"The stick we use to undo the catch is in the broom cupboard just by the loft hatch. It would be easy for anyone to find it and you use the same stick to pull down the loft ladder.....anyone one could have put the gun up there!" Carver shouted, "anyone!"

"Well, which is it David, are you saying we are trying to frame you for murder for some reason, or did one of your guests do it?" asked June.

"Look at it from our perspective for a moment," cut in Reg sliding his chair back from the table so he could lean back and cross his legs. "A man whom you admit tried to blackmail you turns up murdered on a golf-course that is virtually opposite your guest-house. His car is discovered in your carpark, the murder weapon is hidden in your loft and the remains of a home-made silencer is in your rubbish bin. Give us one good reason why we should believe you didn't do it."

The duty solicitor spoke before his client had time to respond. "Firstly sergeant, you don't know that the gun found in my client's loft is the murder weapon and second, I'll give you several good reasons you should believe my client. I haven't known Mr. Carver here very long, less than two hours in fact, but I have already realised that he is not a stupid man."

Carver was about to cut in but the solicitor put a and up to stop him. "So the reasons I think you should believe my client are these, the body was found opposite where he lives, the victim's car was in his carpark and the murder weapon was hidden in his loft. You have to admit it sounds a lot like someone is trying to frame my client, sergeant, otherwise he has to be the most stupid man on the planet and neither of us believe that, do we?"

Reg and June looked at each other and both realised the interview was over. June gathered up the gun and silencer from the table.

"Is my client free to go now, sergeant?"

"No, not just yet."

* * * * * * * *

Back in the main office, Paul stared at the expectant faces before him. "You may or may not be aware of the fact that DCI Blake wants me to charge Carver with Ratchford's murder and I may have to do just that."

"What's preventing you, Guv?" It was June who asked but the question was on all their lips.

"You and Reg interviewed him June, what did you think?"

"I admit he's very believable, but I think he's been careless leaving all the evidence he has because he did things on the spur of the moment. He didn't have time to plan things out the way he did with his wife's murder."

"Well here's another spanner in the works. Phillip and I have been going over the files that were found in Ratchford's brief case. The file folders themselves appears to have belonged to Peter Edwards or more precisely to his father Adrian Edwards who was the solicitor for Sylvia and the rest of the Wagner family.

"The one file appears to have been compiled by Sylvia herself and given to Adrian Edwards for safe keeping and it's really detailed. It confirms firstly, that she did employ Ratchford to follow her husband but that's not the interesting bit. The interesting bit is the details of her father's will and how it was altered. It also deals with the actions of her brother. Phillip, would you like to fill us all in on a bit of Wagner family history?"

Phillip stood up and addressed the team, "The old man himself, Karl Wagner, was of Jewish descent but had managed to leave his native Germany in 1936. He was a wealthy jeweller who obviously had the right friends and contacts to enable him to get out. He had managed to leave with most of his money and the more transportable of his possessions. He set up and ran a modest business in England after the war and met and married his second wife Anne in 1952 at the age of 39, his first wife Helga having died only two years into their marriage.

"Karl seemed destined to be unlucky in his choice of life partner, as Anne also died young in 1980 at the age of 43 after bearing him two children, Marcus in 1959 and Sylvia in 1962. Marcus it seems turned out to be a disappointment to the old-man, he never showed the least bit of interest in jewellery or the family business, much preferring to spend his time tinkering with old cars. The older Marcus became the less he saw of his father.

Sylvia on the other hand was a joy to her father. She not only showed an interest in jewellery, she also had a good business head on her shoulders, something which prompted the old man to set her up in business when she was just nineteen years of age. Something that was obviously resented a great deal by her elder brother.

"Marcus had longed to set up a garage or car dealership but was unable to procure the necessary finances, something his father could easily have provided.

"After Anne's death in 1980 Karl made a new will. Some small bequests to various friends and his loyal housekeeper but the house and contents were to be sold, and the proceeds from that, together with the remainder of the not inconsiderable estate, was to be shared equally between his two offspring. If either of his children were to pre-decease him or their sibling however, the surviving sibling would inherit the whole estate.

"He made an alteration to the will in 1981 when Sylvia married David Carver, stating that if Sylvia were to predecease Marcus, then Sylvia's share would go to her husband David instead of Marcus. This was done in case grandchildren should arrive, but it would seem neither offspring were informed of the changes to the will.

"That being the case, it must have come as a shock to Marcus when his father died, to see half the old man's estate go to David Carver because he would have expected to get the lot under the old will."

Phillip prepared to sit down and let Paul continue but Paul gestured that he should keep going.

"The really interesting files however were Sylvia's files on her husband and brother. There were some bits and pieces about her suspecting David of having an affair and her employing Ratchford to keep an eye on him, but then it gets more interesting. Towards the end of his life, when Karl Wagner had become quite frail and was confined to a wheel-chair, Sylvia had taken to running his affairs and acquired power of attorney.

"When reviewing his bank statements, she noticed several cheques for amounts of a thousand pounds or more each time, made payable to her brother Marcus. She questioned her father about it but he told her that she must be mistaken and that he hadn't made any such payments. Sylvia agreed, to her father anyway, that she had made a mistake but she instinctively knew what had happened.

"She checked her father's cheque book and discovered that the corresponding cheque stubs had not been filled in. Her father had always been meticulous about keeping records and she knew full well that he would never write a cheque and not fill in the stub.

"That no-good brother of hers had been to visit his father on a couple of occasions on the pretext of seeing how he was doing and trying to build bridges.

"She suspected that he had somehow been able to get hold of the cheque book and tear out some cheques.

"When they had been children, Marcus had apparently always been good at copying their father's signature and Sylvia had no doubt that he had revived the practice.

"Sylvia had then begun documenting everything for her solicitor, obviously aware of the possibility that things might get nasty and end up in court.

"She had gone to see her brother and confronted him with it. At first, he had tried to deny it but had then tried to justify it, saying as how the old man had given her plenty over the years and that now it was his turn to benefit from some of the family's money.

"Sylvia had actually felt some sympathy for her brother's position. Their father had always been more generous towards her she knew, but this had to stop. She told him that if she suspected that he had been taking money again she would tell their father and present him with the cheque book for evidence. Marcus knew that if she did that, the old man would most likely cut Marcus out of his will altogether. Remember, neither she nor Marcus were aware of the changes to the will at that time, only Karl's solicitor would have known of that."

Paul stood up and finally took over. "Thank you, Phillip. Well I think you can all see that this actually gives Marcus a motive to kill his sister.

"If she told her father what she knew, Marcus would lose everything. He knew nothing of the changes his father had made to his will so would have thought that he would eventually come in for the lot with Sylvia out of the way; and by robbing her shop he would throw suspicion away from it being personal and he would also benefit from the proceeds of the robbery."

"OK, Guv," cut in Reg. "If we concede that Marcus had a motive to kill his sister back then, why are we saying he killed Ratchford?"

"Perhaps for the same reason we suspect Carver, these files were in Ratchford's possession remember and if Carver was as convincing to Ratchford as he has been to us....well me, anyway; perhaps Ratchford had second thoughts about his guilt as well and tried to blackmail Marcus Wagner instead. Have we been able to trace him?”

“No Guv.” said June, “nobody’s given him any thought. Shall I do it now?”

“When we’ve finished here, June. I may have taken my eye off the ball a bit, I should have thought to contact Sylvia’s brother and interview him about the murder. It won’t happen again.”

Paul cleaned an area on one of the white boards as everyone watched in anticipation. He drew six columns on the board and split them into two sets of three with respective headings of David Carver and Marcus Wagner.

“OK everyone......it seems that we now have two equally good candidates for prime suspect,” he announced. “David Carver who has held that dubious honour since his boat was recovered and now, Marcus Wagner, Sylvia’s brother.”

Paul pointed to each of the names in turn as he spoke them and then proceeded to head each of the three columns under each name with, motive, opportunity and evidence. “Now I think it is a safe bet that whoever killed Sylvia also killed Ratchford, so let’s start with Carver.

“Obviously, there was the insurance pay-out and presumably he would have been in for a share of the haul from the shop as well.

“Then there was the fact that we think his marriage was rocky...if he and Sylvia had divorced he would probably have lost his interest in the business as it was all in his wife’s name......but if she died, he would inherit, as indeed he did. His motive for killing Ratchford would be that Ratchford had something on him and was blackmailing him. Exactly the same motive for Ratchford's murder would of course apply to Wagner."

Paul wrote this all in the appropriate column under Carver's name and moved over to Marcus Wagner's columns. "Now Wagner has effectively stolen money from his old man, thinking he was entitled to something as the old man seemed to be generous when it came to his daughter Sylvia but considerably less so for his son. It looks as if Sylvia found out about the theft and Marcus was afraid that if she told their father about it he would cut him out of his will altogether. Marcus was unaware that his father's alterations to his will had lost him half of it anyway. So both our suspects have motive to kill Sylvia.

"When it comes to opportunity....well, obviously we can put Carver at the scene of both his wife's murder, although he claims it happened after he was taken to the shop by two of the intruders, and we have him on the boat when, or again according to him just before, the two robbers are killed.

"Opportunity is a little more tenuous with Wagner. We don't know if he has an alibi or not for the night it all happened, but if he was the third man who stayed behind to murder Sylvia, he may well have gone straight from there to Carver's boat and been hiding in the cabin when the others turned up. Remember, Carver says he was never allowed in the cabin. It's entirely feasible in that case that Marcus emerged from hiding after the other two had thrown Carver overboard and killed his accomplices. Now Carver doesn't have an alibi for the evening of Ratchford's murder, he just says he was at the hotel, but a lot of that time he was alone so he could have left and come back with nobody realising. We need to interview Marcus Wagner ASAP and find out what he has to say."

"Who's your money on Guv?" asked Reg.

"I need something more concrete on Carver before I arrest him. We can let him go for now. I know I shall take some flak from the DCI but I can deal with that. In the meantime, I have a solicitor to interview."

Paul's interview with Edwards increased the team's knowledge by a factor of zero; other than the fact that Edwards had a problem resisting his clients if they were married ladies and Ratchford knew about it. Ratchford had acquired information about lots of Edwards' clients that he had used in one way or another and it would seem that he left Edwards' office with Sylvia's file after he had tried to blackmail Carver.

It seemed to Paul that if Ratchford had then confronted Wagner the same way he had Carver, then Wagner was looking a strong suspect indeed.

Chapter 8

The sun was trying to find a way through the clouds and into Paul's office when Clive Pascoe put his head round the door. "Have you got a minute, Guv?"

Paul looked up expectantly, desperate for anything that would point the finger at one of their two suspects.

"Sure, take a seat," said Paul. "Have you got something for me?"

"Just an update really, Guv. I've been going through Ratchford's files. It took me a little while to work out his system, but I've got to grips with it now. He started compiling his files before he became computerized and he hasn't yet transferred them all; but wow! What a system, it's as good as anything we've got here.

"Punch a name in and it comes up with all he has on them, name, age, place and date of birth, family history, hobbies and interests, any convictions. But the real beauty of the system is how he cross-references everything. Each name has a coloured tag associated with it, red for any criminal friend or convictions, yellow for homosexuals and lesbians, blue for club memberships, green for any addictions and so on.

"That way, if he wants to find out about someone and he follows them and finds out they belong to a particular casino or they're a regular churchgoer, church attending gets you a brown tag by the way, then he can go to the appropriate colour file and see if he already has someone on his books that also go there. If he has, then he can glean imformation from them about the person he's researching.

"Now, he has a central file that lists everyone on his books and what colour tags they have. It also says whether they are paying him regular sums of money or not."

"Surely, they are all blackmail victims, so presumably they all pay him some money?"

"Not the case Guv. There are a lot who pay him, what in blackmail terms are quite modest amounts of money, around a hundred pounds a month some of them, it all depends what they can afford."

"Blimey! What was he, a bargain basement blackmailer?"

"Far from it Guv. You'd be surprised at the number of people paying him those small amounts, and it mounts up to a tidy sum each month and on top of that, you have some people paying considerably more, either on a monthly basis or just the odd random payment. Some of those payments can be as high as sixty grand or more, depending on how wealthy they are and how damning the secret they're keeping.......One chap stumped up quarter of a million in one payment!

"Now there are also a lot of names with no payments listed against them. Our solicitor friend, Peter Edwards, is one of those. I think he excepted payment in terms of information from them. There may also be some that he hasn't even approached yet, just waiting for the moment when they can help him with something."

"Well, that's really good work Clive. Have you come across anyone we should be looking into?"

"I was just coming to that Guv....there are a couple that stand out. There's a property developer by the name of Andrew Phillips, multi-millionaire. Ratchford has photographs of his car being repaired at a private garage and paint samples taken from a damaged front near-side wing. He also has copies of police reports into a hit-and-run where a sixteen-year-old boy was knocked off his bike. The boy will always need round the clock support because of a brain injury caused in the accident. Now Ratchford not only has paint from the boy's bike that match the sample from Phillip's car, but he also has paint from Phillips car that matches paint found on the boy's bike."

"How the hell did he get the paint samples from the boy's bike? The police must have that locked away somewhere."

"And unfortunately, there's your answer Guv. I've found twelve police officers of varying ranks in his files, none of them pay him any money so I can only assume he pumps them for information when the need arises."

"Jesus!........please tell me nobody from here, nobody we know."

"Sorry Guv," Clive got up from his chair and closed the door to Paul's office before retaking his seat, "one Constable, one Sergeant and one Inspector."

Paul stared at Clive before letting out an enormous sigh, "Go on....tell me who they are."

"The constable and the sergeant are at another station but the inspector........I'm sorry Guv...I know you like and respect him....it's Roy Darnley."

Paul was dumbfounded. He had known Roy Darnley for years. "I can't believe it, I've known Roy for years and I've always thought he was an honest.....always known him to be an honest copper. What did Ratchford have on him? Have you read the file?"

"Yes Guv. It seems Inspector Darnley's son was brought in by uniform about two years ago for joy riding with another lad. One of the coppers who brought him in knew that Roy was in the station at the time and told him straight away. Somehow the two lads were released without charge."

"Is there anything in the file that indicates Roy has made any payments to Ratchford or more importantly, supplied him with information on a case?"

"No payments, Guv. It could be that Inspector Darnley doesn't even know he was on Ratchford's radar."

Paul was quiet for a while thinking but then said, "OK, give me the file and I'll have a think about how best to handle it. You had better log the fact that you have found it and given it to me, you need to cover your back if things get messy."

"That's all right, I trust your instincts on this Guv. I am quite prepared to forget I've ever seen it. As far as I'm concerned, if the existence of the file comes to light....you found it that day at Ratchford's house....I've never set eyes on it."

Paul sat back in his chair staring at Clive and deep in thought once again. "Leave the file with me and if I haven't said anything to you by mid-day tomorrow, log it and cover yourself. You are sure nobody else knows of the file?"

"One hundred percent sure Guv."

"OK, mid-day tomorrow then, I will have spoken to Roy by

then and made my decision about what to do....and thank you Clive, Roy is a good man."

Clive stood and left the office and as soon as he was gone Paul rang Roy Darnley's phone.

"You wanted to meet," said Roy as he entered Paul's office. "it all sounds a bit mysterious Paul, what did you want to talk about?"

"Close the door and have a seat would you Roy, it's a rather delicate matter."

"You, closing your office door, what's the world coming to?" asked Roy taking the offered seat.

"Have you heard about the case I'm working on? A body found up at Lansdown golf course?"

"Yes of course, it's all over the nick, some sort of serial blackmailer I hear, the rumour is that he had a file on practically everyone up to and including the Prime Minister, and your lot are playing it all close to your chests and keeping the files under wraps. Is that anywhere close?"

"Close enough, but if that's the rumour then we haven't played it close enough to our chests, have we?"

"I guess not, a couple of my boys play up there, at Lansdown, they keep asking when the whole course is going to be open again."

"The course will be fully open from tomorrow, the groundsmen are cordoning off the area where the body was found with nets so that balls can't go in and apparently the club is more than happy with the situation because they have had an increase in their membership, along with increased interest from societies wanting to play on a course where a murder victim was found."

"Well that's good, the boys will be pleased when they hear that. Now, what is it you want from me, Paul?"

"I don't want anything from you Roy, I just wanted to know if you had ever come across this chap Ratchford in your cases, anything you know would be helpful?"

"Ratchford, I heard that was the name but no I don't recall the name at all. I'll ask the rest of the guys if you like, but I'm sure it would have come to light by now if any of my lot knew him, what with him being one of the main subjects of conversation at the moment. I'm sorry Paul, I don't think I can help."

"I'd like to show you one of the files we recovered," said Paul placing Ratchford's file on the desk between them.

"Of course, but I can't see that it.....will..." Roy Darnley stared at the name on the file in front of him, "what's this?" he picked up the file and examined it, the colour draining from his face.

Paul watched his every move and judged his reactions, convinced that Roy had no idea about the file and had never had any dealings with Ratchford.

Roy scanned the file. "He was just a kid Paul, my boy, nobody was hurt and the car was undamaged.......how the hell did this Ratchford find out? And actually, there is nothing in the file but hearsay anyway, there's no proof of anything untoward. I can see why this is of concern Paul, and I suspect I'm probably going to be disciplined or even lose my job over it, but I'd like you to know that I have never paid blackmail in my life, hell! I couldn't afford it on my salary."

"We know from Ratchford's own filing system that you have never paid him any money but he didn't always ask for money, sometimes it was information he wanted."

"Oh I see, well that's difficult to prove of course, but once again I swear that I have had no contact with the man and have never given him any information. The thing is Paul, where do you intend to go with this? I presume you'll inform DCI Blake."

"Well Roy, at the moment only three people know about this particular file, Clive Pascoe, you and me. Clive has said that he is quite prepared to forget that he has ever seen it if that's what I decide should happen."

"I wouldn't have given the man any information if he had approached me Paul, I hope you can believe that."

"I've known you since I joined CID Roy, I know you to be an honest man and a good copper. I'll destroy the file and it never gets mentioned again."

Roy slumped back in his chair immensely relieved by Paul's declaration. He had been prepared to face whatever consequences would come from it, but to lose his job under such circumstances would have been nothing short of a catastrophe. "Thank you, Paul, I owe you a great deal and I'll thank Clive personally when I see him, although I suspect he's done it more out of respect for you and your judgement than for me, as we didn't always see eye to eye when he worked with me."

"I didn't know that, Clive has never said."

"Water under the bridge I guess....hope."

The two men stood up and shook hands before Roy left the room and returned to his office, shaken by the revelation that he had come so close to being blackmailed and thankful that his son had managed to go to university and was now a first-year medical student.

Chapter 9

Marcus Wagner worked as a car salesman during the week and was part of an amateur rally team on his days off. He wasn't exactly disappointed with the way his life had panned out. After all, he had always managed to indulge his passion for cars in one way or another but cars were an expensive hobby and money, on the other hand, had always been scarce.

His father had been well off but just as Marcus had never been interested in the jewellery business, his father had viewed his interest in cars as a waste of time and money. Marcus had always been a little bitter about it, the old man could have helped him financially a great deal but chose instead to give all his attention and it seemed love, to his sister Sylvia.

So, he'd made his own way in life and he hadn't made too bad a job of it, he thought. He was a good salesman and as such earned decent commission most months, on top of his salary for selling high end luxury cars. He'd never been able to save because his hobby swallowed money like a drain swallows water, but he had always thought early on that he was in for a decent windfall when the old man finally shuffled off.

He lived in a nineteen sixties semi in a secluded cul-de-sac in Thornbury, north of Bristol, and as he pulled onto his driveway after a successful day at work he was looking forward to watching a documentary on the television about the history of Jaguar cars. He had finished work early at three o' clock, having decided that tonight would be strictly a feet up in front of the telly night. He made it as far as the kitchen with the intention of making a cup of tea and sending out for a take-away when the doorbell rang. He cursed, wondering who on earth it could be, put the kettle back down without filling it and answered the front door.

The man who stood there was unknown to him and he thought at first that he was there to try and sell something. "Sorry mate, whatever it is I'm not interested," he barked and only then noticed that there was a woman with him who now held out a warrant card for his inspection.

"Detective Inspector Paul Manley and this is Detective Constable Kelly. If you're Mr. Marcus Wagner, we would like a word please, can we come in?"

Wagner frowned, puzzled and intrigued to know why two members of Her Majesty's police force should turn up on his door unannounced. He showed them into his front room, which appeared relatively clean but was strewn with magazines, all of which seemed car related.

Both Paul and June had to clear magazines of the chairs they had chosen to sit in and Wagner said jokingly, "Just drop them on the floor, they'll be fine, it's the maid's day off."

Paul found himself sitting opposite a trophy cabinet that was standing in an alcove to the left of the room's fireplace. "You seem to have a lot of trophies Mr. Wagner, you've obviously been very successful, motor racing isn't it?"

"Yeah, I've done a lot of Rallying over the years and I'm not too bad at it, nothing very big internationally though unfortunately, not quite good enough for the big time. It would seem that takes talent and money."

Paul sensed from the bitterness in his voice when he spoke, that he probably thought that he was, or had been, good enough for the big-time but had never been given the opportunity to prove it due to lack of funds.

"Still, you seem to have done pretty well," remarked Paul. As he looked at the cabinet, his eye was drawn to a rather unusual looking walking-stick that was propped against the side of the chimney-breast next to the trophy cabinet. Is that your walking-stick there, I didn't notice you limping or anything when we came in."

"No, I walk just fine Inspector, the stick belonged to my father and I've kept it as a sort of link to the past as it were. My father never gave me anything when he was alive and apart from some money that is now all spent, the stick is the only thing I ended up with when he died; I took it with me after the wake at his house, I don't think the family ever missed it, at least no one has ever asked for it back.

"What can I help you with Inspector? Is it to do with the fact that you have found my brother-in-law's long lost boat? He must be upset, having all that business raked up again after all these years."

"That's right. Forgive me but it doesn't sound as if you got on very well with your brother-in-law. Why was that?"

"I neither got on with him nor didn't get on with him Inspector, I could probable count the number of times we've met on the fingers of my hands. I saw very little of him, or any of the family for that matter. I was eighteen when mum died and I'd never been close to my father, he lavished all his affection on Sylvia. But is this what you've come to speak to me about Inspector, how I got on with my family? I thought it was going to be about David's damn boat."

"That's right, and the fact that there were two bodies discovered on it. What are your thoughts about that? Have you any idea who they might have been? What do you make of it?"

Wagner stared at Paul for some time before answering, "Well, I don't make anything of it....I've never been a man who could solve puzzles Inspector, surely that's your job. So, the question is really, what do you make of it?"

"Casting your mind back to the night of the robbery and the murder of your sister Mr. Wagner, can you tell us where you were?"

Again the pause before answering. "I had a flat in Redland in Bristol back then, I seem to remember I was in on my own watching television, very much like I was intending to do tonight."

"And were you in watching television six nights ago, the 16th of August?"

"Oh dear, this is going to make me sound like a very sad and boring man Inspector but once again, I was home alone watching television yes, why?"

"What did you watch?"

"Well let me think now, I saw the news at six and then there was a quiz show of some sort as I remember, so I turned over to watch a documentary about extreme weather and climate change, after that I think I must have fallen asleep until about ten thirty when I woke, made a drink and went to bed.”

“So you never left the house after six, is that what you’re saying?”

“Yes.”

“Have you ever visited your brother-in-law’s guest-house, up near the golf-course?”

“Golf-course, no, I thought he was in Bath, somewhere near Bath Races I thought.

“The golf-course is adjacent the race-course.”

“Oh really, I had no idea. It certainly sounds like an affluent place to live though, he must have done well out of the insurance pay-out after the robbery and of course Sylvia’s life insurance, and then the inheritance from my dad as well when he went, what a lucky fellow he is to be sure. But then luck isn’t everything is it Inspector? I wonder if he has a trophy cabinet of any sort; do you know Inspector?”

“I don’t know Mr. Wagner, I don’t recall seeing any at the house but it’s possible, he was an open water swimmer remember, he may have some medals or trophies for that, I really don’t know.

“Have you ever had any contact with a Roland Ratchford or does the name mean anything to you?”

Wagner furrowed his brow as if deep in thought, “Ratchford......Ratchford......it’s not ringing any bells Inspector, I’m sorry, would it have been helpful if I had known him?”

“How would you describe your relationship with your sister before she was killed, did the two of you get on?”

"I've already said that I didn't have much contact with the family, but actually, yes Inspector, we did as a matter of fact, despite the fact that my father always favoured her over me."

Wagner shuffled his position in his chair and re-crossed his legs. "I'm sorry, does that sound a little bitter?"

"Did you not get on with your father at all then? What about when you were small?"

Wagner took a packet of cigarettes out of his pocket and offered them. Both Paul and June declined.

"I know it's frowned on these days but do either of you mind if I smoke?" he asked.

"No, go ahead," said Paul watching the man intently for any sign of unease but seeing none, if anything he seemed over relaxed. If this man was guilty of anything he was very cool about it.

Wagner put a cigarette in his mouth and picked up an extremely colourful and expensive-looking table lighter from the coffee table in front of them and lit up.

"My father only cared about jewellery and profit, Inspector. As children, we loved both our parents and mum loved us back. I think our father looked on us more as potential assets for the future. Sylvia worked out well for him, she loved the same things he did, so he invested more time and money in her. I liked different things Inspector; things my father could see no profit in, so he decided not to invest either time or money in me."

"That must have been hard for you. But you say you had a good relationship with your sister, is that right?"

"My sister was no fool, Inspector, she knew which side her bread was buttered and she understood why I felt disenchanted with the family. The only reason I kept in touch with mum and dad was for the sake of any inheritance that would come my way and Sis knew that. I think there were times when she felt sorry for me though, she may even have tried to put in a good word for me with the old man but it wouldn't have made any difference."

"The two of you fell out in the end though, didn't you?" questioned Paul.

Wagner leaned forward and stubbed out his cigarette less than half consumed. It was a gesture Paul considered was done to give Wagner a chance to consider his reply.

"What makes you say that?" he asked, staring at Paul questioningly.

"Sylvia threatened to tell your father that you were stealing from him, isn't that the truth of the matter? She found out that you had taken some cheques and forged your father's signature."

Still Wagner appeared unmoved and relaxed. Paul had hoped that his sudden change of tack would unsettle him and maybe bring forth an unguarded remark, but no such thing occurred.

"Who on earth have you been talking to, Inspector? I never stole anything from the old man. He did write me a couple of cheques though as I recall, towards the end. Has Carver been trying to rubbish me or something, is that it?"

"No, you've never been mentioned in any conversation I've had with Mr. Carver, and why would he try to rubbish you, as you put it? Was there bad blood between the two of you?"

"That man ended up with an inheritance that should have come to me, you bet there was bad blood between us. OK I admit it, he was no blood relation to the old man but he bagged virtually the whole bloody lot."

"Well not the whole lot, you still got your half of the inheritance."

"The old man's will stated that if either Sylvia or I predeceased the other, then the surviving one would get the whole amount. But he changed the bloody thing in favour of Carver and he altered the percentages from fifty-fifty to seventy thirty, Sylvia's share all went to Carver and I had the leavings. So yes, I resent the man."

"You said just now that you neither got on with nor didn't get on with him, now you're saying you resented him, so which is it?"

"Which do you think, Inspector?"

Wagner reached for another cigarette and lit it from the same table lighter. "Look, that was all years ago Inspector, I've moved on since then. I may not be rich but I earn decent money, I own this house and I don't owe a bean to anyone. I wouldn't give Carver the time of day, that's true, but I don't hate him anymore, it's all water under the bridge as far as I'm concerned. I don't know why he would say things like that about me."

"Well like I said, our information didn't come from Mr. Carver, as a matter of fact it came from your sister."

"My sister, what on earth are talking about? How could it have come from my sister, she's dead."

"Well, indirectly from her; she detailed everything concerning you taking the cheques from your father's cheque book and forging his signature. She left the file with her solicitor for safe keeping and now we have it."

Marcus Wagner sat silent for a moment and then said, "O.K. So I took a couple of cheques, big deal, he'd written loads of cheques to Sylvia over the years. I was due something and she forgave me for that Inspector, she knew I needed some money at the time and she knew I was entitled to something from the old man. sShe had received enough over the years."

"So your sister forgave you for stealing from your father because she was sorry for you, is that what you are saying?"

"Yeah, that's exactly what I'm saying."

"Then why the file? Why did Sylvia detail it all out and leave the file with the family solicitor? Isn't it right that she threatened to tell your father about it if you ever did it again?"

"My sister always liked to have more than one string to her bow, Inspector; I expect she created the file in case she ever felt she needed a little leverage, always planned for any eventuality, my sister. It was just in her nature, always planning and scheming."

Paul stood up. "Well we'll leave it there for now Mr. Wagner, but we will want to speak to you again, so don't go anywhere for a while."

"No more holidays booked until Christmas Inspector so I'm not going anywhere. Tell me this Inspector..... did David Carver kill my sister?"

Paul was surprised by the bluntness of the question and decided to be just as blunt back, "Well it's beginning to look as if one of you did. We'll be touch again soon."

Wagner appeared to be deep in thought as he showed his visitors out and Paul was annoyed that he hadn't got more from the interview.

* * * * * * * * * * * * * *

Paul was busy reviewing everything they had on Carver and his account of the events regarding his meeting with Adrian fellows and Clive Lowe, when he became aware that June was standing in the doorway. It was obvious she had something on her mind so he nodded his head indicating that she should sit.

"What's on your mind, June," he asked as she sat facing him.

"I've recently bought some cheap perfume off the man in the flat above mine, Guv. and I'm convinced it's fake."

Since June had joined the team, Paul didn't think he had ever been unhappy with any aspect of her performance. However because of his present mood he was now a little irked that she should trouble him with such a trivial matter when they were in the middle of such a complicated and involved case.

"So tell trading standards and get them to check it out, why bother me with it?"

June was a little taken aback by Paul's sharp response and realised that she had chosen a bad moment. "I'm sorry to bother you with it now Guv. But you know I value your opinion and it's a little more complicated than that. I gave it to David, you know, the chap from SOCO I had a date with the other night, and he said the perfume was definitely Coco Chanel."

Paul sighed in frustration. "Well, if it's not a fake, what are you saying? You think it's been stolen, is that it?"

"David said he would have just given it back and said it was OK, but I had also given him the remains of my last bottle for him to check it against. He said he had both bottles stood on a window sill in the lab and he noticed a slight difference in the colour of the glass, so he examined the bottles more closely and found other very slight differences. He rang and spoke to someone at Chanel and they assured him that all their bottles were specially made for each particular perfume and that it would be impossible for two bottles to be different in any way, let alone colour."

Paul's frown deepened, "Well, wait a minute, are you saying that the perfume is genuine but the bottle it came in is a fake?"

"Yes Guv. That's why I thought I run it by you, it seems so strange."

"Well.....there has to be some rational explanation, what are you saying has happened....that someone has got hold of genuine perfume from somewhere without it being bottled and put it in their own bottles?"

"That's what it looks like Guv. Look I'm sorry I shouldn't have troubled you with at all, especially as we're so busy."

"Well what you're suggesting could only really have happened at the factory where it's made......Look June....whatever has happened here and I admit I am curious to know what that is, it's nothing to do with us, it's Trading Standards. Although, how interested they are going to be if it's the genuine thing I don't know. Perhaps your neighbour had a large bottle and has simply decanted it into some smaller ones."

"No Guv....they're spray bottles and they have obviously been made to look as close to the real thing as possible. There is some kind of scam going on, I just can't work out what."

"Well I don't know what to say June, the ball's in your court. You do as you see fit, but don't get sidetracked with it, I need your full attention on our murders."

"Yes of course Guv. You know you have that."

June got up and left the room trying to put the distraction out of her mind but not entirely succeeding. She wished she had caught Paul in a better mood. She was seeing David again tonight and it was sure to be the main topic of conversation over dinner.

June was still regretting bothering Paul with the perfume conundrum while sat in the restaurant waiting for David and wondering why he was late and not terribly impressed, seeing as it was their first date.

The waiter had just put her glass of wine on the table and she had decided that he had ten more minutes before she left when she spotted him coming through the door with another man.

"Sorry I'm late June," he said apologetically, "but I've chatting to Andrew here about the perfume from your neighbour."

The man accompanying David offered his hand to June and announced, "Andrew Weaver, it's nice to meet you June, I'm from Trading Standards. David rang me about the perfume and I wanted to speak to you both in person, I hope you can forgive me for barging in on your evening like this but we've been working on this for a while and we don't want you upsetting the apple-cart as it were."

"I asked Andrew to join us June, I hope you don't mind, but I thought you would be as intrigued as I am to find out what's going on."

June was a little unhappy that what she thought was going to be a romantic evening had been usurped but on the other hand she was intrigued to know what was going on.

David asked the waiter to set another place, but he suggested that they move to another table that was set for four.

When they were seated at their new table and had given their orders, Andrew began, "Three years ago a large shipment of assorted, top name perfumes went missing, presumably highjacked after arriving at Dover. The police never found the perfume, the lorry or the driver. They all just vanished into the ether without a trace."

David looked sideways at June. "Police are useless aren't they, couldn't find a chair if they were sitting on one, if you ask me."

June just poked out her tongue at David and said, "Well it's a good job nobody's asked for a chair then isn't it," then turning to their guest, "Please go on Andrew and just ignore David's snide remarks."

"Well, a little while later we received some complaints from people who had purchased top name perfumes cheaply at markets and the like, saying that they had noticed that although the packaging looked right, the bottles didn't.

"We investigated and discovered that the perfume was exactly what it was supposed to be. But it kept happening and we were perplexed as to what was going on. Then we had a couple of complaints from people who had purchased these same perfumes from reputable outlets but were disappointed with the product. Well when we investigated these, we found that the product had been contaminated, watered down with a mixture of alcohol and some other chemicals, but everything else was kosher."

Andrew continued, "The diluting agent was quite clever really, it didn't alter the colour enough to be noticeable. The only tangible difference was that the aroma was a little weak and it didn't last very long. The majority of people wouldn't have noticed anything, and if they did, they probably wouldn't do anything about it, and even then, if they did complain to the store where they bought it the store would have sorted out any complaint in-house."

June frowned as she looked at Andrew and said, "So you're saying that the people who hijacked the lorry three years ago are watering down the shipment and selling that in the genuine bottles, and then selling the genuine stuff they take out of the bottles in fake bottles. That's a big undertaking. How can that possibly be worth their while?"

"Believe me, there are huge sums of money to be made in fake perfume but there's more to it. We believe they removed half the perfume from the bottles, watered down what remained, re-sealed the spray bottles and repackaged them so that it appeared to be the original shipment untouched. Then they bribe drivers of other shipments who have to make an overnight stop to divert to their factory for that stop, where they unload the genuine cargo, replace it with the watered-down product and send it on. That way they have another shipment to water down and they can repeat the operation over and over again and again."

"Wow," said David. "They must have a slick operation somewhere to do that, they will need a factory to produce the chemical they use to water down the perfume. They'll need a crew and forklift trucks to exchange the cargo and of course they'll need some source of supply for the various fake bottles. How many different perfumes are we talking about?"

"Six top names that we know of, and we know who is behind it and where the exchanges take place. All we are waiting for is information about when an exchange will take place so that we can be there with the police to catch them in the act. So you can see that we don't want anybody upsetting the applecart at the moment."

"If this is such a big operation," asked June, "how come John is selling individual bottles?"

"I don't know June, but he's only a bit player, so perhaps he is helping himself to some of the product. But I have to say that, if he is, he's playing a dangerous game. The people at the top are a nasty lot, we suspect the original driver may have been murdered."

"Who are the people at the top exactly?"

"You realise that you have to keep anything I tell you to yourselves...yes?"

"Yes of course."

"It's a family concern. The head of the family are a Jack and Marianne Barnes. They have three sons, Alan, Clive and Adrian, all three sons have been done for taking money with menaces and Alan has form for GBH; Mum and Dad have both been done for fraud."

"They sound lovely," said June handing him her card. "Can you keep me up to date with what's happening, I promise to keep out of it but I would like to know, can you do that?"

The waiter re-appeared with their meal and the subject of conversation turned to other things. David dropped June home at eleven o'-clock, because she'd consumed four glasses of wine with her meal. David and Andrew had seemed to hit it off really well and the idea was that David would drive June home in her car, Andrew would follow them and then drop David back to pick up his car.

They kissed and said their good-nights but as David was climbing into Andrew's car the front door opened and John Stubbs came out.

As the three of them watched him walk down the road to his car Andrew asked, "Is that him?"

"Yes, that's him," said June." and walked to her door, stopping briefly to wave back to David before putting her key in the door and letting herself in.

When the two men saw June's front door close behind her, Andrew asked, "Are you in a hurry to get back to your car David, or have you got time for a little adventure?"

David looked at him, not comprehending at first; not until

Andrew followed up with, "I'd quite like to see where June's neighbour is off to at this time of night. Are you up for it?"

"You're in the driving seat."

Andrew Weaver and David Caval followed John Stubbs to a trading estate in Avonmouth, where he pulled into the rear carpark of a firm by the name of Delta Perfumes Limited.

"I thought he might be coming here," said Andrew, "this company, Delta Perfumes, produces a range of cheap cosmetics and perfumes and it's owned by the Barnes family. This is where we believe they bring the lorries to exchange the products. There's little point in us hanging about. I'll drop you off at your car."

Chapter 10

DCI Andrew Blake, known to everyone, although not to his face, as "Blakey" because of his resemblance to the bus inspector from "On The Buses," an early 1970s sit-com, had a good working relationship with Paul. Things were nearly always cordial and friendly between them but today the atmosphere in the room was strained. Paul was fast turning out to be, possibly, one of the best detective inspectors he had but he seemed to be dragging his feet with this present case

"Why haven't you arrested David Carver yet?" asked Andrew Blake. "It seems to me we have more than enough evidence to get a conviction, maybe not for killing his first wife, but certainly for Ratchford......Good God, you found the murder weapon hidden in his loft for God's sake and Ratchford's car in his car park, what more do you need? They have matched the gun found at Carver's to the bullet retrieved from Ratchford, or have I got that wrong?"

"I know Sir, yes they have matched the gun but we have another possible suspect now, the murdered woman's brother. I just don't think Carver would have been stupid enough to keep the gun and leave the victim's car in his car park, it doesn't make sense that he would do that."

"Well, I have to say that I'm disappointed Paul, I thought you would have had this all wrapped up by now. I've had the Chief Superintendent on the phone wanting updates because he lives in

Clevedon and sees it in his local newspaper on a daily basis. If you haven't got any more evidence against this other suspect, Sylvia Carver's brother you say?"

"That's right Sir. Marcus Wagner"

"Well if you haven't got any more in the next twenty-four hours then I expect charges to be brought against David Carver, is that clear?"

"I wish you could give me a little more time Sir, I do think Wagner is worth a closer look."

"Forty-eight hours and that's it, Paul."

"Yes Sir, thank you."

"Don't let me down Paul, forty-eight hours and you charge one of them.....Yes?"

"Absolutely Sir....forty-eight hours," said Paul as he left the DCIs office feeling like he was being bullied into doing something he didn't want to do but pleased that he had at least bought a little more time.

Back at the office he called for everyone's attention. "As you may have all guessed, DCI Blake wants me to charge David Carver with the murder of Roland Ratchford. What's everyone's thoughts on that?"

"We've got more than enough evidence against him, Guv." volunteered Peter Cook.

"You don't think he did it though, do you Guv?" responded June.

Derrick Price cut in. "Before anyone says anything else, I've just received the final report from the team going over Ratchford's car. They can definitely put Ratchford's body in the boot and they can definitely put the car on the golf course. The grass cuttings found in the wheel arches also match the sample cuttings taken from the course. Grass cuttings were also found in the driver's foot well suggesting that whoever parked the car in David Carver's car park drove it there from the golf course."

Paul looked at June. "There were no grass cuttings on any of Carver's shoes when his place was searched, were there, June?"

"No Guv and we definitely checked them all, as well as Mrs. Carver's and there was no sign on any of the carpets."

Derrick continued, "The one thing they have not been unable to do, is to put Carver himself in the car at any time. And to cap it all off, there is no forensic evidence to connect Carver to Ratchford's body either. Apart from Carver's own statement about Ratchford trying to blackmail him when he visited Fairway View, we can't prove that the two men ever met."

"He could have been wearing overalls of some kind." suggested Peter, "maybe that's why there's no forensics in the car."

"What are you saying, Peter? That he was careful enough, not just to wear overalls but to dispose of them effectively afterwards? There were no signs of any overalls recovered from a pretty extensive search, and why would he have gone to such lengths to dispose of those and leave the gun in the loft, the silencer in the bin and the car in the car-park, it just doesn't make any sense. Let's see if we can get a DNA sample from Marcus Wagner; maybe forensics can place him in Ratchford's car."

"Maybe there's another possibility we're all overlooking." All eyes turned to look at John Campbell who had been silent until now. "Everyone has been contrasting the two murders right, saying how clever he had been if he killed his first wife and how stupid he's been if he did this one. Well maybe he hasn't been so stupid after all. Maybe he put the gun in the loft and left the car at his place and dumped the body close by, to make it seem as if someone is framing him, after all....sorry Guv.....he has got our Guvnor thinking that's what's happened."

All eyes now turned back to Paul who just stared back in silence. "Christ! Have I been that stupid? Is he that good a liar?.....If he is, then Blakey's going to have my guts for garters....OK everyone back to work. I need a coffee."

Paul was on his second cup of coffee and trying in vain to clear his head and get his thoughts into some kind of order. He was also thinking that perhaps he might have been a bit short with June over the perfume wondering if he should apologise.

His office was surprisingly warm so he had opened the window to get some air and it was only when Reg knocked and put his head around the door, causing a draft to blow the window blind in and knocking a seldom-used vase to the floor and smashing, that Paul realised he had closed his door.

"Sorry Guv," exclaimed Reg. surprised as much by the fact that Paul's door had been closed as he was by the smashing vase, "You got a minute Guv?"

"I've got just under forty-eight hours Reg" replied Paul, picking up the pieces from the floor and wondering where the vase had come from. "What have you got for me?"

Well with your current dilemma Guv, I don't know whether you'll regard it as good news or bad, but we have managed to trace a Clive Lowe who used to work for Rohan and Pitt jewellery wholesalers back in the 1980s."

"The man Carver said he'd met in the pub with some other man he didn't know....one of the men Ratchford saw him with?"

"Has to be him, Guv. The name is right and he worked as a sales rep for Rohan and Pitt at the time Carver was dealing with them but he'd left their employment at the time Carver had the meeting that Ratchford witnessed. It all seems to fit."

"If he is one of the men Carver met, then Carver wasn't meeting the two men who were found in the boat."

"Unless he's our third man of course Guv."

"Yeah, you're right, he could be the one who did for Mrs. Carver and then killed our two on the boat. Please don't tell me we now have three suspects! I don't want any more."

"Sorry Guv. Shall I have him brought in?"

"As soon as you can Reg. I'm fast running out of time. Blakey's going to go ape if I turn up any more suspects. Where is this Clive Lowe? Can't we just shoot him and dispose of the body?"

Reg laughed, "I don't think that's really an option, Guv."

"No I suppose you're right."

"He's back working for his old firm again, I can have him here in the hour, Guv."

"Do that and let me know the moment he's here, I can't wait to hear what he has to say."

* * * * * * * * *

John Stubbs let himself in to the warehouse and his footsteps echoed eerily as he walked through the main storage area that was piled high with boxes of perfumes, face cream and all manner of cheap beauty products, to what appeared, from the inside, to be the rear wall of the building. He knocked on the central panel and waited patiently until it slid sideways, revealing another large space behind.

The room, although quiet, was a hive of activity where various perfumes were having their packaging carefully removed by two women who then turned the perfume bottles over to a man, who in turn removed the atomizers from their tops. Another woman was syphoning out half the contents and replacing it with a colourless fluid. The bottles were then re-sealed and the packaging replaced as if nothing had happened. John Stubbs worked here whenever he was required to do so by his employers, two of whom walked towards him now.

Alan and Clive Barnes were not men you wanted to be on the wrong side of, both over six foot and fit from exercise in the family gym. They looked more like body guards than business men. As they approached neither of them looked to be in the best of moods.

"John, we need to have a word," said Clive, "would you come with us."

"Sure, what's the problem?"

"Dad wants to see you," he replied, "he'll explain everything when we get there."

John followed the two men out to their car reluctantly, half afraid he knew exactly what their father, Jack Barnes, wanted to talk about. He was driven in silence to the family home, a large mansion in Snead Park, a rich and affluent area on the outskirts of the city. The house stood in five acres of partly wooded grounds with beautifully kept lawns and flower-beds surrounding the imposing architect-designed property.

John was a now a worried man. His brother ran a little market stall selling all sorts of bits and pieces ranging from children's clothes and gifts to CDs and cosmetics.

Fifty percent of the items on his brother's stall were fake and John had supplied him with some of the perfume from the Barnes's operation. If the family had found out, he was in all sorts of trouble.

He was shown into one of the four reception rooms the house offered, where Jack Barnes was sitting in a leather armchair drinking from a brandy glass.

"Take a seat John," Jack instructed, putting his hand out to pat a large Doberman Pinscher who had come to sit beside his chair and stare at John and if he were a tasty snack.

John looked about uneasily before doing as he was bid and sat facing Jack Barnes in a similar chair, trying not to make eye contact with the dog, his heart racing twenty to the dozen.

Jack Barnes leaned back in his chair and brought his hands together gently in front of him, almost as if he was about to pray. The Doberman turned his head to look pleadingly at his master, wonder why the petting had stopped and then back at John wondering if he was the cause.

"My son Alan informs me that you have a brother with a market stall, in Bath he tells me, is that right?" he asked.

John Stubbs was scared and felt sick to his stomach. It was obvious that they knew he had taken some of their product to supply his brother, and the stupidity of his actions was sinking in fast. They weren't the kind of people to let it go unpunished, but he had no idea what they intended to do to him. The dog looked as if it had some options in mind and his blood chilled.

Barnes spoke again, his voice calm, measured, almost friendly as he resumed petting his dog "You look worried John, and yes, I am displeased with you, you've stolen from me and what's worse, you've betrayed a trust."

"I'm sorry Mr. Barnes, it was a one-off I promise, I don't know what I was thinking, it will never happen again, please....let me make it up to you."

Jack almost sneered, "How are you going to make it up to me John? You have nothing to offer me or my family."

Jack Barnes picked up his glass again and took a sip, savouring it like a connoisseur before replacing it back on the small wine table beside him. He rested his elbows on the arms of his chair, bringing his finger-tips together in front of his face once again as if carefully contemplating his next word. "I'm a civilized man John, I know we all have certain frailties and make mistakes. I'm sure there must be some way we can put this right......do you believe we can put this right John?" he asked.

"Yes Mr. Barnes, I'll do anything you want."

"Have a drink with me then and let's talk this over."

Clive Barnes, who had been stood at the drinks cabinet to the right of John's chair, came over and handed him a glass of what looked like whisky. John didn't like whisky or any spirit for that matter but felt he couldn't turn it down, so he took the glass. "Thank you," he said, his hand shaking slightly.

Jack Barnes picked up his glass again and this time swallowed the contents in one go. "Down the hatch John," he said, indicating that John should follow his example.

John looked about the room. All eyes were on him. Reluctantly, he drank the contents of the glass only to have it instantly re-filled by Clive, who he now saw was standing right beside his chair holding the bottle of whisky in his hand, ready to pour again.

"What can I do to make it up to you Mr. Barnes, you just say the word?"

"You say it was a one-off John, is that the truth? Best to make a clean breast of it and tell us now if it's not."

"I swear it was just the one time, Mr. Barnes and I realised how stupid I'd been as soon as I'd done it but it was too late, I had passed it on to my brother."

"Yes I see, well we all make mistakes don't we, the secret is to learn from them. Finish your drink John, you look as it you could use it. Does this brother of yours know anything about our operation here?"

"No no, he knows nothing, I swear."

"He must have asked where you got the product from."

"He asked but he understands that I couldn't tell him anything."

"So he knows nothing about us."

"No, I swear."

"That's good to know John, now drink up." said Jack as he wiped the inside of his glass with the index finger of his left hand, wetting it with the dregs of the whisky and allowing his dog to lick it

John downed his drink in one again but this time he anticipated Clive re-filling it and placed his free hand over the top of the glass saying, "Two's enough for me, really, I have to drive home after my shift."

"Have another one John, Alan will drive you home after, won't you Alan?"

"No really, I'm not a big drinker of whisky, I appreciate the offer, I really do, but..."

"Have another drink John, I insist."

Clive took hold of John's hand and moved it away from over the glass before filling it again, this time to the brim, all pretence of a friendly tipple gone.

Menace hung in the room like a shroud. "What are you going to do to me?" John asked, genuinely worried that Jack Barnes was going to order his dog to attack him.

"I haven't made my mind up yet John, what do you think we should do with you? You know I can't just let you off, what sort of a message would that send to the rest of my workforce?"

"It was only one box, and I'm sorry, you know you can rely on me from now on, I don't think I deserve more than a slap on the wrist," pleaded John. "I'll take my beating if that what you decide but please no broken bones."

"OK then, finish your drink and I'll consider giving you a slap on the wrist. Clive, re-fill John's glass for him will you?"

John looked Barnes in the face and made eye contact. "Please."

"Finish your drink John, it'll ease the pain."

Realising that he would only incur the old man's wrath even more if he continued to refuse to drink and that they would probably force the whisky down him anyway, John reluctantly emptied his glass again. He struggled to down the contents, simply because the glass was so full but the men in the room seemed content to let him take his time. When he had finished it, they filled it again.

* * * * * * * * * *

June was in the process of loading her dishwasher before retiring to bed when she heard the commotion in the hallway and went to investigate.

She looked through the spy-hole in her front door. Because the door had originally been the entrance to the front room of the house it looked across the wide hallway to what was the foot of the stairs and was now the front door to the flat upstairs.

Her neighbour, John Stubbs was in the company of two men who appeared to be supporting him between them. John was unsteady on his feet and June realised he was quite drunk. One of the men took a bunch of keys from John's pocket and used them to open the door, letting all three men into the flat.

It occurred to June that the three of them had been out drinking, but John was considerably more worse for wear than his two companions who, June thought on reflection, appeared to be quite sober. She went back to finish loading the dishwasher but she couldn't shake off the feeling that something was wrong.

* * * * * * * * * * * *

Alan and Clive Barnes had to virtually carry John Stubbs up the stairs and into his flat. "Where shall we put him?" asked Clive, who had no idea what Alan and the old man had in mind for the man, although he feared that as usual, it would be over the top and out of all proportion to the offence.

He loved his father and his brothers dearly but he sometimes wondered if he was truly related to them. Perhaps his mother had been indiscreet at some time in the past and he had a different father, a more understanding and compassionate one. He could always see things from the other chap's point of view, whereas his father and Alan only ever saw things from their perspective and they both had a mean streak in them that scared him sometimes; his other brother Adrian was cast in the same mould.

He remembered when he had been out partying one night with both his brothers when a stranger, who was obviously a little tipsy, backed into Alan at the bar causing him to spill a little of his drink, quite by accident. He gave a drunken apology and Alan appeared to accept it, but when he had seen the man go to the toilets he had followed him out.

He and Adrian had gone along knowing that Alan was going to cause trouble and hoping to minimize it. Once inside, despite there being other men in there to witness things, Alan had hit the man hard in the face, causing him to fall over next to the urinals.

The room had quickly emptied after that and he and Adrian had urged Alan to leave it be, saying that hitting the man so hard had been sufficient punishment. But Alan wasn't finished.

There was a small step up to the urinals and Alan turned the almost unconscious man onto his front, pulled his arm out to the side so that his hand and wrist rested on the step and stomped on it with such force that they could all hear the bones snap. The man had cried out in pain and the three of them had left.

Clive had wanted make sure that an ambulance was called but Alan had just said, "If he needs an ambulance, I'm sure whoever finds him will call one and perhaps next time he gets off his face drunk he'll take care not to bump into anyone."

Clive felt that this present situation was heading for an even more violent outcome and he wished Adrian was there to back him up, "What are you going to do?" he asked.

"Let's get him in the kitchen," replied Alan.

Supporting John between them they entered the kitchen. "Turn him round so that he's facing the door," Alan ordered.

"What are you going to do?" Clive asked again.

"You'll see," said Alan.

Between them they maneuvered John so that he was stood almost upright and facing the door they had just come through. Alan got behind John, hooked one foot in front of John's and shoved him as hard as he could against the door frame. John went down with a crash, banging his head hard against the frame of the door and he lay there quite still, half in and half out of the room.

Clive made to leave. "Hold on," called Alan, "we're not finished yet."

"What are you going to do now, don't you think he'll have learnt his lesson?"

"The old man's been wanting to get rid of him for some time but was worried he'd grass us up if he sacked him, so he wants a more permanent solution. Did you remember to bring the bottle?"

Alan took the almost empty whiskey bottle from Clive that John had been forced to drink from earlier and placed it on the worktop. He then located a glass from the cupboard, poured the last few drops of whisky into it and then knocked both the glass and the bottle over. He then placed a saucepan on the electric hob and filled it almost to the brim with cooking oil from the cupboard. He spread some more of the oil over the worktop next to it, turned on the hob and gestured that it was now time to leave.

Clive looked back at the body in the doorway as he and his brother left and wondered briefly how far the fire would spread before the fire brigade arrived and he hoped that the man they were leaving behind would be dead before the flames reached him. He wondered whether there was anybody in the flat below who would discover the fire quickly and call for help but he was soon accompanying his brother out of the house and walking to their car, wondering what his family would do to him if he ever displeased them.

* * * * * * * * * * * *

Sometime after June had covertly watched John being taken into his flat she found herself almost nodding off in her chair, when she thought she heard a bump from upstairs but she was barely awake and could have been mistaken. She looked at her watch. It was nearly midnight. She would normally have been in bed by this time but she had been so concerned about John's two visitors that she had determined to stay up until she head them leave, and that is what she was hearing now, footsteps on the stairs.

She rose from her chair and rushed to her front door to look through the spy-hole again.

The two men were just closing the door behind them but there was no sign of John seeing them off, something that she would have expected, although John had looked pretty drunk and it was possible his two friends had said they would let themselves out, maybe leaving him inebriated and asleep. Then one of the men did something very unexpected, he removed a key from his pocket and used it to double lock John's front door. He then returned it to his pocket and took it with him when they left.

June took out her mobile phone and went to the front window. Not wanting to draw attention to herself she quickly turned off the flash facility on the phone's camera, drew the curtain ever so slightly to one side and took a photograph of the two men as they left. The delay in taking the picture, caused by her turning off the flash, cost her the chance of a good shot of their faces but fortunately, one of the men turned briefly to look back just at the right moment and she was fairly sure she had a side shot of his face, although she only had the back of the other one's head. She stayed at the window watching as they walked down the road and was rewarded by seeing them get into a dark car.

She was unable to identify the make or model as the car pulled out with the two men inside but the rear number plate was briefly visible in the light from a street lamp and June snapped again with the phone's camera.

Checking the photographs, she was disappointed that she could not make out the number of the car, but she was convinced that, if need be, it could be enhanced.

She was now very concerned about what had transpired upstairs and went into the hallway listening for any sounds from above. There were none. That didn't necessarily mean that there was anything amiss of course, it could well be that John had simply been out with friends and had had too much to drink. The friends had, very thoughtfully, made sure that he had arrived home safely and put him to bed before leaving, but the business with the key worried her; she decided to check that all was well.

"John....John," she called and she pounded on his door. Her actions were rewarded only with silence so she opened the door to the street and pressed John's doorbell, keeping her finger on it for several seconds at a time but there was still no response from above. She knew the bell was working because she could hear it in the street.

Again, it could well be that John was just too drunk to respond but the doubts about his wellbeing remained.

She tried the door to his flat; it was securely locked as expected and when she put her shoulder to it, it was obvious that there was no way she could force it open. She then made a decision that she knew could seriously back-fire on her and make her a laughing-stock at the station, but to do nothing was unthinkable. She called for back-up, explaining that she believed a crime was in progress.

Instantly regretting her rash decision to call in without trying harder to discover what was happening herself, she re-entered her flat and hurried through her lounge-cum-kitchen diner to the back doors. Exiting her flat into the rear garden through the patio doors, she looked up.

The first floor had three windows overlooking the rear garden. The one on the right as June looked at them was a large room that she assumed was John's bedroom, next to it was a small window with obscured glass that was obviously the toilet and bathroom, and to the left of that was another large window that looked out from the flat's kitchen. Below the level of the windows and running the full width of the building was a small, tiled, sloping roof, that extended the downstairs flat into the garden by about eight feet.

At first glance, June thought that there was a light flickering in the kitchen but quickly realised to her horror that she was seeing flames. The kitchen of John's flat was on fire! Thank God she had made the decision to call it in. She got out her phone again and this time called the Fire Brigade as she stared in horror at the window.

June felt helpless. The Fire Brigade were on their way but she couldn't just stand about watching the flames, she had to do something....She had seen John taken into his flat and she knew he hadn't left, he was still in there! What could she do? She had already established that she would be unable to force entry through the front door of his flat. The upstairs windows were the only way but how could she get up there? She was racking her brains.....she couldn't just stand there and watch.

She suddenly realised that the street door and the door to her own flat were shut so she rushed back through the flat and opened them both wide so that the fire-fighters could get through without her having to leave the garden or them having to break them down.

Rushing back out into the garden, she remembered that the garden shed had some stuff of John's in it. Although the garden and shed were the exclusive domain of the ground floor flat, there being no way to get into the garden without access through it, June had allowed John to store some items in there along with her own, mostly tools and decorating paraphernalia.

Amongst those items, she was sure she had seen a pair of steps and she rushed to the shed to check. Sure enough, when she opened the shed door, they were right there in front of her but it was immediately obvious that they were too short to be of any practical use.

She looked around her but all she could see was what was just inside the door. The rest of the shed was in almost complete darkness. She felt around in the dark and her hand grasped what felt like a contender for the world's shortest ladder. She knew straight away what it was. Her father had a set just like them, a telescopic ladder. Dragging it out so that it was visible in the light cast from her downstairs windows, she could hardly believe her luck.

June carried the ladder over to the sloping roof, under what she thought was John's bedroom. Placing her foot on the bottom rung she felt for and released the catches on each side and pulled upwards. The ladder extended by one rung and she repeated the operation several more times until the top rung was above the guttering of the sloping roof.

June looked up at the window above her. It consisted of a large central panel with an opening section on either side - the same as the one in her bedroom. The opening sections she knew were too small to climb through and were probably locked anyway, so she would somehow have to break the large central panel.

Running quickly back to the shed she hurriedly looked, or rather felt around, for a hammer. Just under the shed's small window was an old side-table and it was strewn with various tools that her father had insisted she would need living on her own. She had never been more grateful for her father's fussing. Feeling around on the table top she soon located what she was seeking, a very large hammer. When her father had included it in the items he insisted she needed, she hadn't been sure whether he thought she would have some large nails to drive home or some unwanted boyfriend to fend off. Either way she had a use for it now.

She climbed the ladder with ease, grateful that she was still wearing her work shoes. Quickly assessing the steepness of the roof's slope, she was confident that she could scale it easily and get to the window, and in that she was proved right.

Steadying herself against the brickwork to one side June swung the hammer at the glass as hard as she could and was completely taken by surprise by the force with which it rebounded. She almost lost her balance and cursed to herself but once again her father's words came to her aid.

She couldn't remember the exact circumstances when the advice had been given, only that it had something to do with means of escaping from a burning building.

"It's no good trying to break toughened glass by attacking it in the middle with a hammer," she heard him say. "You have to go for a corner."

She smiled at the irony of the situation, seeing as how she was now using the advice for the exact opposite of how it was intended; that of breaking *into* a burning building. Her father would be horrified if he could see her now.

She had only just managed to keep hold of the hammer after her first attempt at breaking and entering, but this time she was forewarned about the consequences of the intended impact. Her effort this time was rewarded with the appearance of a chip in the corner of the window. She aimed a second blow with the hammer at the same place and was pleased with herself for managing to hit the exact same spot twice in a row. Her accuracy resulted in the entire window exploding into a thousand fragments. June threw the hammer into the room before bracing herself and climbing in after it.

Under the window on the inside was a low ottoman that made it easy to climb down from the window and, June reflected, would make it easy to climb back out. The bedroom door was closed which had prevented it from completely filling with smoke, a situation that June knew would change rapidly when she opened the door. A task that she knew she would have to preform but one that she dreaded.

The door was situated in the far corner of the room to her left, and as was the Victorian custom to ensure maximum privacy for the room's occupants should a servant enter, it opened into the room and was hung whichever hand meant the door would need to be fully open before the rooms interior could be viewed by whoever entered.

She approached the door and grasped the handle with trepidation before slowly turning it. She started to open the door towards herself using it as a shield against whatever was on the other side. The scene from a film she had watched, where a man had opened the door to a burning room only to be instantly engulfed in flame was playing over and over in her mind.

June had no way of knowing if the film's scenario was a likely one, although she had heard of flashovers, where a fire would suddenly leap across a room when supplied with a new source of oxygen, something that she knew would happen when she opened the door.

Fresh oxygen coming through the window she had broken would feed the flames for sure.

She continued to open the door slowly and cautiously, making sure that she was behind it and ready to slam it shut again should her worst fears come to fruition. Fortunately for her and ultimately for John, the half-expected flashover never happened, although there was an influx of black acrid smoke that caught her unawares and made her cough violently. She ducked under the thick layer of smoke and peered into the hall, suddenly aware of the intense heat and the fact that her heart was beating twenty to the dozen.

Both the doors to the bathroom and the kitchen were open and the thick black acrid smoke was everywhere, making it difficult to see anything except the flames in the kitchen which had really taken hold. She reached up and tried the bedroom light but as expected it didn't work. The fire must have tripped the RCD, cutting off all the electricity in the flat. The only light was a small amount of moonlight from the bathroom window, that only managed to slightly illuminate the space below the thick smoke and then there was the light from the fire itself dancing off the walls and floor.

Her eyes, which were beginning to sting quite badly, slowly became more accustomed to the low light levels and kneeling now to keep under the choking smoke, June could just make out the form of a body, lying with the head and shoulders in the hall and the torso and legs in the kitchen. She had no way of knowing whether the person, who she assumed was John, was alive or dead, but she called out to him.

"John! John!" she shouted between coughs, suddenly becoming aware of how noisy the fire was.

There was no response at all from the prone figure and she realised that if she was to save him she would have to venture nearer to the fire.

The heat was overwhelming as she crawled across the hallway causing her to stop outside the open bathroom door. She had never experienced heat anything like it and she doubted that she could go on. She felt as if her clothes would burst into flame at any moment and her courage left her. She changed direction and crawled quickly through the bathroom door.

Just being out of the direct line of the fire was a huge relief but there was no escape from the thick black smoke that was everywhere. She felt around and found two towels, one that had been discarded on the bathroom floor and another that was hanging on a rail. She threw the towels into the bath and turned on the cold tap soaking them in the tepid water. At first, she thought she had turned on the hot tap by mistake but quickly realised that the fire must be heating the water in the pipes themselves.

The thought of hot water made her think about boilers and gas supplies and she had to banish the thoughts from her mind if she was ever to regain her courage.

She put the plug in the bath, preventing the water from running away, making it easier to soak the towels and as an afterthought she did the same thing to the basin, hoping it would overflow and flood the room with water, even though she knew it would be of little use against the raging inferno that was coming.

June wrapped one sodden towel around her neck and draped the other over her head. The relief the wet towels supplied was immense despite the lack of coldness but she realised that when she returned to the hall, this blessed relief would soon be snatched away.

Returning to the hell that was the hall, June was horrified to see how the situation had escalated in the brief time she had spent in the bathroom. The kitchen door and frame were now ablaze, as were John's trouser legs.

Overcome with guilt at the delay and casting aside her fears for her own safety, June now stood up, but crouching to stay as low as possible, she moved quickly forward and grabbed hold of John under his arms.

The heat was so bad that she thought for a moment that she was actually on fire herself. She pulled with all the strength she could muster, boosted by the adrenaline surging through her veins. She didn't stop until both she and John were in the bedroom where she quickly threw one of the still damp towels onto Johns burning lower half, and slammed the door shut.

Coughing and spluttering and weary from exertion she turned to where John lay. She saw straight away that the towel had not completely extinguished the flames and she had to use the second towel that was now almost dry, to smother the last of the flames. She cursed herself for taking so long wetting the towels, but she knew deep down that she would not have been able to stand the heat of the fire without them.

If she hadn't been finding it so hard to breath she would have let out a scream of relief and triumph but her errand was nowhere near over. She checked John's pulse but wasn't sure whether she could feel one or not. If there was one it was very faint. She was just about to check for any signs that he was breathing when she heard a loud crash from the hall. Terrified that there had been some kind of gas explosion, she prepared to drag John over to the window.

At first, she wasn't sure what she was seeing but when she did make out the figure, of what looked like a visitor from another planet in the window, her relief was overwhelming and she burst into tears.

The man was wearing breathing apparatus but he took the mask off to speak and asked in a surprisingly calm voice, "Is there anyone else in the house?"

Almost unable to speak through her tears June shouted "No," in a voice that was anything but calm and she didn't recognise as her own. "Just us two," she continued, indicating the prone body on the floor beside her.

Her saviour placed his mask over her face allowing her to fill her lungs with deliciously fresh air before saying, "Keep low and make your way to the window but don't try to climb out without me, nod your head if you understand and can do that. Are you hurt at all?"

"No I'm OK, it's John....I'm not sure if he's breathing."

"Leave him to me. Stay by the window."

June did as she was bidden, glad not to have the responsibility for the outcome of events any more and more than happy to be close to an escape route.

Just as she reached the window she heard a terrifying noise behind her and she almost cried out in alarm as the bedroom door was opened and another man in breathing apparatus came into the room.

"Come with me miss," the second man called, "we can go out this way," he said, indicating the landing, "it's safe now."

At first June was horrified at the prospect of returning to the landing but then she looked through the open door and could see no sign of the inferno that she felt sure it would now be.

"What's your name?" he asked her.

"June Kelly," she croaked.

The man took her arm and accompanied her out of the room. Once in the hall she could see other alien-looking creatures with hoses in the kitchen, but there was no longer any sign of flames. She marveled at how quickly they had turned the situation around. She had lost all sense of time. One minute, she had seen what she regarded as a preview of what hell must be like, and next, the only sign of a fire was the smell and the black smoke that seemed to have taken up permanent residence. Perhaps she had dreamt it all and would wake up any minute now in the comfort and security of her bed.

Outside it was like a scene from a movie. There were two fire appliances, their flashing lights reflected from nearly every window in the street and their long yellow hoses trailing across the pavement and into the house June and her new saviour were exiting from, and an ambulance with its back door open, around which a small crowd of people had collected, curious about what was happening.

June assumed most of the people in the crowd were neighbours who had come out to help or perhaps just to watch. She reflected on how times had changed. Her parents had lived in a similar place to this when June was a child and they could tell you the names of everyone in the street, whereas June didn't recognise a single face in the crowd. The only one of her neighbours she knew was John.

She made a mental note to herself to change that situation as soon as life returned to normal, if it ever did.

The firefighter who escorted her out of the house led her to the back of the ambulance where a young paramedic greeted them.

"This is June Kelly," the firefighter told her, "and she has breathed in a considerable quantity of smoke."

June started to protest, "No....I'm," she stopped mid-sentence, not recognizing the sound of her own voice and realising for the first time just how painfully sore her throat was.

The paramedic helped June into the back of the ambulance and took a swab from her throat. "Sorry," she said, "I know that must have hurt." She then gave her a small plastic beaker with some liquid in it and said, "drink that for me and then put this mask on and just relax and breath normally."

Whatever the liquid was, it was very soothing on her throat and June was more than grateful for it. She put on her mask and sat quietly for several minutes until John was brought into the ambulance on a stretcher and laid in the bunk on the opposite side to where she sat.

One of the two paramedics that carried him in proceeded to fit a drip into John's arm but he still appeared to be unconscious. June wondered if he was going to make it and once again felt guilty that she hadn't got to him quicker.

She took of her mask and enquired, "How is he?"

"That's my question too," came a voice from the rear doors.

June looked round to see a police sergeant standing in the

doorway looking suitably concerned. The paramedic turned and said, "It's difficult to say at the moment, but he has inhaled a lot of smoke, there is a bump on his head and some second degree burns to his lower legs. I'm not sure how serious the bump to his head is as he also appears to be the worst for drink."

"And what about you?" the sergeant asked, looking at June.

"Just my throat, I think," said June, "but I need to speak to you about the cause of the fire."

The young paramedic, who was still attending to John had heard the exchange, she now turned to June and said, pointing to June's arm, "We'll just ignore that then shall we?"

June looked down at her arm. The sleeve of her blouse had a hole burnt in it the size of a dinner plate and her arm was very red and inflamed, and now that she was aware of it, very painful as well.

"I'll dress that as soon as I'm finished here and we're underway." said the paramedic sympathetically, "and I'll give you something for the pain. Do you think you could swallow some tablets? If not, I'll give you an injection."

June put one hand to her throat and shook her head.

"That's OK, I'll do the injection in your good arm."

"I'll let you get on with things here," the sergeant said to the paramedic," then turning to June, "I'll meet you at the hospital and we can speak there," he said smiling reassuringly, "I take it you're going to Southmead." This last remark had been addressed to the ambulance driver who had just arrived at the back of the vehicle.

"Yes, that's right," he replied and then to his colleague, "are we good to go?"

"Good to go, Jack."

The driver closed the ambulance doors and took his place behind the wheel.

On the journey to Southmead Hospital the paramedic who had treated John explained that she had given him a mild sedative and pain-killers. Although his legs were badly burnt and he had inhaled a great deal of smoke, she thought he had a good chance of surviving his ordeal.

June was pleased but still felt a pang of guilt. If she hadn't wasted precious time getting wet towels from the bathroom, his legs may not have been so severely injured but she had been convinced at the time that the heat would have driven her back.

June's thoughts were still concentrated on John when a voice brought her back to the present. "Let's have a look at your arm now shall we?"

June slipped her blouse down from her shoulder and the paramedic, who it turned out was also called June, looked at her arm.

"That's not too bad. Does it hurt very much?" she asked.

"Yes it does, can you give me something for it? I was unaware of it until you pointed it out, now it hurts like the devil."

She gave June a painkilling injection and said, "It's only a first degree burn but it's best if a doctor has a look and they'll probably dress it. It hurts badly because it would have been best to put cool water on it straight away to take the heat away, but it shouldn't take too long to heal and there's not going to be any scarring or anything."

"Thank you," said June as the ambulance pulled up outside the accident and Emergency Department of Southmead Hospital.

The back doors were opened and between them the driver and the paramedic manoeuvered John onto a trolley and took him inside where he was immediately whisked away by two ladies in white coats and the obligatory stethoscopes.

June pulled her damaged blouse back on and was forced to sit in a wheelchair before being allowed to follow them in. She was closely followed by the sergeant who had been at the scene and had followed the ambulance.

June was pushed into a cubicle and was told a doctor would be along shortly.

Constable Harvey followed her in and when the nurse had left and June was settled he asked, "Do you mind telling me what happened while you wait for the Doc?"

June related to him all that she knew about John, the fake perfume bottles and the events of that evening, "You understand that Trading Standards are investigating these people and will need to be updated about tonight's events." She gave him Andrew Weaver's number.

"Yes, I understand that constable, but this sounds like an attempted murder to me and you know that will take priority over anything else. You were very brave by the way, going into a burning building like that. You should get a commendation."

June quickly made a statement and signed it so that the sergeant could go to see how John was faring. He had instructions to report back to June whatever the news, good or bad. She replaced the mask she had been given and wondered if she could get some more of whatever liquid the paramedic had given her to ease her throat which, after all the talking she'd done, was now very sore indeed.

Half an hour later a young doctor who June was convinced was too young to have left home, but who turned out to have come to England from Poland at the age of twenty six some four years earlier, turned up and examined her.

"Your arm is not too bad," he said in the most perfect English she had ever heard, "just first degree burns fortunately, keep the area clean and take painkillers if and when you need them. The nurse will be back to put a light dressing on it for you. Your face you can just keep moisturized with Aveeno cream and avoid any make-up for a while."

"What's wrong with my face?" asked June suddenly quite scared.

"Oh nothing," the doctor replied realising that he had alarmed her, "it's just a little red from the heat, that's all, it'll be back to normal in a couple of days, it's nothing to worry about, really. I would like to keep you in for observation tonight however," he looked at her chart before saying, "June. You inhaled quite a bit of smoke and although I don't think any permanent damage has been done, there's always the chance of infection and I'd rather be safe than sorry. Just be aware that your lungs and throat are going to need some time to recover. For now, keep the oxygen mask on and try to get a good night's sleep. I'll see you in the morning and we'll assess the situation again then."

June watched the doctor go and wondered briefly about discharging herself but she was very tired and just wanted to sleep so she decided a night in hospital had some merit, although there had been no mention of transferring her to a ward and she supposed that

Southmead was just as short of beds as everywhere else in the country appeared to be. The thought of beds also made her realise that she probably wouldn't be allowed back to her flat that night and would have to go and stay at her dad's place, at least for one night. The thought of explaining to him what had happened filled her with dread.

Another half hour went by and June got the shock of her life when Paul and his wife Margaret turned up. "Guv! What are you doing here?....hello Margaret."

"Jack Harvey called me and told me what had happened. We figured you'd need somewhere to stay, you won't be allowed back into the flat for a while, well not until the repairs are done probably, so you can come and stay with us."

June looked puzzled, "I didn't think the fire had affected my place that much Guv. It was just John's flat."

"Sorry June," said Paul sympathetically, "Firefighters may be good at putting out fires and rescuing idiots that break into burning buildings when they should know better, but they can be bloody careless with water and hoses and the like. I'm afraid your flat looks like a tsunami has been through it, and there's the damage to the front door."

"The front door!...but I opened that specially so they could get in quickly."

Paul shrugged his shoulders, "Firemen and their axes! What can you do."

June was horrified but Margaret intervened and said to her, "They'll make the place secure and the flat is not as bad as Paul likes to make out, although part of the ceiling did come down apparently so you'd be better off coming to us tonight. Are they letting you out soon?"   Margaret suddenly noticed the dressing on June's arm. "What's happened to your arm, is it very bad?"

"No, it's just some first-degree burns apparently," said June, "they want to keep me in overnight though, because of the smoke I inhaled and I have to say my throat does feel pretty sore and my chest is beginning to hurt when I breath. The way I feel at the moment, Margaret I'm glad they're keeping me in."

"Do you want me to pick up some clothes for you from the flat?" asked Paul.

"Absolutely not Guv! But you could get a WPC to it, I've got some toiletries at my dad's but no clothes."

Paul was puzzled. "well I could....."

June looked towards Margaret, who was grinning from ear to ear. "Paul, I think it would be better if you had a WPC pick up June's things for her."

"Why?" Paul asked, frowning

Margaret burst out laughing, "Oh my God! Paul, for a smart detective you can be very slow on the uptake sometimes. I don't think that June wants you rummaging through her underwear drawer is all," she smiled and winked at June. "You can have a rummage through mine when you get home if that's what you want."

Despite the pain it caused in her throat June burst out laughing in unison with Margret.

Paul was now embarrassed. "I just thought....I mean I.....," he stared at June and said in the sternest voice he could muster, "June Kelly, if any of this conversation gets back to the station I swear to God you'll wish you were never born. I'll arrange to have some things picked up by a WPC and brought here for the morning....does that meet with your approval?"

"That would be great Guv, thanks."

"Yes, you do that dear, said Margaret, still laughing, then turning to June, who was now struggling not to laugh because of the pain, "and you'll stay with us until the flat is habitable again and that's an order not a request, isn't that right, Paul?"

"Yes of course," Paul answered, then turning to June, "did you see the men who did this?"

"Through the spyhole in my door Guv, and again through the window when they left."

"And you can identify them?"

"Of course, Guv. I am a trained observer after all."

A nurse suddenly appeared and announced in a cheery voice, "June Kelly, we have a bed for you now," and turning to the porter beside her said, "this is Bert, he'll take you up."

Paul and Margaret said their farewells and asked if there was anything else they could do.

"You could ring my dad in the morning and tell him what has happened, but don't tell him I was hurt or had to stay in hospital."

Paul and Margaret left and June was trundled off by Bert to spend a night in hospital, something she hadn't done since the day she was born.

Chapter 11

Paul and Reg both regarded the man sat opposite them as a sort of throwback to a nineteen-twenties gangster. He had been wearing an old fashioned looking suit with a trilby hat when he had arrived and neither Paul nor Reg would have been surprised to see him carrying a violin case with a machine-gun inside. They had exchanged several questioning glances as they accompanied him to the interview room where they now sat.

"Tell me Mr. Lowe, do you remember having any dealings with a Mr. David Carver back in the late nineteen eighties? Eighty-nine to be precise," Paul asked as he appraised the man once again across the interview table.

"David Carver, well there's a name from the past," said Lowe, "yes I knew him but I knew everyone in the trade back then, Inspector. Carver married into the Wagner family, his wife had quite a reputation in the trade and a fine collection of antique jewellery as I remember."

"Why did you leave your job at Rohan and Pitt?"

"Oh that's easy; I thought I could make it on my own Inspector, I went self-employed for a while but never made the kind of money I was pulling in as a rep."

"When you were self-employed, who did you have dealings with? Did you for instance ever try to sell to David Carver then?"

"Sure.....I tried to keep selling to all my old contacts."

"I asked about David Carver."

"Yeah...Carver and the Wagner's, all of them. They'd been good clients."

"Did you ever meet with David Carver anywhere other than the shop to discuss business?"

"What, at the warehouse you mean?"

"I was thinking more in terms of a social venue, a restaurant perhaps."

"Yeah, it's possible, I sometimes met clients in wine bars or pubs; come to think of it I did quite a lot of business in pubs back then."

Paul gave him the date that Ratchford's file indicated the two men had met. "Blimey! You expect me to remember if a specific meeting took place back in 1989....Can you remember what you were doing on that date? Give me break."

"Look, I'm not interested in what you were up to or planning that night or whether it was legal or not. I'm just trying to establish whether you and another man, possibly called Adrian, met with David Carver, in a pub, on or around the date I've given you. It's of no interest to me what the meeting was about, just whether such a meeting took place."

"With another man, you say. Yes, OK, I have a vague idea we met up around that time, a friend of mine, who shall remain nameless, had some gear he was looking to offload cheap and I put him in touch with David Carver for a small fee."

"And this gear your friend was looking to offload was stolen, yeah?"

"I didn't want to know then and I certainly don't know now Inspector. I didn't ask the question."

"And this friend of yours, who shall remain nameless, are you still in touch with him?"

"Not really, he's moved on, working somewhere up north the last I heard."

"OK Mr. Lowe, I'll get someone to take your statement and it's possible we may need to speak to you again or we may even need to speak to Adrian; so once you've signed your statement and given us Adrian's surname you can go."

"I didn't mention anyone called Adrian, I didn't mention anyone called anything, that was just you, Inspector."

"I repeat, I'm not interested in what you were doing. Just whether you and someone called Adrian ever met with David Carver."

"You're definitely not interested in what we were doing back then? I mean I don't want to get a reputation as a grass any more than you want a reputation as a bent copper, you understand."

"I understand fully. No interest at all,"

"OK, his name is Adrian Fellows, but all I know about his whereabouts is that he moved up north."

"Fair enough."

"I can go?"

"As soon as you've signed a statement, yes."

As Paul and Reg left the interview room Reg acknowledged, "Looks more and more as if our Mr. Carver is being straight with us, Guv. I'm beginning to think your instincts about him have been right all along."

"Yeah, see if you can trace this Adrian Fellows, if he and Clive Lowe are the two men Carver met with in the pub, then they are certainly not the two on the boat."

"How is June, Guv? Everyone's asking when she's going to be back."

"She's doing well, Reg. The Doc wants her to have a week off but I can't see her doing that somehow. I'm half expecting her to walk through the door any time."

"That's good news, she should get some sort of recognition for what she did, a commendation at least."

"I agree with you Reg. and I know the DCI is keen that her actions should be recognised. I've also heard that she might be asked to do an interview on Radio Bristol with the Chief Constable, when she has recovered her voice properly. It's good publicity for the police at the moment and the top brass are keen to bask in her reflected glory. In the meantime, chase down this Adrian Fellow for me, let's see if we can at least tie up that loose end."

* * * * * * * * * * * * * * * *

David and Sandra Carver where sat in their private lounge trying to prevent the frank discussion they were having from turning into a full-scale row.

"Well, who the hell could have put the gun in the loft if it wasn't you?" Sandra asked her husband, in a tone that David interpreted as extremely accusatorial.

"I don't know any more than you do, I've told you for God's sake, someone is obviously trying to frame me......and don't ask me who.....because I don't know who! All I know is that I didn't put the bloody gun in the loft and I certainly didn't kill anyone.....surely you've known me long enough to know I couldn't do anything like that!"

"Well, who can you think of that would have known this Ratchford? If someone is genuinely trying to frame you, then they must have known that Ratchford came to see you....they possibly know that he tried to blackmail you about the murder of Sylvia. Maybe it's one of the men who killed Sylvia......maybe Ratchford tried to blackmail them after he failed with you....that's possible isn't it?"

David was taken aback by the train of thought; maybe Sandra was right. If Ratchford did try to blackmail someone else, that would certainly account for his being murdered, and if that person knew he had been to see him and knew that the police suspected him of his wife's murder, that would explain everything that had happened. But who could it be?

"Have we got Marcus Wagner's number?" David asked.

"Why? Do you think Marcus could have something to do with all this?"

"I don't know. He hates me enough for receiving what he sees as the other half of his inheritance, but I can't believe he would have been responsible for killing his own sister. I'm sure there was some genuine affection between them, at least I'm sure there was on Sylvia's side. But if I speak to him it may trigger some memory or something. I think I need to speak to him anyway. He knows how much I loved

Sylvia back then and he may turn out to be the only person who believes I didn't do it."

"But what if he is the one trying to frame you?"

"I don't know....I just know I have to go and speak to him."

Sandra was in turmoil, one moment she was telling herself that she knew David better than anyone and that it was inconceivable that he could have killed anyone, let alone his own wife, the next minute she reviewed all the evidence the police had against him and she had doubts.

She got up from her chair and went to the bureau where they kept their personal address book. "I think you're wasting your time with this but I'll have a look," she said and after flicking through a few pages she announced, "You might be in luck, we have an address for him in Thornbury, but it's an old address copied over when we combined our two address books, it's years old, he may have moved since then. Do you want his telephone number?"

"No, give me the address. I'm going to go and see him now and catch him by surprise. I don't want him thinking too much and planning what to say to me before I get there, he may know the whereabouts of the reps I dealt with back then. It will help if I can trace them, the police think they are the two bodies found in my boat. If I can prove that they're still alive it should count for something."

David grabbed his coat from the cupboard in the entrance hall and left as Sandra called after him, "Are you sure about this? I think you should call him first, he may not be in, even if he still lives there. And be careful.... If he is the one trying to frame you then he is the one who killed Ratchford."

"Sorry Sandra, I need to do something and a drive will at least help to clear my head, even if it's a wild goose chase."

Sandra returned to their private lounge and sat contemplating her husband's actions. She had never seen him so anxious and upset. He was convinced the police were going to arrest him and charge him with murder and who could blame them after all the evidence they had found. She was reluctant to admit it, even to herself, but there was even part of her that doubted David's account of Sylvia's last day; and if he was responsible for that....then. She mixed herself a drink and sat down to think things through.

The re-emergence of David's boat had changed their lives. Now, even if, or rather when, David was proven to be innocent of Ratchford's murder, the fact that she had doubted him, even momentarily, because of the weight of evidence, would never go away. It would forever lie between them like a river that may have once had a bridge but the bridge had been swept away and could never be rebuilt.

She was still sitting and thinking hours later when she looked at her watch and was astonished to see that it was almost nine in the evening. David had been gone for hours and dinner would have been served and almost cleaned away by now; the kitchen staff would soon be leaving and she had duties to attend to. Why wasn't David back? she hoped everything was all right. She wondered if she should call the police, tell them that her husband had gone to see Marcus and that she was worried.

* * * * * * * * * * * * * * *

June returned to work four days after the fire and seven days before her doctor had recommended. As she walked through the doors she was greeted by thunderous applause from everyone in the room. Walking to her desk everyone in the room took a turn at shaking her hand or slapping her on the back and saying such thing as, "Well done June, that was a brave thing to do, you deserve a medal and good to have you back, June."

She was overwhelmed by the response of the team and had to fight back tears as delayed shock struck her and she herself realised for the first time the enormity of what she had done. The team quietened down and left her to recover her composure when they saw how emotional she was, but Reg brought a bottle of Champaign over to her that had been put into a fire-bucket full of what had, an hour earlier, been ice.

"A little something from us all June, just to say that we are proud of you and really glad to have you back.....Now pull yourself together and get on with your work, we've all been working our socks off while you've had your feet up in hospital and quite frankly it's caused a backlog."

"June pulled herself together and replied, "Right you are Reg, I take it that means nobody has solved the case while I've been away saving lives."

Reg grinned at her and returned to his desk.

The day was a day of frustration for Paul and the team. No new evidence emerged, and DCI Blake was heaping pressure on Paul to get the case wrapped up as the time limit he had imposed was long gone.

Paul was grateful that he had things to do in the evening that didn't have anything to do with work but he wasn't really in the mood for socialising either. He had too much on his mind.

Being under the immense pressure he was to arrest Carver, he was probably going to have to do just that. Paul was well aware of the fact that June's actions had lifted the pressure off him. Her interview on radio with the Chief Constable had highlighted to the public just how brave the men and women of the police service were, and top brass were well pleased. At the moment, the last thing anyone wanted to do was criticise Paul or his team but that situation wouldn't last forever.

What the team had suggested had worried him and caused him to question his own judgement but despite that, Paul still felt Carver was telling the truth.

Maybe an evening with friends rather than colleagues was just what he needed, so tonight he prepared to put work behind him.

Paul's wife Margaret had rung the door bell and it was opened by Elizabeth Drake. Richard and Elizabeth Drake had been good friends of Margaret since she was a child and their daughter Rebecca was like a sister to her. Margaret now worked only part time for Richard in his antique business, whereas she had been full time when she had first met Paul.

Paul had met and married Margret while investigating a case that resulted in two brothers trying to kill Richard. It had been Paul's first case as an inspector and had earned him something of a reputation. They had all become good friends and tonight's little get together was just one of many that had happened since those terrible events.

Elizabeth lead them into the lounge where Rebecca and her husband Daniel were sitting and talking to Richard, each with a glass of wine in hand. Daniel ran his own little business making and selling acoustic guitars and was in the middle of writing a book on antique musical instruments that Richard was helping him with.

Richard got up from his seat to fetch the new arrivals a drink and after nodding a welcome to Daniel and Rebecca, Paul followed him over to the drinks cabinet.

"How's the book coming along Richard, have you sold the film rights yet?"

"It's a reference book you clot, they don't make films out of reference books."

"Sure they do; they just call them documentaries, that's all."

"Yeah, well it's coming along all right. Daniel and I are trying to persuade the Victoria and Albert to let us photograph a couple of their exhibits, if they turn us down we'll have to try a museum in Vienna or failing that we'll have to commission someone to do detailed drawings.

"How's the detecting lark these days, are you on the verge of cracking another big case?"

The two men sat side by side on the small leather settee. "I'll be honest with you Richard, I'm tearing my hair out on this present one. Tomorrow, I think I am going to end up charging a man for murder and I have serious doubts about his guilt."

"Why charge him if you don't think he's guilty? That doesn't sound like you."

"It's not me Richard, but the trouble is, we have so much evidence against him I'm going to look incompetent if I don't charge him, and my DCI will take me off the case and give it to another Inspector who will certainly charge him."

"Surely that's better than you charging a man you think is innocent?"

"I don't know Richard. If Roy Darnley charges him, he'll make damn sure the charges stick and the man will end up inside for sure. Whereas, if I charge him, I can still spend my time searching for the evidence that will free him and convict someone else. Isn't that a better option?"

"Sorry Paul, you do seem to be in a bit of a spot, nothing I can do to help I suppose. Do you have any other suspects?"

"I do as a matter of fact, an Marcus Wagner, a rally driver and all round car nut."

"Wagner? That's not a common name. I used to know a Karl Wagner, but he was a jeweller, a fascinating man, in poor health when I knew him but an absolute authority on antique jewellery."

Paul could hardly believe what he was hearing. "This Wagner you knew didn't have a daughter called Sylvia by any chance, did he?" asked Paul expectantly.

"Yes, he did as a matter of fact. Actually, having said that, it was his daughter Sylvia that I really knew, that must have been back in the 80s. I hadn't been in business all that long and was keen to learn a bit about antique jewellery. Well I can tell you there wasn't much

Sylvia Wagner and her father didn't know. Practically everything I know about antique jewellery now, I learned from them back then."

Paul was astonished to discover that his good friend knew the Wagner family. "Jesus Richard! You knew Sylvia Wagner?"

"Yes, as I said, I knew her and her father....don't tell me they're in some way involved in this case of yours."

"They most certainly are! Do you remember what happened to Sylvia?"

"Well yes....let me think, she was killed, that's right, there was a break-in or something at the shop and she was murdered but I can't remember all the details."

Paul was incredulous. "Let me ask you a question Richard," said Paul, half smiling for the first time since leaving his DCIs office. "Have you read a newspaper in the last week or so?"

"Antique Trade Gazette, regular as clockwork and I have a brief scan through the Telegraph in the mornings to check that we're not at war, why?"

"Because all the local papers have been covering the recovery of David Carver's boat and the nationals have mentioned it as well, how could you have missed it?"

"What, the boat they found with two bodies on? I glanced at the headlines of course but I didn't read the details. What has that got to do with Sylvia Wagner's murder?"

"Well her maiden name was Wagner all right, but her married name was Carver, and it was her husband's boat that they supposedly made their getaway in, tossing him over the side into the bargain, but he survived."

"Oh, that's right, it's coming back to me now. Obviously I followed the story with interest back then because I knew the family. And this boat they've just found is the one they used?"

"That's right Richard, and the fact that there were two bodies found on board pulls into question Carver's version of events. If the two men who had him captive threw him over the side, how come they ended up at the bottom of the Bristol Channel with the boat?"

"Oh! I see....So you now think that David Carver robbed his own shop and killed the two men on the boat?"

"I have to say you're pretty quick on the uptake, Richard. The evidence certainly points to him having planned the whole thing from the start, including the murder of his wife, Sylvia."

"But you just said you didn't think your suspect was guilty."

"I said I have doubts, and there is another suspect."

"Who's that?"

"This goes no further Richard.....yes?"

"Of course," assured Richard completely intrigued with what he was hearing.

"Sylvia had a brother called Marcus," started Paul but Richard interrupted him in his excitement.

"Marcus Wagner, of course, I met him as well, he tried to sell me a couple of things as I recall now!"

"Bloody hell Richard, you seem to know all my suspects. I hope I'm not going to end up arresting you, I came close to doing that once before, remember. Tell me everything you can remember about them."

"But do it after we've eaten," interrupted Elizabeth, who had just returned from the kitchen and caught the tail end of their conversation. "I want you all in the dining room now, I haven't been slaving away in that kitchen for hours so you two can gossip and let it all go cold."

Paul found it difficult not to question Richard further during dinner but stern glances from Elizabeth kept it from happening. As soon as dessert was cleared from the table, Paul dragged Richard away and they went into Richard's office-cum-den. It was in here that he was allowed to keep the things that Elizabeth disapproved of, such as the Navy Colt and Winchester rifle that were mounted on the wall above his desk.

"Tell me all you know about David Carver," Paul pleaded as the two men sat in the chairs they always used for discussions.

"Not much to tell really Paul, it was Sylvia that I knew best. I used to sit in the shop with her for hours discussing the history of jewellery and how to tell a good stone from an average one, or a Georgian setting from Victorian."

"What did you think of him?...David Carver."

"Honestly Paul, I don't think I spoke to the man except to say hello or goodbye, but he always struck me as a decent enough chap, certainly not one who would kill his wife, if that's what you're asking?"

"OK, so tell me about Marcus Wagner."

"Again, I hardly knew the man. I met him once in Sylvia's shop; she introduced us because he had some car bonnet ornaments and some old racing trophies for sale. I bought a couple of items off him initially and for a while after that he kept bringing me stuff all the time. Most of it was next to worthless; I got into the habit of turning stuff down simply to try and get rid of him and in the hope that he would take his stuff elsewhere. It's not that I disliked him or anything, it's just that he only had one topic of conversation, and only turned up when he needed money, which I recall was quite often."

"I noticed a couple antique-looking things at the house when we were there but only a walking stick and a table lighter. Nothing that would be of any value, although having said that the lighter was very decorative and may have been gold."

"Oh, and don't be too sure about the walking stick Paul, some canes can fetch hundreds, even thousands of pounds and I've seen some pretty valuable table lighters as well. What were they like?" Richard asked, genuinely interested.

"Well the walking stick looked as if it was made out of bone or ivory with a silver handle but the ivory bit was all twisted around as if someone had wrung it out like a wet towel."

"Hang on a minute, Paul," Richard raised himself from his chair. The wall opposite the door was covered entirely with bookshelves and it was from one of these that Richard now selected a book.

After flicking through the book, he handed it to Paul. "Did it look anything like one of these?" he asked, after finding a particular page and handing the open book to him.

Paul looked at the illustrations and photographs on the page before him that were mostly of walking canes and parasols and his eye was drawn to one in particular. "Good Lord! Yes, that's almost exactly what it looked like...is it ivory?"

"Yes, but not from an elephant. It's made from a narwhal tusk."

"A what?"

"A narwhal tusk, a narwhal is a whale that lives in the Canadian artic. It used to be known as the unicorn of the sea."

Richard retrieved another book from the shelves, this time on animals but it wasn't a wildlife book. The large, full coloured book was all about the various creatures whose skins or shells have been used for ornamentation of one kind or another, including Turtles and Elephants.

Richard showed Paul a picture of a narwhal. "Strange looking beast, isn't it?"

Paul stared at the picture in amazement. It had obviously been taken from a low-flying aircraft or helicopter and showed a school of several seal-like animals swimming just beneath the surface of a narrow passage of water between frozen icefields. Although they looked seal-like to Paul they were obviously much larger than a seal and each had a long tusk projecting from its head, making them look like some kind of fictional made up creature from a children's book.

"Well, this just shows how ignorant I am about natural history," commented Paul. "I had no idea such a thing existed. It looks like a large seal or something with a huge tusk sticking out of the front of its head. Do these things, these tusks, make any money?"

"They can do. There are some restrictions on the sale of narwhal tusks now, the same as on elephant ivory, but I'll have to confess I'm not sure exactly what they are. I know that the Canadian Inuit are allowed to kill a certain number of narwhals each year and the tusks themselves can fetch hundreds, even thousands of pounds each, depending on their length and how straight they are. How much the cane you saw is worth is impossible to say without examining it, but I suspect it would probably fetch the best part of a thousand pounds at least."

"Blimey! A thousand pounds for a walking stick! What about the table lighter I saw, have you got any illustrations of lighters?"

"Tell me what it looked like."

"Well, it was gold in colour but whether it was actually gold I don't know, I didn't pick it up to look for a hallmark or anything, in fact I didn't look at it closely at all. It was the shape of a teacup bowl without the handle and instead of sitting on a rim at the bottom it had three little legs with claw and ball feet. The top of the cup shape was flat and mounted with what looked like a conventional old petrol lighter mechanism. The main body looked as if it was decorated with different coloured enamels, maybe what you call cloisonné. Are you impressed with my description?"

"Yes, I am, we'll make a dealer out of you yet, Paul."

Richard paid another visit to his bookshelves and after flicking through three or four more books he eventually selected one and took a seat next to Paul so that they could both view the pages together. "Here are some pretty expensive lighters Paul, can you see anything resembling the one you saw?"

Paul turned over several pages and studied the photographs before pointing to a particular picture that showed a large gold egg with a hinged top that revealed a lighter when it was open. "Well, if that one didn't have a hinged lid covering the lighter mechanism, I guess it would be pretty close to what I saw."

Richard looked at the picture Paul had indicated and said, "That one is made to resemble a Fabergé egg when the top is closed. Is it possible the one you saw had a top, although I think it would be more likely for any top to be hinged, it could have had one that just lifted off."

"Fabergé egg.....a lighter in the shape of a Fabergé egg." Paul looked both deep in thought but excited at the same time. Something about the description of a Fabergé egg set bells ringing in his head.

"What's the matter Paul?....you look as if you've seen a ghost."

Suddenly he remembered. "Let me ask you this Richard. If you were writing an inventory of items stolen from a jewellery shop and a table lighter in the shape of a Fabergé egg was amongst those items, how would you describe it?"

"Well I'd describe it as a table lighter in the form of a Fabergé egg, why?"

"A few days ago, I looked at the insurance list of items stolen from Sylvia Carver's shop and I'm sure there was a mention of a Fabergé egg. It caught my eye because everyone has heard of Fabergé eggs. Do you think it could have been a table lighter?"

"That's impossible for me to say Paul, the original eggs, made at the Fabergé factory, hid all sorts of things inside and as I just said, I would describe the item you have in mind as, a lighter in the shape of... not just as a Fabergé egg. In any case the lighter you describe won't be genuine Fabergé; it sounds like something made in the twenties or thirties. Fabergé ceased production in 1917. If it was in the shape of an egg it will most likely be a reproduction or copy of Fabergé made by

Cartier or someone like that."

"I hear what you're saying Richard, but I think it's a hell of a coincidence and I don't think the description I saw was just Fabergé egg, I think it could well have been something like reproduction or imitation Fabergé egg. My God! If I'm right..... Look.... Give my apologies to Elizabeth for me but I have to check this out now. I can't leave it for the morning it's too important."

Paul stood up and was gone, stopping briefly at the door to shout back to Richard, "If I've not been in touch in the next hour, can you order a taxi for Margaret and tell her I'm sorry."

With that, Paul was out of the door and gone, grabbing his mobile as he went to ring Reg.

Chapter 12

The journey from Fairway View to Thornbury was a difficult one. It was early evening and the traffic was a nightmare, coupled with the fact that David was going over and over things in his mind as he drove, trying to formulate some kind of plan to put into effect when he finally got to speak to Marcus.

When he finally arrived at Marcus's house in Thornbury, he parked opposite and wondered if he'd been stupid not to ring first to make sure Marcus was in, but he had been worried that Marcus would refuse to see him if he knew he was coming.

As he stared at the house the question of whether or not Marcus was in was answered when David saw him come out of his front door and drop something into the black rubbish bin that was in front of the garage. He hadn't changed that much in twenty-six years, apart from putting on a bit of weight and sporting some gray hair. David briefly wondered how much he had changed over that period of time and whether Marcus would recognise him straight off.

He didn't get out of the car. There was too much going on in his head to get a clear train of thought. He leaned his head back against the head rest and in trying to relax he found his thoughts drifting back to the events of the 31st May 1989.

He and Sylvia had been just about to retire to bed for the night when the doorbell rang.

"Who on earth can that be at this time of night out here?" asked Sylvia.

Their house was a four-bedroomed detached property situated in a tree lined road in Leigh Wood not far from the Clifton Suspension Bridge, they were not used to late night visitors.

"I'll go and see," answered David, heading for the front door, "it can only be somebody lost and looking for directions or something, or perhaps someone has broken down, you carry on to bed. I'll be up when I've dealt with whoever is at the door."

They left the lounge together and as Sylvia began ascending the stairs, David put the security chain on the door and opened it.

As soon as he had unlocked the door it was flung wide, pulling the chain from its mounting, as two men wearing balaclavas burst in. David himself was pushed backwards against the newel-post of the stairs Sylvia was ascending.

Sylvia quickly turned back when she heard the commotion, "What on earth!" she began and then froze in horror when she saw the hooded man who had so rudely burst into her house. He was now standing at the bottom of the stairs pointing a gun at her. She raised her hands to her mouth in shocked disbelief and stared back at him, unable to move.

Everyone was still for a moment, trapped in time like some grotesque tableau, the only movement being the gentle swinging of the hall light that had been set in motion by the sudden rush of air from outside. The movement causing the shadows it cast to lengthen and shorten in turn, giving the hall an unreal and macabre atmosphere that seemed strangely appropriate under the circumstances.

"Just come back down quietly and nobody needs to get hurt," the man said menacingly to Sylvia, backing out of her way so that both David, who had now regained his feet and Sylvia who was shaking uncontrollably, could walk past him back into the lounge.

"Sit down, both of you," the man ordered, indicating the two-seater settee that faced the television.

"What is it you want?" asked David, holding the back of his head where it had struck the newel-post. He brought his hand away and checked to see if there was any blood, not sure if he should be relieved or not when he saw none.

"Just take what you want and leave us alone," added Sylvia, regaining her voice but feeling extremely vulnerable as she noticed that the one who was not holding a gun was brandishing a baseball bat instead.

He held the handle of the bat in his right hand and tapped the blade casually up and down in his left palm eyeing her intensely.

The man with the gun spoke again. "Now as long as you both do as you are told and answer any questions quickly and truthfully, there will be no need for my colleague here to use that rather ugly looking bat on those rather nice looking knees," he said, looking at Sylvia's legs.

Sylvia grabbed her husband's arm as she pulled the hem of her skirt over her knees and he placed his hand on top of hers to reassure her, despite feeling completely helpless and vulnerable himself.

"Where are the keys to your car, David?" the man demanded.

"On the hall table," replied David, unnerved that the man knew his name.

"How much petrol is in the car?"

"I filled the tank on my way home from the shop tonight. Why?"

"If your wife is to keep being able to walk unaided Mr. Carver, you need to answer questions not ask them."

Sylvia hugged her husband's arm a little tighter.

"Where are the keys for your shop?"

"Hall table as well, with the car keys."

The man with the baseball bat put it down on one of the room's two matching chairs, resting it across the arms; he then produced a roll of duct-tape from his pocket and used it to secure both their arms and feet causing the Carver's anxiety levels to shoot up a hundred-fold. They had both felt vulnerable before but being trussed up awakened feelings of pure dread. They were helpless, unable to prevent these intruders from doing whatever they wanted to either their house or their person.

The man with the gun sat down in the other armchair while his accomplice finished securing Sylvia and David's limbs but then went out into the hall where the Carvers heard him rummaging about before going out of the front door.

After a few minutes, they heard the garage being opened and a car, presumably one of theirs, being brought to the front of the house. The man with the bat got up from the chair and went into the kitchen where he could be heard boiling the kettle and when the first man returned he joined him there.

"What do you think they they're doing?" whispered Sylvia quietly.

"God knows....but it sounds as if they're making themselves a drink," answered David.

"I didn't mean in the kitchen, you fool, I mean what are they doing here!" She almost raised her voice in anger and frustration at her husband's lack of understanding. "What do they want with your car?"

David was about to answer that he had no idea, when one of them returned. He walked up to the terrified pair and checked that they were still securely bound without saying a word, and then returned to the kitchen once again.

"Is that another one?" Sylvia whispered. He looks somehow different, did you notice what they were wearing?"

"No....I noticed the gun and the baseball bat not their clothes, what makes you think it's someone else?"

"I'm not sure, maybe his height or the way he moved, I don't know, there's just something different about him, I think there are three of them now."

It was 1.00 a.m. in the morning when one of the men brought a chair in from the dining room and indicated that Sylvia should sit in that rather than next to her husband on the settee. She was roughly pulled to her feet, dragged over to the chair and made to sit before the duct-tape around her wrists and ankles was cut and she was re-bound. This time her ankles were secured one to each leg of the chair and her hands behind the back of the chair, after which the tape was unceremoniously wound around her upper torso making it impossible for her to move and she was gagged.

Sylvia was terrified that they were planning to hurt her in some way and David looked on with mounting dread. Why had they secured her so tightly now? and why sat upright in a separate chair?

Now it was David's turn to be hauled to his feet, but unlike Sylvia, he had his tape fully removed and was allowed to stand. He took the opportunity of being free to stretch his limbs which were very stiff and realised how uncomfortable his wife must feel.

The man with the gun pointed it at David's head, "Now David," he said menacingly, "it is very important that you understand what is going to happen now and what the consequences will be to your wife if you fail to cooperate."

Sylvia started to cry.

"You are going to drive us to your shop in your car and your wife is going to remain here in the company of our friend."

At this point the third man, whose presence Sylvia had suspected, appeared in the doorway. "Our friend I'm afraid, is not a very nice man, he is also quite impatient. It won't take us long to get to your shop from here at this time of night, let's say half an hour, allow a bit of time for us to get inside and be sure that you have disabled all the alarms for us. I make that to be about 1.50 a.m. So, I will ring here from your shop at 2.00 a.m. precisely. If our friend here doesn't receive that call, then he has instructions to hurt your wife. Exactly what he will do to her we will leave to your imagination but it will almost certainly involve the baseball bat and her knees. Do I make myself clear?"

There was an audible pleading noise from Sylvia as David replied, "Yeah....perfectly clear, I'll do what you want, there's no need for you to hurt anyone. What if we get held up on the way there?....have a puncture or something."

"Well I guess you'll have to buy a wheelchair won't you?"

Sylvia screamed silently into her gag.

"Good, now here are your keys," he said, holding them out for David to take. "Is there anything else you need to get us there and inside both the shop and any safes?"

David took his keys from the man and checked that he had all he needed. "No, I've got everything." Then looking at the man who was to stay behind, "Please don't hurt her, I'm going to cooperate, I promise."

"Good....Let's go."

Sylvia looked on anxiously as the two men escorted her husband out of the room, leaving her alone and helpless with the third member of the gang. David gave one last anxious look back over his shoulder as he left the room and saw the terrified look on his wife's face. He'd never seen anyone look so scared.

Sylvia watched as her minder walked over to the window and pulled aside the curtain to watch the party get into the car and drive away, before strolling over to where she was tied in the chair. She feared for her life and wondered what his intensions were as he approached.

In the car, David stalled as he exited his drive and had to re-start the engine after taking a deep breath. His heart was racing and he wondered if the night would ever be over.

"Try to stay calm David, this shouldn't take us very long and you can be back home to your wife in no time."

Apart from the stalling incident in the drive the journey to his and his wife's jewellery shop in Clevedon was uneventful. Although the days had been pleasantly warm of late, the nights were cold and David shivered as he drove, partly from the fact that the car had not yet warmed up but mostly from fear of what lay ahead.

"Park at the back of the shop, David," ordered the man in the back of the car. He was the taller of the two and the one who had the gun and seemed to be in charge.

David's voice was trembling slightly as he replied, "I have to enter through the front of the shop, there are internal bolts on the back door."

"That's fine David, but we need you to park the car at the back, you can walk around to the front to enter. Turn off all the alarms and then open up the back door, one of us will come with you. Just remember that your wife's ability to walk depends on your cooperation."

"I haven't forgotten."

At the back of the row of shops where Sylvia and David's business was located, there was a delivery and utility area with its own access road. It was like a courtyard and had designated areas marked out with different coloured lines, white for car-parking bays, yellow for delivery trucks and blue for rubbish bins. An urban fox that had been looking for a free meal scurried away as they drove in and watched the unscheduled activity with interest from the relative safety of the bins.

David was about to drive his Ford Granada Estate into one of the four parking bays assigned to his shop but man in charge, as David now thought of him, barked, "Reverse in David, and use the bay directly outside the rear door."

David did as he was told without question and was then escorted around to the front of the premises by the man he not only took to be the boss of the odious threesome but the one he feared the most, the one who could order an assault on his wife.

The fox, who was anxious to resume his search for food, watched them from the cover of two large black rubbish bins, indifferent to David's plight and anxious for them to be gone.

The main road at the front of the shop was quiet as they stepped out from the access road. David looked at his watch anxiously. They had just eight minutes before the call to his home had to be made.

It had rained earlier in the evening and the pavements glinted in the light from the street lights. The front of the shop was fitted with a roller security shutter and after unlocking it, David rolled it up just high enough to be able to unlock the shop door. The harsh metallic sound of the shutter being raised sounded ten times louder in the stillness of the night than it ever did during the day and both men looked about them to see if it had attracted anyone's attention.

A torch was thrust into David's hand and the man spoke quietly as if the world was listening. "Remember, no lights until we are all inside, turn off all the alarms as soon as you are in and I'll pull down the security shutter behind us."

They both ducked down under the shutter and entered the shop. After an agonizing few seconds, when fear momentarily made him forget the numbers, he shut off the alarm and hearing the closing of the shutter behind him he made for the back door, acutely aware of how fast time was passing.

David and his minder opened the back door and let in the second man who was stood in the shadows outside. They closed the solid wooden back door behind them and pulled down the blind on the bolted and barred rear window so as not to show a light. Only then did they use the shop lights to illuminate their surroundings.

The back room that they were in was used as a kitchen and dining area for the staff with a sink and microwave oven one end of the room together with a small table and four chairs the other.

"OK," the one in charge ordered, "let's get to work David," and then turning to his accomplice, "don't go smashing cases open, use the keys, we don't know if anyone is out walking past so we don't want to make any more noise than we have to." Then turning to David again, "What's in the rooms upstairs? Is there any jewellery?"

"You have to ring my house now, quickly, you have to stop him hurting my wife, it's almost time!"

"As soon as you answer my question. "What's in the rooms upstairs? Is there any jewellery?"

"No, the one room at the front is our office, the one at the back is a workroom where we do small repairs and the other two are filled with packaging and other types of stock, clocks, watches, some silverware and trinkets, that sort of thing. Anything of any great value is always put in the safes overnight. Now please ring my house!"

The man stared back at David, spreading his hands questioningly and asked calmly, "Where's the phone?"

"There's a small room behind the main counter in the shop."

"And where are the safes?"

"In that room as well, please come quickly."

David led the men to the room he had just described. Inside were three large safes, each six foot tall and approximately three feet wide.

"There on the desk.....please phone"

Much to David's relief, man in charge picked up the phone and dialled the Carver's home.

The other man pointed to another door. "What's in there?" he asked.

"That's the staff toilets, I don't think you want anything from there." Said David unable to keep the contempt from his voice.

"Careful.....smart ass remarks like that could cost you dear. What have you got that we can pack the jewellery in?"

"There are lots of boxes and things upstairs, some secure metal boxes specially for transporting jewels, there are velvet bags inside."

"Go and get some, but don't try anything stupid when you're up there. Remember dear Sylvia, we can always make another call."

It took no more than half an hour for the three men to load David's estate car, not just with the valuable stock from the shop but also with Sylvia's personal collection of antique jewellery, much of which would be in a special display cabinet during the shop's opening hours. The collection was of some importance and was well known nationally, having been featured in several magazines along with other items owned by her father.

The collection was in fact, partly hers and partly her father's, much of which he had amassed over his many years in the jewellery trade and had managed to bring with him from Germany, at great personal risk, in 1936.

"What now?" asked David anxiously, as he settled himself once again behind the wheel of his Granada.

"Now you need to drive us all to your boat."

"My boat! That's in Portishead....what on earth do you want with that?"

"You're not forgetting the rules are you David? Just drive."

David's boat was moored along with seven others at a privately-owned jetty in Portishead. The jetty was owned by a wealthy business man and was located below his house on the headland. He rented it out to a small number of leisure craft owners who had access to it via a narrow private road that ran down past his home to a large boathouse. The jetty projected out to sea from the side of the boathouse and David's boat was moored about half-way along.

David's boat was an old but well maintained thirty-foot-long four berth motor cruiser. It cost a small fortune in mooring fees each year, but it provided David and Sylvia with all they ever wanted in regard to holidays and weekend breaks. Occasionally they would stay on it overnight in Portishead just as a break from their normal routine.

At high tide, the water would lap around the base of the boathouse enabling the vessel within to be launched straight out. At low tide, unlike the unlucky boats at the jetty that would have to content themselves with sitting on mud, it could be winched down a ramp from the boathouse into the sea and still sail out into open water, possibly laughing at its inferior neighbours left behind lop-sided in the mud.

David was forced to give the two men a hand transferring the boxes of jewellery and the whole of Sylvia's collection from the back of his car to the boat and was then ordered aboard.

"What do you want with me now? You have what you came for. When will my wife be released?"

"Your wife will be released soon but we are hardly going to leave you here so that you can call the police the moment we're gone, now are we?"

"When do you intend letting me go?"

"We have to pick up our friend down the coast, when we do that we will let you off...now get on board!"

David reluctantly climbed aboard his boat and sat on one of the padded benches behind and to the side of the steering wheel, below which were stowed four life-jackets, some marine distress flares, some spare rope, a can of diesel and a picnic hamper.

David was in real fear for his life now. The two men could have tied him up and left him in the shop to be discovered by the staff when they came in at ten to nine in the morning. Bringing him along in the boat could only cause them more hassle.

They had started the boat's engine and cast off as if they knew what they were doing, causing David even more cause for concern; he could have understood them bringing him to the boat if they had needed help with it but they could clearly manage without him. If they were reluctant to let him go now in case he rang the police straight away, why would they release him when they picked up their friend?

He looked at his watch. It was just before 3.45 a.m. They had timed everything well; the tide would be perfect for leaving the jetty and heading down the Bristol Channel. Fear for his own wellbeing and consequently that of his wife was now growing by the second.

He estimated that they had been underway for no more than ten minutes when one of the men beckoned him over to where he was staring down at one of the boxes. "What's this David?" he asked.

As David bent forward to see whatever it was that had been the focus of the man's attention, he saw a lightning bolt shoot across his vision; it was accompanied by a jolt of excruciating pain, after which all was dark.

When he began to come round some time later, he had no idea how long, he was suffering the worst headache he could remember; it was so bad that he had to stop himself from crying out with the pain. Luckily, his survival instinct had kicked in and was operating well; he decided it would be in his best interest to ignore the pain and lie still.

The two men on his boat, who he could hear talking somewhere on deck, obviously wanted him unconscious, so unconscious was what he'd give them; he had no desire for another smack about his head with the butt of a gun, for he now had little doubt that is what had happened.

He had no idea how long he had been out. All he knew was that they were now well out at sea because, although the engine noise was much the same as before, the motion of the boat was quite different, the water they were in now was less choppy but had more of a swell.

All of a sudden, the boat slowed a little and there were hands taking hold of him, some at his feet and others under his arms. He was about to be moved. Were they about to take him into the cabin? That seemed unlikely, why would they do it now? Indeed, if they wanted him moved, why not just get him to walk there before knocking him out?

Sudden realisation hit him like another blow to the head....he knew exactly what they were about to do....they were going to throw him over the side of the boat like so much jetsam!

His immediate instinct was to fight but what could he possibly gain by that? There were two of them; they would simply knock him out again and he would be thrown into the water unconscious and drown. Far better to be conscious when hitting the water and have at least a fighting chance of survival. After the fear and uncertainty of the last few hours, he was surprised by how calmly and logically he was thinking.

There were some things in his favour. He was an experienced open water swimmer for a start, one of those strange people who swim in the sea all year round no matter what the weather or the temperature of the water ,and the sea temperature had been reported as being above average for the time of year.

Before he had any more time to speculate on his fate, he felt himself propelled through space and he prepared himself for the shock he knew was coming.

When the shock of entering the cold water of the Bristol Channel hit him, it brought with it two unexpected benefits; it brought him fully to his senses and it took away the bounding pain in his head, a benefit that he fully expected to be only a temporary respite.

He had reason to be grateful for several things that night. He was grateful that the sea was remarkably calm and that the temperature was warm for the time of year. He was grateful that he was in peak physical condition having been in training for a particularly challenging race and he was grateful that the sky was clear.

He was able to stay quite calm considering his predicament. He didn't think they could have travelled that far down the channel, so he reasoned that he even if he was in the middle of the channel he wouldn't be more than five miles or so off the coast.

Under normal circumstances that would be no trouble for him but these were anything but normal circumstances and he was well aware that if he panicked, he was lost.

He floated on his back for a while thinking, and at the same time divesting himself of his shoes and woollen sweater. He debated whether he should lose his trousers as well but decided to see how much they hindered his progress before making that decision. They would not get as water-logged as his sweater, which would certainly have been a hindrance.

Studying the night sky, he tried to work out where he thought the moon should be if it was, as he suspected, somewhere between four and five in the morning.

With just his head out of the water the horizon was no more than yards away so there was no chance of seeing the coast. He would have to make a judgment call about which direction in which to swim.

In the end he was reasonably confident about the direction he had chosen but the tides and currents in these waters were horrendous. He looked in the direction he had determined was his best chance of landfall, picked a particularly bright star in that part of the sky and struck out for what he hoped was the shore. He realized that as the current took him, the star he had picked would move in relation to his hoped for landfall, but it was the only strategy he could come up with.

He swam at a calm leisurely pace. His main problem was his attire and the cold. Normally when swimming in these conditions he would be wearing a wet-suit, not a shirt and trousers.

People think that if you are in cold water it is better to keep moving vigorously to get warm but in fact the opposite is true; he knew that he would lose body heat faster the more energy he used. Keeping still means that you lose vital body heat less quickly and hypothermia was more of a threat to him than running out of stamina. He had to strike a compromise between making progress through the water and not exerting too much energy.

If he was swimming against a strong current then he was lost anyway, unless he was lucky enough to be spotted by the crew of a passing boat, so he just kept swimming in the direction of his selected star and hoped for the best.

It was impossible to keep track of the passage of time, so he had no idea how long he had been swimming, but it was well over one hour and possibly approaching two. He felt he was still progressing at a steady rate but he was now very cold indeed, colder that he could ever remember being in the water before and the confidence he had felt when he had first summed up his plight had largely evaporated.

His headache had returned, not even the numbing cold could hold it at bay any longer and he was now seeing lights before his eyes and he assumed this meant he was losing consciousness.

No...wait a minute.....the lights were coming and going, that was strange. The swell of the water had increased he knew and the lights seemed to be in harmony with the swell, they were gone when he was in a trough and appeared when he felt the swell lifting him up. The lights were in a row as well...a row of yellow lights!

Suddenly all the numbness and the negative thoughts vanished in an instant. The lights weren't in his head....they were street lights! He was within sight of land! Even close to land, judging by the size of the lights he was seeing and it wasn't just land either, it was land with a coast-road and streetlights!

During his epic swim, he had speculated about what sort of coastline he would encounter should he make it to shore. Rocks had been his biggest fear. How ironic would it have been to survive the long haul to land only to be pounded to death on rocks in the end. Undergrowth was a largely unknown outcome. If he could climb over or through it that would be OK but what if it proved to be impenetrable; would somebody at a later date find his remains hanging there like some grotesque Christmas tree ornament? Mud, well that could be even more of a hazard than the sea.

As things turned out he was the luckiest man on the planet. Within what seemed like only seconds of this enormous realisation that he was near his goal, there was ground beneath him. No, not just ground....sand! He had made landfall on a beach! He had never been a religious man but he thanked God anyway, just in case there had been some divine intervention in this case.

How lucky had he been, the odds of landing on a sandy beach must have been very small. But then, after a moment his thoughts turn back to Sylvia. What did the fact that the men who had taken them captive had tried to kill him mean for Sylvia's fate? Anguish washed over him like a sudden downpour. Why would they leave her alive if they intended to kill him?

He tried to get to his feet but found that his energy had been sapped far more that he thought, so he just rolled onto his back and literally thanked his lucky star. He had never had much of an interest in the heavens, despite his connection with the sea but he made up his mind then and there to find out the name of the star that had guided him home in such style.

His thoughts then turned back to the fate of his wife again. The men who had entered his home had clearly planned all along to kill them both, would he be in time to save her? He thought not and he felt true despair.

He tried to stand again and this time, urged on by the concern for his wife, he managed to stagger to his feet and look about him. He could hardly believe his eyes...not only had he been incredibly lucky and landed on a beach, he now knew exactly which beach. Alongside him and no more than 300 metres away was the unmistakable sight of

Weston-super-Mare pier. The lights he had seen had been those of the promenade. He staggered up the beach and no more than a minute after regaining his feet a young couple, who had either been strolling romantically in the moonlight or engaging in some other activity under the pier, came to his aid.

"Are you all right?" they asked excitedly.

"I need to ring the police," David replied, "what time is it?"

Chapter 13

Marcus Wagner was doing what he did most Mondays, housework. As a car salesman, he worked every Saturday and every other Sunday so Mondays were dedicated to shopping and housework. Having lived on his own for most of his adult life he was used to looking after himself. There had been a brief period, probably no more than two years in fact, when there had been a woman sharing his life but it had ended acrimoniously and he had been reluctant to repeat the experience. In his job, he got to meet a fair number of women, so there was no lack of sex in his life, just companionship, and his upbringing had prepared him well for that.

The ring on the front door bell was more than unexpected, it was downright unheard of. Nobody other than delivery people and cold callers rang his door bell, well, except for the police the other day.

When Marcus finally opened the door, it took a few moments for him to realise who was standing there.

"David Carver! Well this is a surprise, what can I do for you? Have you come to give me my inheritance at last?"

"Well you could ask me in for a start."

Marcus took a step back and ushered David into his hallway. "Sure, come in, the lounge is through there," he said indicating the door on David's left. "It's not very palatial I'm afraid but as long as you don't mind slumming we can talk in there."

In the lounge David sat in the same chair that Paul Manley had occupied only two days before and his eyes instantly picked up the table lighter on the coffee table in front of him.

Marcus saw the direction of his gaze and said, "Beautiful, isn't it?" It was obvious from the expression on David's face that he recognised it so Marcus continued, "a family piece from way back, I can't remember when I acquired it, and I've no idea if it's worth anything. What do you think?"

David instantly recognised the piece for what it was and said so, "That was part of Sylvia's collection! How on earth did you get hold of it? It was amongst the item stolen from the shop!"

"No no, you must have your wires crossed there David. I've seen a list of all the items stolen from the shop...they were all listed on the insurance manifesto and I can assure you there was no table lighter on there or a lighter of any description if it comes to that."

Marcus was desperately trying to think of a way of explaining how he acquired the piece. "Maybe there was a pair, and the old man had this one, yes I'm sure the old man gave it to me."

David just stared back at him in silence for a moment feeling as if he'd suddenly been encased in concrete. After a moment he regained the power of movement and said in a calm and measured tone, "You never did have any idea about the business or any appreciation of jewellery or Objet d'Art, did you, Marcus? You were almost as ignorant as me. That table lighter is incomplete, the top cover is missing, it's a copy of a Fabergé egg made in the nineteen twenties by Cartier. Where's the top gone Marcus? Did it get lost overboard, is that it?"

"Look I don't know what...."

"Don't try and deny any of it," shouted David, now shaking with rage, "because it won't wash..... the only way you could be in possession of that is if you were in on the raid."

David picked up the lighter from the table and examined it. "Look," he cried. "you can see where the hinge was attached, it's been broken off, you can still see a trace of solder, this is definitely Sylvia's Fabergé egg. The very idea that there may have been a pair is ridiculous."

Marcus took the lighter from him and examined the imperfection that David had pointed out. "Oh yes, I just thought it had some damage, it never occurred to me that it might have had a top. It was left in the bottom of one of the sacks I put some of the stuff in to store until I could sell it on. One of the feet got caught on the inside of the bag as I tipped the contents out. I suppose the lid became detached and only the top came out when I emptied the sack."

David suddenly grasped the full implications of what he'd just discovered. "My God!.... I'm right....you must have been in on the whole thing from the start.... Did you know they were going to kill Sylvia?....My God! Of course you did.....you wanted her dead....your own sister for God's sake... and you tried to kill me! You bastard!"

David had never been so angry. All the pent-up emotion that had been lurking below the surface for years suddenly reared up like a wild animal threatened.

"You murdering bastard! Why?!" David was in a near blind rage by now, standing in front of Marcus bellowing at the man and trembling from head to foot.

Marcus realised there was to be no calming David down the state he was in. He expected him to physically attack him at any moment.

Marcus's emotional state was in complete contrast to David's. As he collected his thoughts he said, "Calm down David, you have to look at it from my point of view. Sylvia had it all, the old man had lavished gifts and money on her all her life, all I ever got was contempt and a stern look. I knew the old man's will split his estate between the two of us but I needed money before that, and surely I was entitled to the same as my sister, a little influx of money now and again would have been a big help in my life.

"So, when the old man's mind started going I figured he might let me have a bit. But I should have known better, mind going or not, he wasn't going to let me have anything until he was in the ground, so I took the opportunity to take a few cheques out of his book. I'd always been good at copying his signature and he was loaded....he wouldn't miss a few grand here and there.

"Well, Sylvia found out and threatened to tell him didn't she. Why would she do that, she knew how unfairly I'd been treated. Well I couldn't let that happen.... He'd cut me out of his will completely for sure if she did that. The added bonus of course was that I thought, with Sylvia gone, the whole estate would come to me... that's how the will was set up originally. I had no idea that he changed his will when sis got pregnant and stipulated that her half should go to you if she died first."

David was still angry but he wanted to understand what had been going on in Marcus's head, "So why try to kill me as well if you thought it would all come to you with just Sylvia gone?"

"Why not? It just seemed the natural thing to do, kill the two of you, call it tying off loose ends if you like.... Who knows, I might have ended up with the shop as well."

David had stopped shaking but was incredulous at the revelations he was hearing.

"Why on earth did you hang on to the egg? You should have got rid of it as soon as you found it in the bag."

"I don't know...perhaps I needed some kind of material reminder, anyway, I had the stuff in a rented lock-up for a couple of days until the man who bought it all turned up.... Call me a thief! I think I ended up with a tenth of what it was all worth."

"That's what happens when you sell stuff that's not yours to sell," sneered David wondering if his brother-in-law had any remorse in him at all.

"Anyway, after he'd gone I was clearing out the lockup and found that table lighter and two watches left in the bottom of one of the velvet bags. I was going to chuck them in the river but then I obtained a list of the stolen items from a local pawn-broker I know, the list had been circulated to anyone who might have been offered the goods. It was impossible to identify the watches from the list. There was nothing remarkable about them, and there was no mention of any lighter, so I hung on to them as a sort of memento if you like. I sold the watches some years later but I've got used to having the lighter around."

During Marcus's explanation of his motivation back then, David had sat back down in his chair, his initial rage at what had happened all those years before melting into a resigned acceptance, but Marcus had gradually moved towards the kitchen door and now entered it. "Let me make you a drink David... tea... coffee, something stronger perhaps?"

David, more in control of his emotions now, realised he could be in danger, after all, the man had tried to kill him before. He seized the opportunity of Marcus's absence to leave by standing up and headed for the hall door, intent on getting far away from this madman's lair and summoning the police, but Marcus re-emerged from the kitchen almost straight away and now he was brandishing a shotgun. David stopped in his tracks. He could only assume the gun was loaded and for a moment he thought Marcus was about to fire.

Marcus waved the gun indicating that David should re-take his seat. "Don't go just yet David, I was enjoying our little chat, they say confession is good for the soul don't they, do you believe that David? that confession is good for the soul, well even if you don't, at least it has cleared the air between us."

"So, what happens now? You can't just keep me here," stated David as he reclaimed his seat. "And if you shoot me, it'll take some explaining to the police."

"Well....that's true, I shall have to give some careful thought to what happens next, won't I?"

Marcus sat in the other easy chair facing David and rested the shotgun across the arms in front of him.

"What happened that night?" asked David. "How did my boat end up at the bottom of the sea with two bodies on board?"

Marcus looked at his watch. "OK, there's no harm in you knowing now and we seem to have some time on our hands. I'll tell you the full story if you like."

"I'd like to know your side before the police come for you."

"I'd been planning it for some time, ever since Sis threatened to tell the old man I'd pinched some of his precious money. I knew a couple of reprobates I could enlist and I told them they could keep all the proceeds from the robbery if they agreed to dispose of you. You've obviously realised by now that I was the man who stayed behind and killed Sylvia. You may not believe me David, but it was the most difficult thing I've ever had to do."

"Had to do! What are you talking about? You didn't have to kill anyone....let alone your own sister! You must be some kind of evil twisted bastard to do that. You put a bag over her head you bastard, you didn't even have the decency to do it painlessly...why did you have to make her suffer?"

"Oh... sticks and stones David, I couldn't shoot her at that time of night could I, it would have made too much noise and anyway it was quite quick....I don't think she suffered for long; anyway we're getting sidetracked."

Marcus took a packet of cigarettes from his pocket and put one in his mouth before getting out of his chair and lighting it with the table lighter that had given him away.

Resuming his seat he continued, "As I was saying, after seeing to things with Sis, I drove the car we had hired straight to your boat and hid in the aft cabin, it wasn't difficult to open. I remained in there while the three of you loaded everything onto the boat, I didn't see any reason to exert myself by helping and it was better if you still thought someone was with Sis.

After the two idiots had thrown you over the side I emerged from hiding and shot them...it was as easy as that. You should have seen the look on their faces before I pulled the trigger, it was priceless."

"So you had a gun as well as them?"

"No, there was just my gun, they had it when they took you to the shop and when I emerged from hiding I asked for it back. They were so surprised to see me they handed it over without question, it was really quite amusing. "What are you doing here?" they asked and "What have you done to the woman?" That's when I pointed the gun at them and ushered them into the cabin. They had to go down with the boat you see. Having your body wash ashore somewhere was fine but I didn't want their corpses turning up, that would have caused too many questions."

"How did you get to shore?"

"Well how do you think, we had a little tender with an outboard motor tied to the back of the boat. The plan they were following had them sinking the boat after dealing with you and then picking me up in the tender from Ladye Bay, where I was supposed to be waiting with the car."

"Why all the business with the boat at all?....Why not just get away in the car? It all seems such a waste of time and effort."

"I know, perhaps it was all a bit overelaborate but the idea was that when the police discovered we had got away in your boat, they would assume we had made our way across the channel into Wales and concentrate their search there. It also meant that we had an easy way of disposing of you."

"What about Ratchford...what's the story there? I presume it was you that killed him and set me up for it."

Marcus ignored the question, "Where did you park your car David?"

"Why?"

Marcus stood up and indicated that David should do the same, "Through that way," he said, pointing to the kitchen, "this is just like old times David," he joked.

Marcus led David at gunpoint through the kitchen into a small lobby area between the back door and the door into the garage. Putting both barrels against the back of David's head he told him to open the door to the garage and go inside.

Once inside Marcus switched on the lights and retrieved a role of duct-tape from above his bench.

"Put your hands behind your back," he demanded, and proceeded to secure David's hands together.

The large garage housed Marcus's pride and joy, a 1965 Mark1 Ford Cortina GT. He opened the boot and after getting David to sit in it he proceeded to tape his feet together and gag him. David was terrified for the second time in his life and both times, it was now apparent, at the hands of the same man.

Marcus rummaged through David's pockets until he located his car keys, manhandled the now panicking David into the boot of the

Cortina and shut the lid. It had been a tight squeeze to fit him in and he had had to slam the lid shut, an action that solicited a cry of pain from inside. He could just hear David inside the car, thrashing about as much as the confines of the boot would allow and making muffled sounds through the gag, but he was confident nobody outside the garage would hear the noises.

Leaving him in the boot he left his house in search of David's car. Operating the remote locking button on David's key he readily located the car, a Toyota Avensis, parked just two doors down on the other side of the road from his house. He needed to get it out of sight as soon as possible and hope that none of his neighbours would remember it parked there.

Marcus still rented the lockup that he had used all those years before to house his ill-gotten gains from the robbery. He used it as a workshop when working on the old cars that frequently came his way. Fortunately for him it was temporarily vacant. Checking that nobody he knew was watching, he got in and drove David's car to the lockup in order to hide it until he had figured out what to do next.

With David's car safely out of sight he walked back to his house, a journey that on foot took him no more than half-an-hour. Once back he reviewed everything in his mind and began formulating a plan.

It was obvious that he had to finish what he had started so long ago, and permanently dispose of his deceased sister's husband. But how?

It was clear that the police believed David to be responsible for

Ratchford's murder, at least they should do after all the effort he had gone to. Although it bothered him that they had not charged him yet.

Well, a suicide seemed the obvious solution....but what manner of suicide? He had David's Toyota of course...if he drove him into the country somewhere and connected a hose to the exhaust, there seemed every chance the police would accept that he had done it rather than face going to prison for the rest of his life. That's what he'll do then.... tonight, after all the neighbours have gone to bed, and where, well that that was obvious.... the golf course.

Satisfied that his plan would work, he cut a length of hosepipe from the reel he used to water the garden and tried it in the Cortina's exhaust, making sure he had enough to reach from there to the rear window of the car. David's car was an Avensis and bigger than the Cortina but the length of hose needed would be about the same.

He would need to secure it in place so he hunted on the shelves until he found the end of another reel of duct-tape. What else would he need?

Mentally he went through a dry run of what he would have to do and realised that where the hose would have to go through the rear window there would be a gap and he would need something to plug it and stop the exhaust fumes from escaping. He would need to take a cushion or something from the house for that. No, on second thoughts the police might wonder where the cushion came from if it didn't match any at the Carver residence

Next, he went to his bedroom and fetched an almost empty bottle of sleeping tablets from his bedside table He wished he had more but they would have to do. He knew David would prove to be a handful and had decided to get him to take the tablets. They would make him groggy at least and much easier to handle.

He went back to the garage and got David out of his car boot before bringing him back into the lounge and once again placing him in the seat that he had occupied before. David was now in some pain; the boot of the Cortina was not very large and being trussed up in it for nearly an hour had been torture.

As David looked on, wondering what his fate was to be, Marcus fetched a glass of water together with some writing paper and a pen which he placed on the table before David. He cut the tape that was binding David's hands and pointed the shotgun menacingly at him again.

"You're at your wits end David," he said, "the police are closing in on you for Ratchford's murder and there is nowhere for you to hide. You need to write a suicide note explaining your actions to your wife. There's a pen and paper there," he said pointing, "get writing."

"No."

Marcus had anticipated David's reluctance to cooperate and explained, "Look, there are several ways you could end it all David, some are quite quick....like maybe blowing your own brains out with a shotgun," he raised the shotgun in one hand to remind David that he had it, "some are painless," he continued, "like carbon-monoxide poisoning; but I'm sure if I put my mind to it I could come up with something that would be both painful and take a long time, if that's what you'd prefer?

"So, it's up to you....have you ever considered drinking household bleach for instance? I'm sure I have heard of people doing that, although for the life of me I can't think why they'd choose such an unpleasant method. I've got some bleach in the kitchen you could try if you want. Or maybe you'd prefer dousing yourself in petrol and setting yourself on fire, I'm sure I have a can of petrol at the lock-up."

David was horrified, "My God, what sort of a man are you?"

"Well, a sort of desperate one at the moment David, it's your own fault for recognizing that damned lighter. What the hell did you come here for in the first place anyway?"

"Ironically, I was looking for some support from someone who wouldn't think I had killed my wife.... Look we can work this out surely?"

"I don't see how...get writing."

David picked up the pen and looked at Marcus, "What do you expect me to write?"

"You could just put, sorry for everything and sign it, that will do."

David did as he was bid, carbon-monoxide poisoning sounding considerably preferable to the other alternatives he'd been given and he figured the longer he could delay things the more likely an opportunity for escape would present itself. After he had finished writing he decided to play for more time. "Tell me how you did for Ratchford."

Marcus studied his watch for a second time and then replied, "OK, if you really want to know, I guess it can't make any difference now. But I want you to take these first," he said handing David the sleeping pills.

"Just something to make you drowsy and calm you down."

"I don't want to take them."

"Well I'm afraid it's not up to you. Don't make me have to repeat my threats again, David."

David reluctantly swallowed the six tablets that remained in the bottle, washing them down with the glass of water. Marcus had been meaning to replace the bottle of whisky he had recently finished but hadn't got round to it. It was a shame because he could have forced David to drink that along with the tablets, but now they would just have to do.

"Are you going to tell me about Ratchford or not?"

Marcus sat back in his chair and recounted the recent events that had led to his killing for the fourth time in his life.

"Ratchford came to see me," Marcus began as he recalled the events.........

He had answered his door expecting to have to turn away yet another cold caller trying to get him to buy something.

The man who stood there was unknown to him and he thought at first that his suspicions had been right and the man was going to come out with some sales patter or other, even though his style of dress spoke more of upper management than salesman.

"Sorry mate, whatever it is I'm not interested," he barked.

The stranger stood his ground, "Oh I'm not selling anything Mr. Wagner, no, I knew your sister Sylvia and I'd like a little chat if that's all right."

"A chat about what….Sylvia's long gone."

"Yes I know but now they have found David's boat haven't they…….Look, do we have to do this on the doorstep, what I have to tell you won't take very long…please…" Ratchford gestured with his head towards the interior of the house, "can't we discuss this inside?"

Marcus was both irked at the intrusion but also a little curious about what the man actually wanted, "Oh come on then," surrendered, Marcus indicating the front room with his arm and closing the front door behind the stranger who he now looked at more closely.

The man appeared to be in his mid-fifties but sported more hair than most men of that age; he was dressed in a suit like a salesman but it was a far better cut than most and must have cost a pretty penny, Marcus surmised. He was becoming more intrigued and found that he was now anxious to know what the man wanted.

The two men sat facing one another in the two chairs of a three-piece suite that constituted the bulk of the room's contents.

"What is it you have to tell me, Mr….?"

"Roland, please, we might as well be on first name terms, I think it's much nicer, you don't mind if I call you Marcus do you?"

"Well what is it you have to tell me then….. Roland?"

"Well as I say, I knew your sister; in fact, she employed me in my capacity as an enquiry agent some years ago."

This man didn't fit in with Marcus's idea of a gumshoe or private detective, if anything Marcus would now put him more in the James Bond court.

"Sylvia suspected that her husband David was seeing someone else and she wanted me to find out for sure, one way or the other you understand."

"Sylvia thought David was cheating on her? My God, the old dog, I would never have thought he had it in him... was he? Cheating on her I mean."

"Yes, he was as a matter of fact, but that's not what this is about. It wasn't long after I started working for her that the robbery of her shop took place and she was tragically murdered, I say tragically because of course it meant I didn't get paid and that must have been a terrible time for you and the family. Now you must understand that I never had any real evidence at the time but I have to tell you now that I suspected David was involved!"

"What! You mean you thought David killed my sister....well why didn't you go to the police?...and what made you think he had anything to do with it? David said a man stayed behind at the house with her...he was taken to the shop and then they tried to kill him for God's sake. No....What you're saying doesn't make any sense."

"Well it made sense to me back then and I have to be honest, when I heard the other day that they had found David's boat and that it had been sunk with two bodies on board.....Well....I thought that was the clincher."

Marcus was deep in thought and silent for a few minutes but then said, "Well it's true, the fact that the two men who robbed the shop were still in the boat does cast doubt on David's story, and I suppose that does implicate him in the whole thing. My God! to think that he might get away with it, what can I do?"

Ratchford shook his head in dismay, "No! no you misunderstand, I said it made perfect sense to me back then. Now of course, I know about you taking money from your father and Sylvia threatening to tell him about it. He'd have cut you out of the will for sure if Sylvia had told him…don't you think?"

Marcus stared back at the man in disbelief, "Who the hell told you a cock-and-bull story like that. What are you saying? That you can't get the evidence against David so now you come trying to pin it on me? You start making accusations like that and I'll have you in court for every penny you've got. Now I think you had better leave."

Marcus was now a worried man. How on earth had this man gained so much knowledge of the family, and blackmail. There was no way Marcus was ever going to succumb to that.

"Oh no," Ratchford replied, "I'm not going anywhere just now, we have a lot more to discuss yet."

"I don't think we have anything to discuss, now if you don't leave I'm going to call the police."

"Well, that would be rather silly. If you involve the police I will be forced to hand over the files I've acquired."

"What files?"

"Your sister's files, proving that you stole money from your father's account. She documented it all and gave it to her solicitor for safe keeping."

"Safe keeping! Doesn't sound like they were very safe if you've got hold of them. How did you manage that I wonder?" Marcus's mind was working overtime now. "What is it you want? Money I suppose….is that it? Well hard luck I haven't got any bloody money."

"Oh, over one and a half million each wasn't it...that's what you and David inherited from the old man? Don't tell me you've spent it all on cars."

"Well hard luck Mr. blackmailer, whatever your bloody name is......that's exactly what I did with it....so you're out of luck aren't you, and your wrong into the bargain. David got over two million and I received less than one."

"Don't give me any of your sob stories, they won't wash with me. I thought twenty grand was a fair price for you to pay to stay out of prison, at least to start with."

"No...I've told you, the money's all gone."

Ratchford stood up as if to leave, "Well that's a shame for both of us then isn't it. Do you think many of your rallying friends will come to visit you when you're inside?" He made his way towards the door. "I understand you get used to the food after a few years."

"Wait," said Marcus in a panic, desperate to prevent the man leaving. "Look, I might be able to put my hands on five grand, that's all, but it's better than nothing, right?"

Ratchford turned back to face Marcus as he pulled open the front room door to leave. "Five grand, I don't think so, I'd rather do my civic duty and turn you in than settle for a paltry five grand. Sorry Marcus, but I'm sure you'll have a lovely time with all your new mates in there, I'm sure they can't all be bad people."

"Wait a minute," Marcus called, thinking on his feet, "I've got something in the back garden that might interest you, at least have a look and see, what have you got to lose?"

Ratchford sighed. He didn't think there could be anything is this man's garden of interest to him. He was probably going to show him some beat-up old classic car that he is in the middle of restoring, but curious, he asked, "Which way?"

Walking back past the room they had been in Marcus instructed, "To your left into the kitchen." Marcus followed close behind.

Ratchford entered the kitchen and stood at the kitchen sink staring out of the window wondering what on earth he was doing. There was no car to be seen or anything else other than a lawn in need of cutting and some washing that he surmised had been hanging out for at least two or three days.

Marcus had followed Ratchford into the kitchen at his wits end; he just couldn't think of any way out of his predicament. Reaching to his right he picked up the heavy cast iron frying pan that lived permanently on top of the cooker and swung it as hard as he could towards Ratchford's head.

Ratchford never knew what hit him and never regained consciousness. Whether he died instantly or only after the injury to his brain and subsequent bleeding had caused his body to shut down Marcus neither knew nor cared. Neither did he spend any time regretting his actions, he couldn't have allowed the man to go to the police. Well now he had other things to worry about. Killing the man had been a spur of the moment action. What would follow now would require thought and planning.

Marcus had no idea if anybody knew of Ratchford's plan to blackmail him or of his visit to the house but he suspected not. Blackmail is a solitary as well as an illegal business. His biggest worry was that somebody had seen him call at the house, but if they had, they had, there was nothing he could do about it now so there was no point in fretting about it. The only piece of advice he ever remembered his father giving him was, "Never worry about things you can't control, if you have no influence over it, then worrying about it is simply a waste of time."

He closed the blind in the kitchen, not that anybody was likely to call around the back and look in, but it made him feel more secure. Reaching into one of the kitchen cabinets he took out a glass which he then took into the lounge and after filling it half way to the top with whisky he sat back in the same chair he had occupied earlier and began to think.

He mentally listed the things he would have to do. One, he would have to locate the car Ratchford had arrived in and get it out of sight. Two, he would have to remove all trace of Ratchford from his house and that of course meant disposing of the body. That was his biggest problem; what was he going to do with it?

One thing at a time he told himself. He returned to the kitchen and searched through Ratchford's pockets, finally locating the man's keys and going through his wallet to see who it was that he had just killed. The first of his problems arose straight away but it was a minor one. He planned to back Ratchford's car into his garage to get it out of sight but the garage was occupied with his own vehicle, so his first action was to drive his car out and park it on the road.

Outside the road looked deserted. It was one of the benefits of living in a cul-de-sac, so after getting out of his car he walked slowly and casually along the pavement and every time he passed a car he didn't recognise, he activated the unlock button on Ratchford's car key. All the houses had driveways and garages which meant there were few cars parked in the road so when Marcus operated the key for only the second time the lights flashed and beeped on a Ford Mondeo facing down the road on the opposite side.

Marcus looked around to make sure the road was still clear and got quickly into the car. After adjusting the seat position, he drove Ratchford's car just past his house and reversed it back into the garage. Closing the garage door, he turned on the light and satisfied himself that he had enough room at the back to open the car boot and manhandle it's owner inside.

There were two doors into Marcus's kitchen, one from the hall through which he and Ratchford had entered, and a second that led into a small lobby that was situated behind his garage separating it from the garden.

He had underestimated how difficult it would be to manoeuvre a dead body out of the kitchen across the lobby and into the garage, let alone lifting it into the boot of a car, but after some considerable effort he manage to achieve both.

Marcus was far happier once the body was out of sight in the boot. There was some blood to be cleaned up in the kitchen but that hadn't taken long so Marcus once again found himself sat in his lounge, whisky in hand, planning his next move.

Something that Ratchford had said earlier gave him the inkling of an idea. Ratchford had said that he had first suspected Sylvia's husband David of planning the whole thing and that the finding of his boat with two bodies in it had reinforced that idea. The police were probably likeminded, and their enquiries would be geared towards gathering evidence of David's involvement.

Was there any way he could dump the body and maybe plant evidence somewhere that would throw suspicion onto David Carver? Not only did this seem like a feasible option, but seeing Carver arrested for the murder of this man and also possibly for the murder of Sylvia would brighten his day enormously.

He knew that Carver lived in a guest house or hotel that catered for people on golfing breaks and there was a golf-course just the other side of the main road running past his place. It should be easy enough to dump the body somewhere on the course. Then he would have to think of something that would point the police in David's direction.

He still had the gun that he had used to shoot Neil and Trevor Pobjoy, the two lowlife brothers he had recruited all those years ago. It occurred to him that if he now shot Ratchford with the same gun and somehow managed to plant it where it would incriminate Carver he would be home and dry. The day wasn't turning out so bad after all.

At three o' clock in the morning Marcus drove Ratchford's car onto Lansdown golf-course which he was reasonably familiar with, having played it on at least three occasions with friends from the South Gloucestershire Rally Club. There's a road running across the golf-course off the main road that leads to the entrance to Lansdown Racecourse, and it was into that road that Marcus turned.

Half way along the road he turned off onto one of the fairways on his right. The weather had been quite dry for several days and the ground was firm under the wheels of the car.

The moon was quite bright that night but the sky was cloudy which meant that visibility was good at times but could change quickly when the moon was obscured. He remembered a small copse of trees that one of his friends had been unlucky enough to hit his ball into and he drove the car as close to the copses as he could get.

Although the moon was hidden by cloud as he approached the trees Marcus nevertheless felt that his every move was being observed by some unseen audience who would summon the police at any moment. The hairs on the back of his neck were stood on end and he was constantly looking over his shoulder. He didn't remember being as nervous as this the first time he had taken a life, wasn't it supposed to get easier? Lifting the body from the car boot proved to be only slightly less arduous than lifting it in but that accomplished, he dragged it into the copse and let it lay where it fell.

Earlier he had made a crude silencer for his pistol by cutting the bottom four inches off a plastic coke bottle, gluing some bubble wrap to the interior wall and then forcing the cut end of the bottle back inside the bottom section and securing the two pieces together with sellotape.

He hadn't seen the need to dispose of the gun after shooting his accomplices before, simply because he was confident their bodies would never be found and therefore no bullets to match to the weapon. Now of course he was very pleased he had hung on to it. He had bought the gun, a Walther PPK, from an army friend who had returned from a tour of duty with several small arms. He had never asked how his friend had acquired them and his friend had never questioned why Marcus wanted one. In truth, Marcus had no idea why he had purchased the weapon. Maybe it was just because he was young and it felt macho to own a gun. It had always been hidden away with the small amount of ammunition it came with, until of course he had put it to use all those years ago.

He now forced the neck of the bottle over the muzzle of the pistol and secured that with tape. He had no idea whether his improvised noise suppresser would work or not but he had seen it done in some film or other and just hoped that it would have the desired effect.

Pointing the gun at the prone body before him he crossed the fingers of his left hand and pulled the trigger with his other.

The noise produced by the firing of the gun seemed very loud indeed in the extreme quietness of his surroundings. It disturbed a myriad of sleeping birds that had settled for the night, causing such a commotion that for a while, he was convinced that police cars and helicopters were going to descend on the scene at any moment.

At length, he consoled himself with the thought that the shots had sounded much louder out in the middle of the Bristol Channel on a small boat all those years before and even if somebody had heard this one, he doubted anyone would come to investigate at that time of night, thinking that it was most likely a car back-firing or maybe a farmer shooting a fox.

Making no further attempt to conceal the body he checked around to make sure he hadn't dropped anything that could be traced back to him and got back into the car.   He drove back out onto the main road with only his side-lights illuminating his path. It was tricky following the road at first but he wanted to be sure that nobody witnessed a car joining the main road from the golf-course and for that same reason he turned off even the sidelights when he reached the junction with the main road. The road was deserted and the moon had put in another appearance so once back on the road he drove the short distance to the entrance of Carver's guest-house without lights and turned into the driveway.

He had never visited Carver's place but having viewed it with the aid of Google Earth earlier in the day, he knew that the house itself was set back from the road by some two or three hundred metres. The driveway went up one side of the building where it split in two. One branch of the drive curled round to a drop-off point at the front of the house with a circular turning space and the other continued to a carpark for as many as two dozen cars at the rear.

Marcus drove only a short distance on the drive and then turned off the engine, not wishing to awaken anybody from slumber in the house. He pushed the car the rest of the way into the car-park, thanking his lucky stars that most of the driveway had been tarmacked rather than laid with chippings like the area in front of the house.

Once in the carpark he pushed it alongside another Mondeo that was parked there. He then removed the gun and silencer and walked away. He had not been able to come up with any brilliant plan concerning the planting of the gun as evidence so he just quickly looked around for some place to put it.

To the right hand side of the carpark was a large well-maintained garden that was obviously for the use of guests staying at the house, and in one corner of the garden was a large pond with a waterfall. There was no water cascading down the fall at that moment and Marcus surmised that it was only turned on when guests were there to appreciate it. He walked to the edge of the pond trying to judge its depth. He decided against dropping the gun into the pond, hoping that a better plan would come to him in the morning, but on his way out he dropped the home-made silencer into one of the black bins he had passed on the way in. He briefly considered dropping the gun there as well but for all he knew the bins could be collected early in the morning and the police would miss finding it. He left the property on foot, taking the incriminating gun with him.

Planning had been everything and he now had a relatively short walk to the layby that he had visited in his own car earlier in the evening. Once there, he retrieved the pushbike that he had hidden in the field behind some bushes, and steeled himself for the most gruelling part of his plan; a cycle ride back to his home in Thornbury some twenty or twenty-five miles away.

It was almost four in the morning according to his watch; he would have to make good time to get back before his neighbours were up and about.

In the end, it had taken him a little over two hours, two hours of worthwhile therapy as it turned out. He actually enjoyed the ride home, the night air and the wind in his face cleared his head and relaxed him and he let himself back into his house at ten minutes past six.

If anyone had seen him return they might be curious about his early morning bike ride so he resolved to go cycling early for at least the next week or two. He could tell anyone who was interested enough to ask that he was endeavoring to keep fit; he didn't fancy getting up and cycling every morning, despite enjoying the ride home so much, but it was a small price to pay if it averted suspicion.

It was too late to get any sleep and in any case, he had things to do. He had thought he would feel tired but in fact he had caught his second wind and felt more alert and alive than he had for a long time. Perhaps a life of crime and murder was what he was truly good at.

Early that morning after a light breakfast and when he thought the school traffic would have cleared, he returned to David Carvers guest-house with the gun concealed under his coat and wrapped in a clean rag.

He was taking an enormous risk; he knew that, but he had to plant the gun somewhere. Ratchford's body would undoubtedly have been found by now, a fact confirmed when he caught sight of some police vehicles in the golf-club carpark.

He drove into the Carver's carpark for a second time, fully prepared to abandon his mission if there should be any sign of a police presence there. The only person who could possibly recognise him, other than the police who visited him, was David Carver himself and they had met only two or three times, briefly, many years ago. If he was confronted about what he was doing, he would simply brazen it out, give a false name and say he was looking for somewhere to stay.

As things turned out he needn't have worried. As he slipped inside the building, a woman whom he took to be the new Mrs. Carver was talking to one of the cleaners or maids in the hall and neither of them even looked his way as he ascended the stairs. As he looked about on the first floor a woman was just leaving one of the rooms, so he quickly ascended another flight of stairs to the top landing.

The top landing was almost a perfect copy of the floor below except that there were no more stairs going up. Where the stairs would have continued had there been another floor there was instead a door labeled, STORAGE AND LAUNDRY.

Opening the storage cupboard with a view to putting the gun in there somewhere he immediately spotted a long handle with a hook on the end that could only have been the means of opening a loft hatch. Marcus looked up and spotted a large hatch in the ceiling that was obviously access to the loft.

After listening carefully for the sound of anyone approaching and with his heart beating much faster than was good for it, he picked up the handle and opened the loft hatch. There was nobody on the stairs and still no sounds coming from any of the rooms so he took his chance. He pulled down the loft ladder, quickly went up far enough to put his head into the loft space and located a light switch. Trembling now, he took out the gun, still wrapped in freshly laundered cloth and pushed it under the loft insulation to his left.

After turning off the loft light and almost falling down the ladder in his haste, he wiped the hatch pole clean of finger prints with his sleeve and returned it to its home in the cupboard; he then made his way back down the stairs as quietly as he could while still listening out for the sounds of approaching feet. On reaching the reception area again he was relieved to find it void of all life and simply re-traced his steps to his car and drove away, surprised and exhilarated that he had managed to achieve so much without having been spotted even once.

He heard nothing the rest of the day and that night he slept the deep, undisturbed slumber of one who is innocent.

Chapter 14

As Wagner finished recounting the events surrounding the murder of Roland Ratchford and the framing of David Carver, he was acutely aware of the fact that he had to go through a similar process again and he wondered if he could do it.

He had killed four people already and was now about to make it five. He hadn't killed because he enjoyed it, he had killed the first time out of a combination of frustration, anger and self-preservation. He'd been younger then and had visions of a long and prosperous life doing what he enjoyed; now he was older and more resigned to a life of hard work and loneliness that maybe didn't warrant the same extreme measures to preserve it.

He had killed Ratchford on an impulse purely because he felt threatened by him, and he had framed Carver, partly because it drew suspicion away from himself and partly because he still blamed Carver for what he considered his paltry inheritance money.

Having to kill Carver now made it seem as if the necessity to kill would never go away and it made him weary, but he could see no alternative. He hadn't set out to be a bad person. He was a victim of circumstance. If his father had loved him like he had Sylvia, things could have been so very different. But he couldn't change the past and there was no time for brooding. He had things to do.

Wagner looked at the clock on the mantelpiece; it was eleven o'clock and he thought maybe it was time to put his plan into operation. He knew from experience that the cul-de-sac in which his house was situated was as quiet as the grave by this time. His neighbours would be tucked up in bed and the golf course as well would be long devoid of players or ground staff.

For the second time that evening he marched David Carver at gunpoint into his garage, gagged him and shut him in the boot of his car. He noted with some relief that Carver appeared groggy and was much more compliant this time, but he still wished he had more tablets or some whisky.

Marcus drove his Cortina out of the garage and closed it behind him before driving back to his lock-up where David's car was waiting. He reversed his Cortina up to the front leaving just enough room to open the up-and-over door.

The most dangerous part of his plan, and when he was going to be most vulnerable was now, he felt. Checking that there was nobody in sight he opened the boots of both cars and then reversed his Cortina back until the two boots were almost touching. There was just enough room for him to stand between the two cars and as he did so he dragged David, semi-conscious from the one and into the other.

David almost felt some relief. His new prison was far more spacious than his previous one and his groggy and disoriented mind almost laughed at the thought of his taking comfort from that fact in his present predicament.

As Marcus closed the boot lid on his prisoner he glimpsed his bike hanging on the far wall and briefly wondered about taking it with him. He could easily devise some method of tying it to the roof of David's car but in the end, he decided against it for two reasons. First, it would be difficult to prevent it scratching the paint and the police might find that suspicious and second, if he passed anyone on the way there, they would be much more likely to remember a car that had a bike tied on the roof.

After swapping the cars around and locking the garage Marcus set off for the golf-club in David's Toyota, it's owner an unwilling passenger in the boot.

In the foreboding darkness of the boot Carver was at his wits end; this man, his brother-in-law from his first marriage, was going to kill him in the same cold-blooded way he had killed his own sister all those years ago. As he lay tied and gagged, this time in the boot of his own car, he tried to figure out exactly what Marcus was intending to do but his mind was fuzzy, the tablets Marcus had forced him to take were beginning to have an effect and his head was slowly filling with cotton-wool.

It seemed reasonable to suppose, from Marcus's remarks earlier, that he was going to stage a suicide by driving him somewhere remote, probably the golf-course, and sitting him in the car with a hose pipe attached to the exhaust. At least he hopped that was his plan. The alternatives he had suggested filled him with horror.

Marcus must realise that he would not be compliant and would put up a struggle, and that was why he had made him take the tablets. Perhaps he intended to keep him tied up or unconscious or both until he was dead and then stage the suicide, but that would mean him hanging around until the deed was done; would he risk that? The alternative seemed to be to just leave him unconscious in the car and hope that he didn't come around until it was too late.

Whatever scenario Marcus chose, David considered his chances of getting away as very small unless he could somehow escape his bonds now. He hands had been secured behind his back so there was no chance of attacking the tape around his wrists with his teeth, and he would not have been able to reach his ankles even outside the confines of the car boot.

David Carver began to weep. He wonder if he was somehow paying for sins he had committed in some past life. Why else would he have to endure the indignity of being hit over the head, tied up and have someone try to kill him twice in one lifetime? He hated the fact that not only was he going to die but he was going to die with everyone, including Sandra, believing that he had killed Sylvia, and not just Sylvia but others as well; he began to wonder if there was anything he could do to make it obvious to the police that he had been murdered and not taken his own life.

His body was in conflict with itself, the motion of the car and the tablets he had taken were trying their best to send him to sleep but fear and the adrenalin it was producing in him was keeping him awake. He knew that his only slim chance of survival lay in his ability to stay awake and alert but all the time something inside was telling him to just accept his fate and that there would at least be peace in the grave.

The journey from Marcus's house in Thornbury to the golf-course at Lansdown took just under an hour and Marcus was pleased to see that, as expected, everywhere was quiet and deserted when they arrived.

He took the same entrance road to the race-course that he had previously with his other victim, but it was a much darker night than it had been then. The night sky was cloudy, blotting out the moonlight to such an extent that he was able to see only what fell within the scope of his headlights. He was afraid of getting lost if he ventured too far away from the road, so instead of trying to locate the small copse of trees again, which he was sure would still be cordoned off with police tape, he stayed on the road all the way to the race-course entrance.

Outside the main entrance and turnstiles of the race-course there was a large tarmacked space that served as a turning area for large delivery vehicles and horse-boxes. There was also room to park some twenty cars or more and there were three large horse boxes on the far left along with the usual assortment of various coloured rubbish containers and waste bins.

Marcus was a little concerned that there might be a night-watchman on duty but he could see no sign of one. The area was lit to some extent by some low-level lighting positioned at each end of the row of turnstiles and Marcus suspected that motion sensors would trigger floodlights if he got too close to them. There may even be CCTV for all he knew. How much security racecourses regarded as necessary was not a subject he had ever contemplated.

He was beginning to think that he may have acted in haste and that it might have been better to hang on to his victim overnight so that he could check the lay of the land in daylight. He actually considered driving back to Thornbury and doing just that but he was anxious to wrap things up quickly so that he could put the whole dreadful business behind him.

In the end he decided to park away from the turnstiles on the left, between two of the large horse boxes. Luckily the largest of the boxes was far enough away from the other two to allow him to park the car between them and still have enough room to open the doors on either side. Having done that, he turned off the car engine and lights and sat waiting to see if anyone would approach him to ask what he was doing there at that time of night. No one did and none of his actions had triggered any floodlights. He breathed a sigh of relief and sat still for a few more moment hoping his heart would slow to a more normal rate.

The night seemed to get even darker despite his eyes becoming more accustomed to it and it took him a moment to realize why that was. The race course was so high up, low level cloud was drifting in and he began to feel the chill of the night air.

The deathly silence was broken only momentarily by the squeal of a small animal in its death throes as its short, brutal life was ended by a predator. A scenario not too dissimilar to what was about to be enacted here on a human scale.

Still no night watchman or guard-dog put in an appearance and apart from the squeal of the unfortunate animal, the only sounds that disturbed the silence came from the boot of the car where David Carver shuffled about as best he could in the confined space, both in an effort to ease the growing pain in his limbs and to stay awake. He also had the vain hope that he might locate something with which he could somehow free his bonds.

When Marcus eventually felt it completely safe to extricate his victim from the boot, Carver was taken by surprise and totally unprepared after the total inactivity of the last sixty minutes. He was also surprised when the boot opened to see that it was almost as dark outside as it had been in the confines of the boot. Perhaps he was dead already! No, he was aching all over from being trussed up for so long in such a confined space and in such utter despair that when Marcus man-handled him out of the boot and into the back of his car, he put up no resistance at all.

He had gone through a cocktail of emotions since he was first held captive. Incredulity at discovering Sylvia had been murdered by her own brother, anger that he had got away with it for so long, fear at the thought of his own violent death and now, strangely, a resigned acceptance of his fate, no matter how unjust and unfair it was. He just wanted it to be over.

He neither assisted nor struggled as Marcus, once again with some difficulty, manhandled him out of the boot and onto the back seat of the car.

Somehow sensing that his victim no longer had neither the will nor the ability to escape, Marcus retrieved a length of hosepipe from the passenger footwell together with some stiff cardboard and a roll of duct tape.

If only he had more sleeping pills he could have left David to his fate, but now he would have to hang around until David at least succumbed to the fumes of the exhaust so that he could remove his bonds. No one would believe he had committed suicide if he was found bound hand and foot and similarly if he knocked David unconscious it would give the police reason to doubt that it was suicide.

He stuffed one end of the hose into the car exhaust and secured it in place with some of the duct tape. He then opened the passenger door window just enough that he could feed the other end through and likewise secure it with tape. Once that was done he used the cardboard and tape to cover the remaining gap left by the partially open window and stepped back to inspect his handiwork.

During the whole of the time Marcus was preparing the improvised gas chamber, David lay motionless on the back seat like a frightened animal caught in a trap. He could see no way out, he could barely move, he could barely stay awake.

He felt as if he was a child again, sat on a comfortable seat in front of the television, desperate to stay awake and watch the end of the film but the television seemed to get further and further away and his eyelids were so heavy. On those occasions of course, the next thing that he would remember would be waking up in his bed in the morning with not the slightest idea how he had got there, or how the film had ended. He knew however, that this time, there would be no waking up in his own bed, no waking up at all, no morning.

Marcus went over things in his mind, putting himself in the position of the police finding the car and working out what had happened. They would surely assume that David had prepared the car with the hosepipe the way it was and then got into the driving seat and started the engine before getting out again and getting into the back through the opposite door to the hose to take the sleeping pills. He'd almost forgotten the pills. He took the empty bottle from his pocket and dropped it in the rear foot-well together with a half empty water bottle.

Perhaps he ought to put David in the driving seat, would that seem more usual? If he did it now and propped him up in the driving seat David might be able to open the car door, maybe with an elbow or something, a task he was unable to perform in his present position, hogtied on the back seat. Marcus decided against it, maybe he was over thinking the whole business.

He suddenly remembered the suicide note he had forced David to sign and walking around to the other side of the car he opened the door and placed it on the passenger seat in plain sight. All he had to do now was start the engine and wait for David to die. He would have preferred to have been able to leave but with David still half-awake it was impossible

He briefly thought about smothering him so that he could untie him straight away. He could then remove all signs of any restraint and make his way home. It wasn't too long a walk into Bath and he could get a taxi to somewhere, maybe not straight home but perhaps to where he could walk to another taxi rank and get a ride home or he might even be able to hitch-hike. He wished now that he had brought the bike.

He realised that he wasn't thinking clearly any longer, fatigue was setting in. He hadn't hitchhiked since he was a teenager, and if he was lucky enough to get a ride, whoever picked him up would remember him for sure. As for smothering David, well that would be pretty stupid he decided, if he smothered him he wouldn't inhale the carbon-monoxide and suicide would be dismissed by the police straight away. He stood up straight and took some deep breaths trying to clear his head. There was just too much going on in there and his thinking was becoming confused.

Returning to the off side, he sat in the driving seat and started the engine. As he got out of the car and shut the door he caught a brief glimpse of the frightened figure staring back at him from the rear seat but quickly turned away and looked about him for somewhere he could rest until he was sure his gruesome task was accomplished.

The low cloud had moved away a little, slightly improving visibility. He didn't want to go any nearer the racecourse, still a little concerned that he might trigger some camera or security light, so he wandered back the way he had come, wondering just how long it would take a man to die of carbon-monoxide poisoning in the confines of a car. Only then he realised that perhaps he wouldn't have to wait that long.

David didn't actually have to be dead he realised, he would only have to be unconscious enough for Marcus to remove any signs of restraint, he could then leave. He had to decide whether he was going to turn the engine off while he removed David's restraints and then re-start it or whether he could risk doing it while the engine was running; but the last thing he wanted was to be overcome by the fumes himself and throw up or something.

He was turning these things over in his mind when he suddenly became aware of car headlights approaching over the golf course.

Damn! who the hell could be coming to the race-course at this time of night?

Chapter 15

When Paul got through to Reg on his mobile phone he was surprised to discover that he was still at work. "What the hell are you still at the station for Reg? I was thinking I would have to apologise for calling you back in so late."

"No problem, Guv. I find it easier to catch up on paperwork when the place is quiet and I'm supposed be on a day off tomorrow remember. As it happens I was just about to ring you. Mrs. Carver's been on the phone, she's worried about her husband, said he went off hours ago to see his brother-in-law, Marcus Wagner and she's been unable to contact him since."

"Right Reg. Get over to Marcus Wagner's house straight away and take someone with you for backup. I'll meet you there and fill you in with developments, but I have a nasty feeling Mrs. Carver is right to be worried."

Paul actually arrived at Wagner's house ten minutes before Reg because Richard and Margaret's house was nearer to Thornbury than the station. He arrived at two minutes to midnight. The house appeared empty and the only person who had responded to Paul's banging on the door was Wagner's next door neighbour, who poked his head out of an upstairs window and demanded to know what all the noise was about.

Paul flashed his warrant card. "Police....have you seen Mr. Wagner today?"

The man was rubbing his eyes having just been woken from sleep. "He was there earlier, his car was parked on the drive as usual when he gets home from work, but he treats that car as if it was a baby, as soon as the engine has cooled down he puts it away in the garage so it may be in there or he may have gone out, I don't know. Why, what's happened?"

"What car does he drive, do you know the registration number?"

"It's an old Cortina, mark 1 I think but I've no idea what the reg is."

"What colour is it?"

"It's white with a green flash down the sides, has something happened or can I go back to bed now?"

"Yes ...sorry, thank you, you've been helpful."

The man closed his window and his light went out just as Reg and Constable Ben Horrocks turned up.

"Reg, I think David Carver may have been abducted by Marcus Wagner, and if he has I don't think he intends anything good to happen to him."

"You think he intends to harm him Guv....why?"

"When June and I were here I noticed a distinctive table lighter. I've just been talking to Richard Drake and I now believe the lighter to be part of the haul from David and Sylvia's shop. If I'm right and David has been here he may well have recognised it."

"I'll get a call put out for his car, Guv."

"Yes, do that now.....wait, put a call out for David's car as well, have you got the registration of his Toyota?"

"Not off hand Guv. But I'll get it checked and get the registration of Marcus Wagner's car as well. I'll put out an alert for both vehicles."

While Reg was organizing a search for the cars, Paul was deep in thought. When Reg was finished Paul said, "It's possible Marcus has either killed David and is deposing of the body as we speak, in which case, if he is doing it in his own car, then where is David's? I can't see it nearby. I think it is more likely he has taken David somewhere in his car, but where?"

"Do you think he may be going to stage a suicide, Guv? Hosepipe from the exhaust maybe, that sort of thing."

"My God! I think you could be right Reg. He knows that we suspect Carver and it now seems likely that he planted the evidence on him, so it would make perfect sense for him to now kill Carver and make it look like suicide. We have to find him before it's too late."

"It may already be too late Guv."

"I know, if only I had arrested Carver when Blakey asked me to. Where would he take David to stage a suicide?"

All three men looked at each other and said in unison, "The golf club!"...Paul said, "It has to be, come on you two. we'll go in mine. Ring for backup."

* * * * * * * * * * * *

When Marcus saw the car headlights approaching he assumed it was somebody turning up to the racecourse for some reason, or maybe he had somehow triggered a silent alarm and it was the police, but the car stopped and three men got out with torches and headed towards the copse of trees where he had left Ratchford's body.

He realised then that it must be the police looking for him and wondered how on earth they had got on to him and what had brought them here. They obviously hadn't heard the car engine and were looking in the wrong place. Glad now that he had parked between the containers, he returned to see how things were progressing. Perhaps he had time to remove Carver's restraints before whoever it was came searching here.

"There's no one here Guv. We must have got it wrong."

"No wait," said Paul holding up his hand to indicate that they should be quiet. "I can hear a car's engine running."

Reg and Ben listened intently. "You're right Guv. It's coming from over towards the racecourse."

The three men ran back to Paul's car as fast as they could and drove swiftly into the grounds of the racecourse. As they exited the car they could hear the engine quite distinctly.

"This way," called Reg running in the direction of the noise and spotting the car parked between two large horse boxes. Reg instinctively opened the driver's door and turned off the engine. Paul ran to the back of the car, opened the rear door and pulled the still tied David Carver out, hoping and praying that he was in time.

"Call an ambulance Ben," Paul shouted as he began to give CPR to David Carver, struggling to remember the correct procedure. It was difficult to administer the CPR because David's hands were tied behind his back with duct-tape.

"Get me a knife or something to cut this tape Reg quickly."

Reg. produced a knife from his pocket and Paul turned David briefly onto his side so that Reg could cut the tape.

"Not a very convincing suicide Guv. If you leave your victim with his hands tied."

"My God! You're right," cried Paul excitedly, "we've interrupted him....he must be still around here somewhere close......where the hell is that backup! Have a look round you two, he can't be far."

Marcus was watching events from behind a large sign that informed those people leaving the racecourse that they were crossing a golf course and to watch out for golfers. He thought about his options. The police were obviously on to him and if David was still alive, he was sunk. If David was dead however, and he had been in the car with the engine running for some time before the meddling police got him out, then they would still need to prove that he was the one who tried to kill him.

If only he had untied David earlier he might still have got his plan to work, but that was water under the bridge now. He had to get far away from here as quickly as possible and hope that David was already dead.

He started to make his way as quickly and as silently as he could towards the main road but there were more cars entering now so he turned right towards the clubhouse carpark hoping he could get out that way.

As he approached the carpark another police car with its blue lights flashing parked across the entrance preventing any vehicles from entering or leaving. The lights of the police car had a strange ethereal corona around them caused by the low cloud and giving the whole scene an unworldly appearance.

To his left was a low drystone wall separating the course from a wide grass verge that followed the side of the main road.

Marcus kept low and followed the wall almost to the carpark where he hopped over it unseen. If he was to make his way to Bath he would have to get past the car that was blocking the golf-course entrance so he made his way across the main road to a similar verge the other side.

The foggy conditions caused by the low cloud was proving to be valuable ally, and after passing the golf-course entrance on the opposite side of the road he felt confident enough to stand upright and make his way into the city of Bath. As he did so an ambulance with lights flashing and siren blazing came to a stop at the entrance to the golf club. Marcus paused to watch, it was difficult to make out what was happening but he assumed the driver of the ambulance was receiving instructions from the uniformed officer next to the car.

After a brief period, the ambulance continued along the road and turned in to where Ben was now waiting, so Marcus continued on his way, wishing he had worn more suitable clothing.

Paul was still giving David CPR when the paramedic from the ambulance arrived and began to examine him.

Paul explained what had happened and the paramedic immediately called to his colleague," he needs oxygen and we need to get him to hospital as soon as."

"How long was he in the car, do you know?" the paramedic asked.

"I have no way of knowing." replied Paul, "how bad is he?"

They lifted David onto a stretcher and the paramedic answered, "Difficult to say but it's not a good sign that he's unconscious. Do you know if he's vomited at all?"

Paul thought back to when he had pulled David from the car and there had been a faint smell underlying the exhaust fumes, "Yes I think he vomited in the back of the car."

As David was placed in the back of the ambulance, Paul asked, "Which hospital will you take him to?"

"Bath United," replied the driver as he started the engine and drove away, the sirens once again disturbing the eerie silence of the night.

As the ambulance left the race course the rest of the team started turning up together with several uniformed officers, word of what was happening having circulated amongst them.

Paul quickly organized a more extensive search of the area, convinced that Marcus couldn't be far away. He then got the team together and filled them in with the events that had taken place.

"Which way do you think he would have run when you and Reg turned up Guv, back towards Bristol or would he have made for Bath, it's a lot closer," suggested Derrick.

"We need to figure out what he intends to do now," said Paul. "what are his options?"

"Do you think he knows David is still alive Guv?"

"He would most probably have heard the ambulance even if he didn't see it, so he must know there is a good chance David survived."

"In that case Guv if it was me," said June, "I'd want to make sure David didn't come round."

"You're right June, if he is to stand any chance at all of evading justice he has to finish what he started. Let's get to the Hospital. Phillip, I'd like you to stay here and continue the search with uniform and fill SOCO in when they turn up, we need to be able to put Marcus here, preferably in the car with Carver."

"OK Guv."

Once inside the entrance to the emergency department of Bath United Hospital Paul declared, "Clive, you go and baby-sit with David, June, can you speak to security, see if they have somewhere where we can monitor the CCTV cameras, and find out from them how many entrances there are to the building. Just because we came in the front doesn't mean Marcus will. Peter, as soon as we know how many entrances there are, I want you to make sure they are all covered, call for more people if you need them, but not uniform, I don't want to scare him off. I want to catch him going for David, so if he is spotted nobody is to arrest him, just let me know he's here, is that clear.

"Yes Guv."

"Good, make sure everyone is aware of that. Reg, you come with me.

* * * * * * * * * * * * *

Marcus had made good progress and as he descended the hill from Lansdown, the cloud had provided him with cover disappeared and the air felt warmer and thankfully drier.

He heard the ambulance approaching and was aware that he was more visible now that he was below the cloud base so he stepped back behind a tree as it rushed past him.

It was obvious from the vehicle's urgency to get its patent to hospital that David must still be clinging on to life.

What was he to do now? His plan was in tatters. If David survived to tell his story then he was facing spending the rest of his life in prison, certainly not an option he was in favour of. His only hope was that David should die, at least then the police would have to prove that he was the one who framed him and tried to kill him. He would have some chance of freedom.

He tried to think what evidence they might get from the car. His DNA was the most likely as he was almost bound to have left some trace there, but who was to say that he hadn't been in David's car at some other time? No, if David died, he still had a chance, maybe a slim one but a chance nevertheless.

Well then, his next step was obvious, he had to ensure that David died. The ambulance must be taking him to Casualty at Bath Royal United. He racked his brains trying to think how to get there. He had some knowledge of the geography of Bath and he looked at the road to his right, Sion Hill, the hospital was in Combe Park he knew, he was convinced he wasn't more than a couple of miles away.

Striding out with more purpose now he crossed the road and entered Sion Hill looking at his watch, 4.30am. it would be light soon. Looking at his digital watch made him think for some reason about his phone. He had recently updated it to one of the new smart phones and the man in the shop had said something about there being maps on it.

He took his phone from his pocket and quickly scrolled through the apps. He had no idea what most of them were for but one caught his eye. It was simply called maps and he opened it up.

Crikey! New technology, there on the screen in front of him was a map of his present location. It even had a little marker to show exactly where he was on the map, he couldn't believe it. He studied the map for a few minutes to locate the hospital and started walking again. After having to consult the little miracle that was his mobile phone only once more, he arrived at the entrance to the hospital forty minutes later, tired but slightly less pessimistic about his chances.

He walked up the small entrance road to the hospital to find the emergency department on his right, a low flat roofed structure in front of which was a waiting area for ambulances and there were two parked there. He had no way of knowing whether one of them had been David's saviour but it was of no consequence as far as his intentions were concerned

He walked cautiously towards the double doors, half expecting the interior to be filled with police. Inside, there was a large waiting area with a reception desk on the right and although his fears about some police presencs appeared unfounded, he realised that he still needed a reason to be there.

Marcus approached the receptionist who, although not appearing to be very busy, took her time looking up and acknowledging his presence.

"Yes...can I help you?" she snapped.

He assumed that she was towards the end of a difficult night shift. "Yes, I've had a terrible pain on the right side of my gut, it's been getting worse all night and I can't stand it anymore, I have to see a doctor."

The woman slid a piece of paper and a pen across the desk and said, "Fill this in and wait to see the triage nurse. The wait at the moment is about thirty minutes, please return the pen when you have finished with it."

"What should I do with the form?"

"Well yes, return that to me as well, obviously, please fill the form out over there," she continued, pointing at the chairs furthest from her desk, clearly not wanting him even in her eyeline any longer than necessary.

Marcus did as he was told and sat in the chairs furthest from reception. He filled out the form with false information and took it back to the grumpy receptionist. He would have loved to have wound her up a bit but the last thing he wanted was to stand out to anyone, so instead he thanked her politely and returned to his seat.

He looked around. There were three people in the waiting area besides himself and one of those left in the company of a young nurse when she materialized from somewhere and asked, "Mr. Strong, we're ready to do your X-ray now, would you like to come with me?"

Mr. Strong was in fact a rather weedy-looking teenager in motorbike leathers who, judging from the way he looked at the nurse, wanted to follow her very much indeed, but judging from the way he was cradling his arm he didn't think the nurse would have too much bother.

Not long after the rider had left for his X-ray a far less appealing vision in uniform appeared and called for Mr. Jones. It took Marcus a second or two to register the fact that he was the sought after Mr. Jones, so he quickly stood up and followed her. She led him into a little room on the right of a corridor that led past Grumpy at reception.

"Take a seat Mr. Jones, we don't seem to have a file on you, have you been here before?"

"No, I live in Newcastle," Marcus lied, "I'm just down for a couple of days on business."

"I see, and what seems to be the trouble?"

He concocted a story about suffering increasing abdominal pain through the night trying to make it seem like a probable burst appendix and eventually he was told to re-take his seat and that a nurse would call him.

Marcus noted that at the end of the corridor there were double doors that had restricted access. It looked as if you needed to punch in a code or swipe a card to get in and he assumed this was where the emergency cubicles were located. If David was alive and in this hospital, there was a good chance he was in there.

It was another half an hour before yet another nurse, this one in her mid-forties he guessed, and looking much more professional and in charge, came to get him.

As he suspected would be the case, she led him through the double doors that he had seen earlier, into a large room with a square of desks in the centre behind which were two men and three women. Only three of the five wore white coats but all five had stethoscopes around their necks.

Marcus looked around as he was lead into one of the cubicles that lined the far wall. It seemed to be a quiet time in the department as only five of the ten cubicles were occupied. It was the cubicle on his far right that caught Marcus's eye. The curtains were pulled across the front to give the occupant privacy and outside it a man, who wouldn't have fitted any other role than that of a policeman, sat in a chair reading a magazine.

He was told by the nurse that he could sit in the chair or lie on the bed, whichever he preferred and a doctor would be along shortly. Before leaving she wrote his name on a whiteboard that was mounted on the wall above the bed and added underneath, abdominal pain.

All the cubicles were numbered and had a curtain at the front. They contained a bed, a bedside locker, a large reclining chair, an equipment trolley cum medicine cabinet and a large stack of monitors of one sort or another mounted on a wheeled frame.

Each cubicle was separated from its neighbour by white partitioning panels, and the curtain that could be pulled across the front and wrapped around inside for a few inches to ensure maximum privacy.

Marcus stood at the front of his cubicle with the curtain only half closed and surveyed the room. Opposite his cubicle and a little to the right was the central desk area where most of the rooms activity was concentrated. Beyond that were the double doors through which he had entered. To the right of the doors there where some small rooms, the exact purpose of which was not obvious to him, maybe specialised treatment rooms, maybe offices or a combination of the two he thought.

To the left of the double doors, towards the end of the room in which he was convinced was David's cubicle, there were several wash hand basins with the usual arm operated taps and next to them was a door with a toilet sign on it.

As he watched, the policeman from outside David's cubicle got up and ambled down the room. A nurse carrying a pile of dressings passed him en-route and he casually remarked to her, "Just stretching my legs, those aren't the most comfortable chairs in the world, are they?"

The nurse just smiled at his remark and carried on but the policeman continued up to the desk area and engaged in conversation with one of the women. She appeared to be looking something up on the computer, maybe for him, Marcus couldn't tell.

He decided that he would be lucky to get a better chance than this one of David being left alone, so leaving his cubicle, he made his way swiftly to David's. A quick look over his shoulder to make sure Mr. Plod was still occupied at the desks and he slipped inside.

The interior was exactly the same as the one he had left except that the patient in the bed had wires attached to his chest and a drip in his arm. His face was obscured by a large oxygen mask, he also had a towel or dressing covering his eyes, presumably shielding them from the very bright overhead light.

Marcus glanced at the whiteboard on the wall above the bed for reassurance that he had the right cubicle. Sure enough, emblazoned in thick blue marker pen was, *David Carver, carbon-monoxide poisoning, Dr. Ratcliffe. 100% Oxygen, nil by mouth.*

There was a spare pillow on the reclining chair next to the bed so Marcus picked it up. Stepping backwards he used his free hand to open the curtain just enough to peer out and confirm that the police officer was still engaged in conversation at the desk. Then he deftly whipped away the oxygen mask with one hand and replaced it with the pillow with the other. Once in place Marcus used both hands to apply pressure to the pillow pushing down with all his strength.

Marcus was completely taken by surprise at what happened next. No sooner had he placed his two hands on top of the pillow then two arms appeared from either side of the bed and grabbed his wrists. The patient in the bed struggled to sit up, causing a plastic tray which had, for some unfathomable reason, been left at the foot of the bed to crash to the floor, causing an almighty din. At what seemed like the same time, the curtain at the front of the cubicle was pulled aside and two men rushed in and grabbed him, pulling him away from the bed. His hands were pulled behind his back and as he was being handcuffed, the man he had tried to suffocate sat upright in the bed.

Marcus knew then that it was all over. The occupant of the bed was now standing beside it and he could see that not only was he fully dressed but he bore no resemblance to his brother-in-law whatsoever.

Paul released his grip on Marcus's arms and explained, "Sorry Marcus, you seem to have chosen the wrong cubicle. David's in the one the other end of the ward."

"Is he going to be all right?"

"No thanks to you, all the signs are that he will make a full recovery."

As Paul, Reg and Clive led Marcus out through the casualty waiting area the rest of the team had assembled and two uniformed officers took Marcus out to a waiting car whose blue flashing lights had just replaced those of a departing ambulance.

"Well done Guv" was the cry as there was a round of mutual congratulations on a job well done.

"Does anyone know how David Carver is doing?"

"He's poorly at the moment Guv but he's going to recover, you and Reg got to him in time."

June's comments had started a second round of applause but Paul put a stop to it by looking at his watch and saying, "Right you lot! I'll treat you all to breakfast if we can find somewhere open."

Phillip took out his phone. "I'll see if I can find somewhere local, shall I Guv?"

Paul looked at his watch for a second time, "You do that Phillip, but you'd better make it snappy, we've all got to be in work soon."

Chapter 16

Six Months Later

Ron Kelly was surprised when he heard the door-bell. It was Tuesday and as far as he was aware all his friends knew Tuesday was the one day in the week that he reserved for cleaning the house. He and his wife Irene had always worked on the house together on Tuesdays ever since he had retired and when she had died he saw no reason to abandon the routine.

He was not expecting a delivery so he speculated that someone was collecting for some charity or other. As he walked to the door he felt in his pocket to see if he had any loose change.

As soon as he had unlocked the door it burst inward throwing him backwards and causing him to fall heavily. He was fit and healthy for a seventy-six-year-old but any kind of fall at that age can have serious consequences and in order to stop himself falling to the ground he reached out, trying to support himself against the wall. This maneuver resulted in him half twisting and impacting with the wall before sliding to the floor.

He had pain in his hip where he had landed awkwardly and that concerned him and his head also hurt where it had hit the wall. He wanted to just sit for a moment to assess his injuries but the two men who had entered so violently shouted to him to get up as they closed the front door.

"Just give me a moment," he pleaded, "I think my hip is broken."

He didn't actually think he had broken his hip but he did want to sit and saw no reason why he should do as they wanted just because they shouted at him. Who did they think they were, bursting in like that!

It appeared to him that the men lacked patience as well as good manners as one of them caught hold of him under one arm and dragged him to his feet, unconcerned as to whether the maneuver would cause any more pain or injury.

He cried out in pain, not because it had hurt particularly but because he wanted them to think he was injured. It would give him an excuse not to comply too quickly to any other orders they would see fit to give him, he was so angry at the way they behaved.

The two men were wearing balaclavas and the one who had lifted him from the floor so unceremoniously now dragged him towards the stairs.

"I hope you don't expect me to climb those," he said trying his best to simulate a convincing limp when they finally got him to his feet. "What is it you want anyway, there's very little money in the house?"

"Just shut your mouth and get up the stairs old man, before I take something heavy to your knees or make certain your hip is broken."

After that last remark, Ron decided it would be better to comply with their demands rather than defy them, his knees hadn't been too good lately and they were the only two he had.

He wasn't scared particularly, he'd been in a few scrapes in his time in the police and before that in the army. He'd even tackled a group of youths armed with knives on one occasion, but he had to admit he'd been younger and fitter then.

He made as much of a meal of getting upstairs as he dared, frustrating the two men who appeared to be in a hurry and that served to give him some satisfaction.

They forced him into his bedroom and he almost laughed when he found himself thinking that he was pleased he had made the bed and that the room was tidy. Irene would have been upset at strangers seeing the place untidy.

One of the men made him sit on the little bedroom chair that his wife had bought in an antique shop the year she died. The other one crossed the room and pulled the curtains, enveloping the room in semi-darkness.

"Where's your mobile?" one of them asked.

"Yes thank you, I'm normally quite mobile," Ron replied, now pretending to be hard of hearing as well as injured.

He was rewarded with a fierce backhander across the face that almost sent him to the floor for a second time, and he reconsidered his decision to try and wind them up.

The man waited only seconds before repeating his question.

"On charge in the kitchen," he replied tasting blood in his mouth. He was furious with the intruders but also more concerned now because, as the one who had hit him had swung his arm back Ron had seen the butt of a gun protruding from his belt.

This was not just some aggravated burglary; these men were here for a specific purpose and that purpose would appear to involve his mobile phone in some way.

"What's June's number?" the man asked as he returned to the room with Ron's phone.

Ron's heart sank. Oh hell, this involves June in some way he thought, now very concerned indeed about the way things seemed to be going. If they thought for one minute that he was going to ring his daughter and ask her to come over, they were very much mistaken. They could knock him from here to kingdom come and he wouldn't do that.

"June's number? I'll not ask again."

"June......who's June, are you sure you've got the right house?"

Ron was hit again, harder this time and he spat out his bottom denture together with one of the few teeth he had left and which the last blow had dislodged.

The one who had hit him turned to his accomplice exasperated.

"Her number will be in the phone," he said, "scroll through."

The second man did as was suggested and eventually said, "Yeah, OK I've got it."

He pressed the key and rang Constable June Kelly.

When June answered he said, "Just listen June, we have your dad and his wellbeing....or lack of it....depends upon the evidence you give in court today. Know that we'll hurt him badly if you go identifying anyone in court today. He's an old man, he may not survive a beating, speak to him if you like, he'll tell you."

He held the phone so that Ron could speak into it. "Tell your daughter to keep her mouth shut in court Ron. Tell her how nasty we are."

"June...I'm fine, don't do anything these bastards want...Love you."

The phone was snatched back angrily. "Your old man's got some guts June, I'll give him that, so don't give us reason to spill them all over the floor, you just tell them you can't identify anyone and he'll be fine, if you don't.....well I don't think he can take much more.." He hung up.

"My daughter's not going to lie in court, she'd lose her job, it looks to me as if whoever it is you want to protect is going down and if you had any sense you'd get the hell out of my house before the peelers turn up in the guise of armed response."

"Shut the old fool up will you," one said.

"My pleasure," the other responded and this time took out his gun and hit Ron over the head with it, causing him to fall to the ground and lie very still, bleeding profusely from a nasty gash on the back of his head.

* * * * * * * * * * * * * * * * * *

Roy Darnley entered the room and asked Reg who was nearest to the door, "Where's June? we have to be in court by 10:30 a.m."

Reg pointed across the room to where June had just answered her mobile.

Paul came out of his office at the same time and greeted Roy with a smile. "You've come to pick up June have you Roy, she said you were going together."

"That's right Paul, I'm not sure which one of us is giving evidence first but we've both been told that we will be called at some time in the proceedings today. Well done by the way, I hear that Marcus Wagner got the life sentence he so richly deserved."

"Yes, that's right, It was a good result for the team."

"It was a good result for you."

Both men looked over towards June as they heard her cry into her phone, "Who is this?....Dad!" but then she turned off the phone looking as white as a sheet and on the edge of tears.

She stared towards Paul and Roy with a look of pure horror on her face. "What on earth is wrong June? You look as if you've seen a ghost or something, are you all right?" asked Paul worried, he had never seen June look scared, but that was certainly the impression he had now, that she was very scared.

"Paul!" she almost screamed, "I need to speak to you privately."

The team all looked on, concerned, None of them had ever heard June use the Guvnor's first name in work before, something must be very wrong.

Paul followed June into his office and looking back over his shoulder said to Roy, "You'd better go on Roy, make sure you're not late, tell them June will be there as soon as possible and I'll make sure she gets there."

"Ok Paul, ring me if there's a problem or anything I can do," said Roy, shrugging his shoulders at those who looked to him questioningly as he left.

In his office Paul pulled out a chair for June to sit in. "Do you want a drink or anything?" he asked. "Water, something stronger if you want?"

June shook her hand, trying to compose herself, "No," she answered.

Paul made sure the door to his office was closed and took a seat at his desk facing June.

"What's happened June? Tell me."

"They've taken my dad!"

"What! Who's taken your dad, what do you mean?"

"The Barnes's, the man on the phone said that they had my dad and that he would come to harm if I identified Alan and Clive Barnes as the two men at John's flat on the night of the fire. What the hell am I going to do, Guv? I can't let them hurt my dad...I'll have to perjure myself in court, but everyone will know I'm lying."

"Try to stay calm June, did the man mention Alan and Clive Barnes by name?"

"No, but I'm not identifying anyone else in court today. How can you expect me to stay calm, they have my dad and I think they intend to kill him if I don't lie under oath in court."

"Where did they snatch him from, do you know that?"

June took some deep breaths and said, "Today is Tuesday, it's the one day of the week he stays home to do housework, every other day he's either fishing or playing snooker at his club."

"So, he was home?"

"Yes, he must have been."

"Well then, they will probably have broken into the house rather than have snatched him off the streets, so they are most likely keeping him there as well."

"I know Guv, but they may have taken him somewhere else, and if we raid the house and he's not there....they will know I've spoken out and they could kill him!"

"Who is the judge presiding over the case, do you know?"

"Judge Wheatherhead, why?"

"I have an idea June, trust me, I'm going to do everything I can to ensure your dad's safety. I'll get you to the court and you're not to say a word to anyone about your dad being taken, not even to Roy Darnley, is that clear?"

"I guess so, but what are you going to do? I don't want my dad put at risk in any way."

"Best if you don't know, I think it has a better chance of success that way. Now listen carefully, the single most important thing to me at this time is your dad's safety. If you haven't had a signal from me by the time you have to give your evidence, then you have to assume that my plan hasn't worked and that they still have your dad. Then I'm afraid you must do whatever you feel is right. I know if it was my dad, I'd probably lie through my teeth to save his life, nobody here is going to blame you for doing that, and you shouldn't get into hot water over it either because you have done the right thing in telling me about it."

"You won't tell me what you're planning to do?"

"No June, like I said, I think it stands a better chance of working if you don't know."

"OK Guv," said June, still fighting to hold back the tears. "You will save my dad, won't you? I don't care what happens to me as long as dad is safe."

"I'll do my best June, you know that but just remember that it is up to you if you don't get the nod from me in time, and don't tell anyone about your father being held."

Paul drove June to the courts and after some difficulty arranged an urgent meeting with Judge Wheatherhead. As he left the judge's chambers he looked at his watch and saw that it was 10:15 a.m. The trial was due to start at 11:00 a.m. and Paul needed to get things in place quickly. He rang the station.

* * * * * * * * * * *

Ron Kelly's house was a mid-terraced property half way along Longfield Road in the St Andrews area of the city. The rear garden backed onto the rear garden of a house in the street behind. Constable John Campbell and Constable Peter Cook pulled their car in, a few doors down on the opposite side of the street from the house, at the same time as Constables Derrick Price and Clive Pascoe in one car with Phillip Strange and Reg Evens in another, parked at either end of Longfield Road itself. Just two roads away, four armed officers sat chatting in the back of a police Land Rover, ready to go at a moment's notice.

Reg took the call on his mobile and confirmed to Phillip, "The people opposite June's dad are Jack and Gillian Pearce, they've been contacted and are willing to let us in. They will greet us at the door as if we were old friends.”

“Good, let's go. ” The two men exited the car and walked to the house opposite Ron Kelly's. They knocked on the door knowing full well that their every action was probably being observed from the upper window of Ron Kelly's home. The door was opened by Mrs. Pearce who took them both by surprise as she greeted each of them in turn with a big hug and a kiss on the cheek.

“Lovely to see you both,” she said in a loud voice as she stepped aside to let them in.

Once inside they were shown the way to the front bedroom overlooking Ron's house.

Mr. Pearce said to them as they ascended the stairs, “I had Gillian go up and close the curtains as soon as I'd spoken to your lot, I hope that was the right thing to do.”

“Yes, thank you, that's good thinking Mr. Pearce,” replied Reg as he retrieved a pair of binoculars from beneath his coat, “I hope this isn't too much of an inconvenience for you both.”

“Not at all,” said Mrs. Pearce excitedly. “This is the most exciting thing that has happened to us in years, can I get you both some tea or would you prefer coffee? I've got some jammy-dodgers as well if you'd like.”

As the two men set up surveillance of the front of Ron Kelly's house and Mrs. Peace went to make coffee, John Campbell and Peter Cook were setting up their surveillance of the back of the house at the home of Miss Giles, a ninety-year-old spinster who had lived in the house all her life.

"What can you see from the front Reg?" asked John on his mobile.

"Nothing, it all looks quiet but the bedroom curtains are closed and that's odd if June's dad is up and about, most people open their curtains as soon as they're dressed. What about the back?"

"Same here, it all looks very quiet, so do we think they're holding him here or have they taken him somewhere else?"

"We are just to watch at the moment and not do anything unless we hear from the Guvnor."

"Hang on," said John, "there's a postman delivering at the end of the road. I've got an idea, I'll get back to you."

John left the house and hurried across the road. Peter Cook watched with interest as John spoke to the postman who was obviously on his rounds, "Have you delivered to Longfield Road yet?" he asked showing his warrant card discreetly.

After chatting to the postman for no more than a couple of minutes John returned to the house and rang Reg. "I've just arranged for the postman to deliver a letter to Ron's house, luckily he has some circulars to put through the door anyway. You let me know when he is at the door and I'm going to ring Ron's mobile. I've told the postman to delay a little fumbling with the mail and to listen for a phone ringing in the house."

"Well that's a great idea John," said Reg, "but what will you say if one of them answers Ron's phone?"

"Don't worry, I'll go into unsolicited call mode, I get so many of those I can quote them in my sleep.....we understand you have been involved in an accident that wasn't your fault."

"Blimey John, that was brilliant, I almost hung up on you. I'll let you know when to make the call, our postman has just entered the end of the road."

The postman took to his clandestine role like a natural, continuing his round and if nothing had happened but as soon the he reached Ron Kelly's house Reg gave John the signal and he rang Ron's phone. The arrangement was that if the postman heard a phone ringing in the house as he delivered the mail he would make a play of arranging things in his bag as he left the house. But almost as soon as John had rung Ron's number he hung up and announced.

"It's no good, they've obviously turned Ron's phone off, it's unavailable."

"Never mind John it was a good idea anyway," said Reg, but they all shared in the disappointment.

* * * * * * * * * * *

As June took the witness stand she was trying desperately to stop her hands from shaking. She looked around and was surprised to see Paul sitting in the visitor's gallery. She had supposed that he would be off doing whatever it was he had planned to do but then reasoned that he must have put his plan into operation with the rest of the team and be waiting for confirmation that all had gone well so that he could give her the nod that her dad was safe.

After she had been sworn in, the prosecuting counsel stood up and addressed her. "Constable Kelly, could you describe to the court the events that took place on the night you so bravely entered a burning flat to save your neighbour?"

June relayed the events of that evening in as calm a voice as she could muster, but it must have been obvious to one and all that something was wrong. Those that didn't know her assumed she was just nervous giving evidence in front of so many people.

After she had finished her account the councilor asked, "You say that you twice had the opportunity to observe the two men at close quarters, once through the spy-hole in your front door and again through the window as they left. Is that correct?"

June hesitated and looked over at Paul who shook his head indicating that there was no news.

"Constable Kelly....is that correct?"

"Yes."

"And could you please point those two men out to the court?"

June looked over at Paul again in desperation, but this time Paul just shut his eyes and bowed his head. June was close to tears. "Well.....No....not really."

"Constable....may I remind you that you are under oath, now I'm going to ask you again, can you identify the two men you saw that night?"

"Not really no, the spy-hole in my door is a fish-eye lens to take in a wide area, the view you get is quite distorted."

"But even if that is true, you say that you saw the two men again through the window as they left, that is what you said isn't it?"

"Yes....but that was mostly from behind and I was fiddling with my phone, trying to get a picture without the flash going off.....I'm sorry....no I can't identify them."

As the prosecuting counsel sat down in disbelief the defending barrister, who the court had been told was a last minute replacement due to a sudden illness, shot up.

"Your Honour, I believe that the evidence of this witness forms the bulk of the evidence against my clients, the rest is just speculation and hearsay. In which case I would like to make a motion to dismiss the charges against my clients, Your Honour."

The judge looked over towards the prosecuting counsel, "Do you have any more evidence to submit to this court?"

"Well Your Honour, we were expecting this witness...."

"Councellor, Do you or don't you have any more evidence to put to this court?"

"No, your Honour."

"Then I don't see that I have any choice other than to dismiss the charges against the accused." He looked over at the dock. "You are free to go."

Paul had been watching the public area closely and now followed a man who seemed anxious both to leave and to make a phone call.

The two Barnes brothers high fived each other as they exited the dock and were approached by a man who introduced himself as The Court Bailiff.

"If you would like to follow me gentlemen," he said, "there are just a couple of formalities and some paperwork to go through before you can be formally released."

The brothers wrapped their arms around each other as they followed the man out of the courtroom and into a small office. "Just wait in here for a moment would you, I just have to go and get the necessary forms to fill in. I shouldn't be long."

In the corridor outside the courtroom Paul watched as the man he had followed made a call on his phone while making his way to the exit.

Paul also made some calls and the waiting began.

June was approached by one of the court bailiffs and taken to a room next to the one where she and Inspector Darnley had waited to be called to the witness box.

She was left alone and fully expected that the next person to enter would be an officer to arrest her for perjury. She didn't care, she just needed to know that her father was safe. She tried calling Paul several times but his phone was always busy. What was happening...where was her father?

* * * * * * * * * * * * * * *

Reg and Phillip in the upstairs window opposite and Derrick and Clive in the car at the end of the road, had their eyes glued to the front of Ron Kelly's house where Adrian Barnes and one of his father's henchmen, Greg Kite waited for news.

Adrian was pacing up and down and beginning to get on Greg's nerves when his phone rang. Greg watched Adrian's expression change from one of frustration to one of joy in an instant and realised, with a slight tinge of disappointment, that he wouldn't have to beat anyone to death today after all.

"Looks like good news from your expression, boss." he said.

"Yeah ... that's right." He looked over at June's dad who was once again conscious and tied in the chair his wife had bought, now with his mouth taped.

He approached Ron menacingly. "Looks as if that daughter of yours loves you after all....isn't that nice. We'll be leaving now, you'll forgive me if I don't untie you before we go but I want you to have some time to think over how stupid it would be to go to the police. Your daughter has put her career on the line for you, you wouldn't want her to do the same with her life, would you? Keep your mouth shut and we'll leave her alone.....Have a nice day."

They left the house in a good mood but that soon changed when, only yards from the door, they found themselves surrounded by police shouting, "Armed police...lie face down with your hands behind the back of your head...now!"

Adrian Barnes and Greg Kite lay in the road as instructed as an officer patted them down and removed the gun from Adrian's belt. As the two men were led away to a police van, Reg and the others broke down the door of Ron's house and entered calling his name

They began searching the house and it wasn't long before Reg entered the bedroom to find a somewhat damaged but much relieved Ron Kelly doing his best to smile behind the tape that covered his mouth.

"You have to tell June I'm safe," he shouted at Reg as soon as the tape was removed, "before she has to testify, quickly man."

"Calm down Ron, my Guvnor's got it all under control, there's no need to worry."

Reg took out his phone and called Paul. "We've got him Guv. it looks as if he's had a nasty bump on the head so we'll get him to hospital but tell June he's smiling."

"Can I speak to my daughter?"

"Sorry Ron not just yet, but my Guvnor will let her know your all right. We need to get that bump on your head looked at."

"Sod the bump on my head....I hope you hurt the bastards when you took them down, they deserve it."

Reg smiled, realising where June got her bottle from. "I'll see what I can arrange, shall I Ron?"

Ron winked at him, "That's a good lad."

Paul walked into the room where June was sitting, resigned to her fate now that she had stopped crying. "Christ June," he exclaimed, "you'd better get yourself cleaned up a bit, you have to give evidence in court soon. Oh! and by the way your dad is waiting for you to call him."

The only bit of what Paul had said that had got through to June was the bit about her dad. "Is he Ok have they let him go?"

Paul called Reg and asked him to put June's dad on the phone before handing it to June and warning, "He's been taken to hospital because they hit him over the head, but he's absolutely fine and can't wait to tell his story down the snooker hall."

June spoke to her dad for several minutes while fighting back the tears until he said, "Sorry June, but an extremely pretty nurse wants me to go with her now and she has a bit of a glint in her eye, God knows what she's going to do to me. If you haven't heard from me in the next forty-eight hours come and get me. Love you."

June wiped away the tears and Paul put his hand on her shoulder. "He is all right isn't he....June?"

June took a tissue from her bag and blew her nose, "By the sound of it Guv, I'd almost have to say he sounds as if he bloody well enjoyed the situation...wait till I see him!" then suddenly transported back to reality, "Am I going to be charged?"

Paul found that he was actually enjoying the situation now things had been resolved. "Charged ....charged with what?"

"Charged with perjury.....you were there. I lied on the witness stand."

"Oh that! Don't go worrying about that."

"But I lied to the court."

"No you didn't.....well yes I suppose you did.... But not really, anyway it doesn't count."

"What do mean it doesn't count...I don't understand."

"Well you haven't given your evidence in court yet, that was just a sort of rehearsal."

June was at a loss for words. "A rehearsal? What do mean...tell me...I don't understand."

Paul took a seat beside her, "I'm sorry June but I do think it all went much better with you being in the dark. I spoke to Judge

Wheatherhead and told him the full story. He agreed to postpone the trial for a couple of hours. We told the defence barrister and solicitor and they went off to do whatever they do in these situations.

"In the meantime, we collected some random people to play the part of the jury and staged a rehearsal for the sake of anyone with an interest in what you were going to say. We told a white lie about the defence counsel being ill and having to be replaced. You did your bit and your dad was released....quite clever I thought."

"How on earth did you get the judge to agree to a deception like that and what are the consequences going to be? Was it legal even?"

"I'm not sure how much flak there is going to be but Judge Wheatherhead agreed because he has this thing about people who try to interfere with his jury or his witnesses, he hates them with a vengeance. Not very impartial for a judge I suppose, but I like him. And of course, the most important thing is that your father is OK."

June did a very unprofessional thing and gave her boss a hug. "Thanks Guv, I knew I could count on you, what now?"

"Now I have another very enjoyable task to perform."

Paul, accompanied by an officer of the court and two large uniformed police officers entered the room where Alan and Clive Barnes had been waiting expectantly.

"About bloody time!" shouted Clive as they entered. "We've been waiting here ages, let's get these bloody papers signed so we can go."

"Go," said Paul smiling broadly, "go where?"

"Home, out of here....where do you think?"

"Well I'm sorry to disappoint you gentlemen, but there's the little matter of a trial to get through yet."

"Christ! Does nobody communicate around here, the trial is over, the charges have been dropped, we just have to sign some papers and we're out of here!"

"Ah...look I'm sorry, but it seems to be you two that have been left out of the loop. What you went through just now wasn't the real trial......neither your barrister nor your solicitor are ill and that wasn't the jury, just some people we found in the street. I'm afraid it was all a little charade to get your family to release the witness's dad. And it worked like a charm too, your family fell for it hook line and sinker. You'll be pleased to know that the whole of your family are going to be in prison at the same time. It will be just like Christmas for you, having all the family together like that."

Alan's temper got the better of him and he lunged at Paul, who half expecting something of the sort stepped aside, allowing the two officers to restrain him and escort him, along with his brother, out of the room still protesting. An hour later, prosecuting counsel asked June Kelly for the second time, "Constable Kelly, can you identify the two men you saw that night.

"I most certainly can." she replied.

The End.

Other books by Colin Holcombe

featuring

Inspector Paul Manley

First Time Hard

ISBN   987 - 1518677519

The Moving Finger Writes

ISBN 978 - 1518776144